Cut to the Quick

JOAN BOSWELL

Cover art/design: Jennifer Harrington

LE CONSEIL DES ARTS DU CANADA DEPUIS 1957 | THE CANADA COUNCIL FOR THE ARTS SINCE 1957

We acknowledge the support of the Canada Council for the Arts for our publishing program.

RendezVous Crime
an imprint of
Napoleon & Company
Toronto, Ontario, Canada

Printed in Canada

11 10 09 08 07   5 4 3 2 1

Library and Archives Canada Cataloguing in Publication

Boswell, Joan
        Cut to the quick / Joan Boswell.

ISBN 978-1-894917-47-6

        I. Title.
PS8603.O88C883 2007   C813'.6   C2007-900503-9

For Nicholas, Katherine, Francis and Trevor

I would like to thank my critiquing group, The Ladies' Killing Circle, Vicki Cameron, Barbara Fradkin, Mary Jane Maffini, Sue Pike and Linda Wiken. As always their help was invaluable. Thanks too to my publisher, Sylvia McConnell and editor, Allister Thomson, who patiently smoothed the rough edges. And love and appreciation to my supportive family.

One

Something was wrong with Manon. Usually she sparkled and flashed; today she spoke in a monotone and sagged like a doll that had lost its stuffing.

"It seems as if we joined the campus French club just last week. Can you believe it was twenty years ago?" Manon pushed the restaurant menu to one side and raised her glass. "Here's to our friendship—I'm glad you're here today and even happier you'll be in Toronto for three weeks this summer." Her warm words contrasted with her flat voice.

"And may we always be there for one another." Hollis Grant gave what had become a traditional reply. Today the words had new meaning. *Being there* meant identifying the source of Manon's unhappiness. Better not to ask directly. Manon hated pointed questions: she said they made her feel defensive and uptight. Instead Hollis would update Manon on her own life while she decided how to find out what was bothering her friend.

"I had a hundred end-of-term academic things to attend to," Hollis sighed. "I've held this trip out as a carrot to keep myself going. This first year as a widow has been rough, but I've reached a turning point in my life. This course will be a litmus test for my future." She hadn't yet shared what she was about to say with anyone, but it was time she did. "When it's over, I'm deciding whether or not to give up my academic career and paint full time."

Manon's eyes widened. "That is definitely news. Give up teaching. What a major, major change. Can you support yourself?"

"I've crunched the numbers. It's possible."

"You're a terrific painter." She examined Hollis. "To change the subject—you look great. I like your hair—strawberry blonde suits you." Manon reached up and smoothed her chestnut brown chignon. "I've always envied you those curls."

"And I've yearned for straight hair. Funny how we're never content. Next to you I've always felt like a cart horse."

Manon's smile seemed more genuine. "Statuesque, imposing, stunning—adjectives no one applies to small women like me. And your new glasses are smashing—I'd *never* be bold enough to buy red." As she talked, she repeatedly tapped the table with perfectly manicured crimson-tipped nails, a new nervous mannerism.

"I thought they suited a tall, big-boned woman like me. I'd look ridiculous in tiny glasses." Hollis tucked her un-manicured hands out of sight. Did she subconsciously pick showy jewellery to detract from the leathery skin on her face and hands? But it wasn't time to think about herself.

Their warm scallop salads arrived.

Hollis risked a direct but generalized inquiry. "How are *you?*"

"*Mon Dieu,* is this an innocent question—has today gone okay, or has clinical depression struck again?" Irritation edged Manon's voice.

"So much for *trying* to be subtle." Hollis tried for a light touch.

"Sorry for sounding cranky. I know you care. We've shared a lot. But you've never been subtle. You've always spoken your mind—and acted impulsively, I might add."

"Thank God, or I wouldn't have dragged you down to the Canadian National Exhibition Midway to meet Rocco," Hollis said.

"Or told me you planned to drop out of university to run off with the world's sexiest man."

"He was gorgeous and exotic." Hollis shook her head, thinking how close she'd come to ruining her life.

"And when I locked you in your room to stop you, your fury scared even you."

"An understatement. I'd never before and have never again been that angry."

"Or so grateful when you regained your sanity." Manon finished Hollis's sentence.

"And realized you'd quite literally saved my life. Now it's my turn. Confession time. Tell me. How are you?"

"Since I'm taking my meds faithfully, I'll say—'as well as I ever am', and that's not bad."

She might be physically and mentally well, but something was wrong. Hollis removed her glasses and polished them on her napkin. That something could involve work, but more likely it related to her home life. "You said Etienne couldn't decide whether to play baseball or soccer. I bet he's doing both? Eleven's a terrific age. You're competent and independent but not mired in a hormonal swamp. He's a great kid."

"I agree. You're right. Baseball and soccer keep him busy. He's also enrolled in a July astronomy day camp." Manon's eyes crinkled, and her expression softened when she spoke about Etienne.

"And your stepsons?"

"Ivan's about the same." She thought for a moment. "Not true. He's more secretive. He's seldom home. He's still employed part-time at the Buy Right Supermarket on St. Clair. And now he's out most evenings working for Catering Plus. When he drifts in, he hardly talks. I don't blame him. Curt is always on his case."

"You didn't tell me he had a second job."

"Nothing to tell. I only know about it because the company phones every so often to leave a message. Anyway, Curt nags him to shape up and do something significant with his life. Ivan listens, agrees and leaves it at that. He never defends himself."

"How come he still lives at home?"

"Good question. A year ago he said he planned to move out but something, I have no idea what it was, changed his mind." She tapped her dessert spoon to punctuate her comments. "Since it seemed he didn't intend to leave, we converted the third floor into an apartment for him and Tomas. I think Ivan needed privacy. After all, he *is* twenty-three. But I worry about him. Even though he and Tomas have always lived part-time with us, Ivan's never allowed me to get close. I know inconsequential details—how he prefers button-down shirts, is allergic to wool, hates anything made with tofu, but nothing important."

"What about Tomas? How did his second year at UNB go? What's he doing this summer?"

"He's finished exams and came home last Friday. He didn't try for a summer job relating to his engineering course—he's working at a fast food restaurant. But that's okay because he's swimming competitively, and shift work allows him time to practice." She grinned. "He wants to swim Lake Ontario."

"Now *that's* a serious ambition," Hollis said. She enjoyed hearing Manon speak about her son and stepsons. Her voice and expression reflected love and affection. Whatever bothered her didn't involve them. That left Curt, Manon's husband.

"How's Curt? Painting twenty hours a day?"

"He's not..." Manon paused and laid the spoon down, "great." She aligned her water glass with her dinner knife. Her shoulders slumped, and her voice dropped.

"In what way?"

Manon sighed and moved her plate a fraction. "It's his heart."

"His heart," Hollis repeated.

"After Christmas, he started taking afternoon naps. And his grey skin—it scared me." Manon picked up and examined a fork. "I gently suggested he see a cardiologist. He not only refused, he shouted at me. He said I obsessed about health, my own and everyone else's. Told me to worry about myself and leave him alone." She pushed the fork's tines into the table cloth. "One day in February, he was in his studio talking with Sotheby's in New York—they had three of his paintings in an auction. He gasped and stopped talking. Whoever he was speaking to heard him whisper '911'. She called Toronto. Minutes later, paramedics whisked him off to St. Mike's."

"My God, what was it? How bad? How is he now?"

"A heart attack, one totally blocked artery. Angioplasty isn't an option. He's waiting for bypass surgery." Manon stopped fiddling and looked at Hollis.

"Waiting—you're kidding." What must it be like to cope with a heart attack threat on a daily basis? Constant worry. Every pain, no matter how small, possibly the beginning of "the big one". What a way to live.

"He waits because, according to triage rules, he's not as badly off as others. He keeps his little nitroglycerine spray bottle at the ready. Actually, that's not true. Spray is new, but he doesn't like it because you're supposed to sit down for five minutes after you use it. He said he couldn't do that and returned to pills. He always carries them and has extra bottles stashed everywhere."

"How awful for both of you. He must be furious."

"You've got it." Manon pointed a scarlet nail at herself. "He's mad at me because he didn't listen to me, and I was right." She tapped the table. "Mad at his body because it let him down. Mad at the medical system because they can't fix him yesterday. He's mad, mad, mad. Etienne, Ivan, Tomas and I—we understand why he's short-tempered and angry. It doesn't make living with him any easier."

Hollis reached across and grasped Manon's hand to still her fingers. "I wish you'd told me. Does he have any idea when he'll move to the top of the list?"

"Next fall."

"That's two or three months away. The waiting must be affecting his daily life."

"He pretends that it isn't."

The waiter hovered, ready to remove their salads. Hollis waved him away. She released Manon's hand and plunged her fork into the last juicy scallop. She felt guilty about asking, but she needed to know.

"Is he well enough to give his course?"

"He's determined to pretend nothing is wrong and carry on with his life."

"Another question—are you sure we won't be too much trouble? Three days, let alone three weeks, is a long time to entertain visitors, especially when one is a dog."

"You *know* I love dogs. Etienne has pressed me to buy a puppy since Beau died." Manon paused. "Visitor?" She raised her hand with her palm facing Hollis. "I officially adopt you. You *are* family. If God had given me a sister, I would have wanted one just like you." A lilt had returned to her voice. "I need an escape—something to look forward to. We'll see a million movies—foreign films, chick flicks, whatever takes our fancy." She grinned. "And jazz at Hugh's Place. They have a great summer line-up. Maybe Shakespeare in High Park. And it will do Curt good to have you there. He's always liked you. When will you and MacTee arrive?"

There was no question any longer of refusing such a heart-felt invitation. "We'll arrive on Tuesday morning, in time for me to make it to class at two." Hollis leaned forward. "And it will mean that…"

A shrill cell phone rendition of "Mon Pays". Manon dove for her handbag and fumbled for her phone. A fanatical Canadian Federalist, she'd agonized over using "Mon Pays", the Quebec separatist anthem, for her ring. Her love for the song overruled her reservations about its political associations.

She pushed "talk", said "I'll call you back" and excused herself. Other diners glared at her as she left. Prominently displayed notices requested patrons to turn off their cell phones. Hollis checked her purse—hers was off.

While she waited, she picked a second roll from its napkin-wrapped nest, bent forward and inhaled the yeasty fragrance. She should resist temptation, but who could ignore the siren call of warm rolls? After buttering a small piece, she raised her eyes, gasped and shot to her feet.

Manon's hand anchored her to the frame of the doorway from the hall. Her skin, always pale, was ashen. Her eyes appeared unfocused, as if she couldn't quite remember where she was.

Hollis rushed to her friend, who stood rooted and apparently unable to move.

"He's dead," Manon said.

"Curt's dead?"

Manon slowly shook her head. "Ivan."

Sure she had been about to learn about Curt's death, it took a second for Hollis to reorient herself. "What happened?"

"A motorcycle crash. That was Curt at Sunnybrook's trauma

centre." She shook her head and blinked rapidly. "I'm going right now. Poor Ivan. I can't believe it. He always drove so cautiously. And I'm afraid for Curt. What will this do to his heart?"

"It certainly won't do it any good, but if something goes wrong, he's in the right place."

But what about Manon? She coped badly with stress. Ivan's sudden death. Curt's heart. If ever there was a time to be a friend, this was it. "I'll come with you?"

"No." Manon approximated a smile. "I'll need you later. Go to our house." She glanced at her watch. "Etienne should be back at school by the time you arrive. Break the news to Nadine. She'll be devastated. Ivan was her favourite. They spent hours cooking and talking about food. She needs to hear the news before the others come home. I don't know what we'll have to do at the hospital, but we'll come home as soon as we can." She bit her lower lip. "I hope I'll be the one to tell Etienne, but you'll have to do it if I'm not back."

Hollis liked Nadine. She was much more than a housekeeper—she was a strong right arm and emotional support for Manon. Sharing the news would be horrible, but it had to be done. "I'll wait with you until you get a taxi."

Manon grasped Hollis's arm as they huddled together in warm early summer sunshine. "Stay with us until this is over?" she pleaded. Her voice quivered.

What would a stay in Toronto involve? Nothing that couldn't be arranged with a few phone calls. She knew first-hand how much it helped if a friend assumed some of your responsibilities. Elsie, a church stalwart, had taken over the day-to-day running of the manse following Hollis's husband's murder. She remembered how grateful she'd felt. But it was more than that. Hollis had never believed she'd adequately repaid Manon for saving her from running off with Rocco.

"As long as you need me," she said.

Hollis returned to the restaurant after Manon had slipped into a taxi and headed to Sunnybrook. She retrieved her suitcase from the cloakroom. Outside again, she hailed a cab, hoping the cabbie wouldn't want to talk. She needed time to pull herself together. Her hands shook, and she felt nauseous. Although she hadn't been close to Ivan, learning that anyone you knew had died violently shocked you. Seeing her husband lying murdered on the road in the opening moments of Ottawa's National Capital Marathon flashed onto her mind screen. Sudden death—she knew all about it. She locked her hands together and breathed deeply. To be useful, she'd have to use jogging and meditation to maintain her composure. It wouldn't be easy, but she'd do her best.

Inside the Winchester Street house, she followed Nadine, the housekeeper, to the kitchen. The smell of a freshly baked pie filled the air. Silver lay on the counter along with polish and clothes.

Hollis expected Nadine to be alone. Instead she found Etienne and Tomas sitting at the kitchen table. Etienne clutched a half-eaten sandwich in one hand and a glass of milk in the other. Tomas, tipped back on a chair, gripped a beer can. A calm, happy domestic scene.

"How come you're back? I thought you and Maman were having lunch and going to the art gallery," Etienne said. "Where's Maman?"

"We did. I was..." How did she do this? Oh, God. There had to be a protocol. How did you tell two young men their brother was dead? But she had to do it—she couldn't stand here pretending nothing was wrong.

"There's been an accident..."

Tomas rocked forward. His chair's front legs banged down

on the tile floor, puncturing the silence that had followed her announcement. "What kind of accident?" Tomas said and lurched to his feet.

Etienne placed his sandwich down as if it were made of the thinnest crystal. His body stiffened, his eyes widened, and he appeared to hold his breath.

Nadine, her hand covering her mouth, looked from one to another.

Tomas stepped forward. "Who, *who* had an accident?"

"Ivan," Hollis managed. Her tongue seemed far too large and felt glued to the roof of her mouth.

Tomas, Nadine and Etienne stared at her.

"What happened?" Tomas said.

"He crashed his motorcycle."

Her announcement sucked life and air from the room. Her body language probably told them to expect the worst, but maybe not. Naturally they'd try to deny it when they first heard the terrible news.

"Where? How badly was he hurt? Where's Maman? Does Papa know?" Etienne leaned toward her. "Tell us."

Hollis didn't want to tell them, didn't know how to do it.

"Your mother and father will be back soon. They're at the hospital."

Tomas considered her words. "If Ivan's critically hurt, they won't leave," he said in a measured tone. He narrowed his eyes. "It's worse, isn't it?"

Hollis nodded.

"Oh, no," Nadine cried.

Etienne's face appeared to be made of soft putty that formed and reformed as his gaze flipped back and forth. "What do you mean—worse?"

She didn't want to pronounce the words that would bring

their worlds crashing down.

Tomas's shoulders slumped. He dropped his head forward as if he were about to pray. Perhaps he was. "Ivan's dead."

"Yes," Hollis said.

They reacted as if the single word had turned them to stone. Finally, Nadine began to cry. "Such a nice young man. Never any trouble. Never."

Etienne whispered, "Is it really true?" He pushed his chair back, rose then looked confused, as if he wondered what to do next.

"I'm afraid it is," Hollis said and couldn't say any more. Tears ran down her cheeks. She stepped to Etienne, held out her arms, drew him close, patted his back and made meaningless, consoling sounds.

Tomas, still holding his beer can, took a long drink. "Ivan hated his bike—maybe he was psychic. Maybe Dad should have let him sell it." Tears filled his blue eyes and glittered on his long black lashes. "Shit. I guess it's up to me to go and tell Mom."

Clearly he wanted Hollis to say "no", to tell him someone else would do it.

She felt helpless but wanted to do something. Her friend, Kas, had made her drink sugared coffee after Paul's murder. "A cup of tea or something hot and sweet will help," Hollis said to Nadine.

Nadine collected the kettle, filled it and set it back on the stove.

"Nothing will help," Etienne sobbed.

The back door opened.

Curt and Manon came in, looking like shell-shocked refugees staggering away from a bomb blast. Hollis hadn't seen Curt for several months. Always an ectomorph, he was now skeleton-thin. His skin was grey. There were dark circles under his eyes. His tall frame stooped. Every feature on his face sagged. His thick, silvery mane stuck up in wild disarray. He stared at them, but not as if he really saw them. Finally, heavy-footed and deliberate, he headed to the cupboard above the refrigerator, reached up with shaking hands and pulled out a bottle of rum. Without turning, he said, "Who wants what to drink?"

Etienne ran to Manon, who remained beside the door as if she didn't have the will or energy to move any further. She hugged and rocked him like a much younger child. Tears streaked her makeup. "Nothing for me," she said.

"Dad, I don't want anything either. Are you going to tell Mom, or should I?" Tomas asked. He stood with his legs apart as if to steady himself on a rolling ship's deck.

Curt swung around, clutching the bottle. "My God, poor Lena." His gaze moved from one to another. "You don't know the worst."

"What could be worse than Ivan's death?" Hollis said almost to herself.

"Someone cut the brakes. Ivan was murdered."

TWO

Midmorning—Rhona Simpson sorted through her paperwork. She surreptitiously surveyed her environment—the Homicide Division of the Toronto Police Service headquarters on College Street. A year earlier, she'd left the Ottawa police. She wouldn't be sitting here now, the newest appointee to Homicide, had she not been a woman who knew the right people and had a Cree grandmother. Nevertheless it felt great. She'd work like hell to prove the appointment hadn't been a mistake.

"Join me for an early lunch? I have court this afternoon."

She looked up and met the gaze of Zee Zee, a tall, elegant black woman who'd introduced herself several days earlier. She could have been a princess or modelled for a Modigliani painting. The combination of elongated head, cropped hair, fine features and almost breastless body created a regal image. Her voice rose at the end of each sentence, making each statement into a question.

Food's siren call, morning, noon or night, she could never resist. "Love to."

Entering the cafeteria a little later, Zee Zee said, "I'm not sure who your Homicide partner will be."

Again the rising voice implying a question. She made you want to provide an answer. This vocal characteristic must be useful in interrogations.

"Before he or she is assigned, I'll fill you in on a few things you need to know," Zee Zee explained. She led them to a cafeteria table away from other officers. "No point in having to whisper," she said.

Should she agree? No, it had been a statement. Rhona looked down at her tray. She'd chosen a salad, tomato juice and black coffee. When she'd moved to Toronto, she'd resolved to do something about the weight collecting around her middle. Because she was short and compact, every extra pound showed immediately. Body types resembled apples or pears when it came to excess weight distribution—she was definitely an apple.

Zee Zee, who had selected cream of mushroom soup, an egg sandwich, apple pie and a soft drink, surveyed Rhona's tray. "Has the boss already given you his food lecture?"

"No, what is it?"

"He's a health food nut. Actually, Frank Braithwaite is one reason why we're having lunch—I'm sure you want the lowdown on his major and minor fixations? I expect because he was forced to take you, he's ready to give you a hard time. You'll need ammunition, won't you?"

Should she have come? Never a big fan of gossip, she wanted to tread carefully in her new workplace. No help for it; she was here.

"You're wondering why I'm doing this, and if you should find a reason to leave?"

"Either I'm transparent, or you're good at figuring people out."

"You found out in Ottawa that the *old boys'* police network is a powerful force?"

Rhona nodded. She was getting used to the woman's questioning voice.

"Don't you think it makes women police officers' jobs harder than they should be? I'm talking to you as an *old girl.*

You must agree that we need to hang together and help each other? That's why I'm filling you in. You'll need to recognize and avoid landmines."

Rhona grinned. "Sounds good—I'm all ears."

"First, you'll want to know about the boss? Frank is forty-three, and divorced. He's a university science grad and gung ho about technology—wants us to be Canada's most up-to-date police force. Don't tell him you have a hunch or a feeling about anything. It's all science and high tech with him."

Zee Zee sipped her drink. "Now you'll want to hear the interesting stuff that isn't in the records? It explains his fixations. His wife, a high-powered financial analyst, left him four years ago. No kids, so it should have been okay, but it wasn't. Bet you can't guess why?"

Rhona, who had gobbled her salad and still felt hungry, shook her head.

Zee Zee spooned up several mouthfuls of soup and munched a bite of sandwich. "No guesses?"

"No—tell me."

"His wife left without warning, at least that's what Frank says. Didn't she prop a note on the kitchen counter informing him she'd moved to Calgary? That would have been shocking, but okay, except she crated his dog, Bailey, and took him with her. Frank loved that dog. Did his wife know that and figure he wouldn't risk looking silly going to court to get the dog back? Probably, and it broke his heart. Hadn't he taken him to classes for obedience, retrieving and who knows what else, and entered him in field trial competitions? The dog's a retriever, and they do that." She smiled. "Believe me, being Ethiopian, I know zippo about dogs. But didn't Frank bore the hell out of us by giving every detail of his trials, tribulations and triumphs as he trained Bailey?"

"I sympathize. I have a cat, Opie. She's an overweight, neurotic pain in the butt, but I'd sure miss her. "

"He kept Bailey's photo on his desk for ages."

"So I shouldn't talk about dogs?"

"Or about older guys who live with young girls."

"How young?"

"Not jail bait—he *is* a police officer. Twenty-somethings. Blondes with start-up jobs and..."

"How do you know this?"

"Isn't my mother's best friend his cleaning lady? If you think cleaning women don't know what's going on, think again. Wouldn't we be smart to use them as undercover officers? Anyway, she says a young woman moves in and establishes herself as if she figures she's there for the long haul. She puts her health foods and vitamins in the kitchen, leaves her birth control pills in the bathroom and her yoga mat in the bedroom. Then, six months later, isn't she gone? Soon a new one, a clone of her predecessor, moves in."

"Weird."

"Isn't it? Who knows why he lives that way? Is he a misogynist? I suspect he is. I'm pretty sure he doesn't have any use for women police officers, although he's careful about what he says."

"Terrific. How do you cope?"

"Mostly, ignore his innuendos. Early on, didn't I let it be known that I'm prepared to file a grievance if I have cause? Does he want a black woman grieving? I don't think so. But, to be fair, results count for Frank. He would never permit his personal feelings to jeopardize a case's outcome." She shook her head. "Never." She pointed at Rhona's tray then at her own pie. "He's nuts about keeping fit and eating right. Whatever he's doing agrees with him. Isn't he a handsome guy, with that mop of brown hair and those green eyes?"

"Almost a pretty boy—he dresses like Mr. Preppy."

"I think you've identified one of his problems—he still considers himself a young preppy swinger. As I started to say, he has a thing about Tim Hortons. He despises the doughnut-eating cop stereotype. Don't ever suggest picking up anything there."

Rhona considered dumping sweetener in her coffee, but she'd read that every kind but Splenda pickled your brain. Hers needed all the help it could get. She was cultivating a love of black coffee but finding it difficult. "Thanks, I'll remember no dogs, no bimbos, no hunches and no doughnuts."

Zee Zee impaled a chunk of pie. She considered it. "Later I'll fill you in on the others. A good bunch, but not as enlightened as they should be."

"Since you're the source of all knowledge, what do you know about me?"

Zee Zee pushed her half-eaten pie to one side and leaned back. She tilted her head and contemplated Rhona. "Really want to know?"

After Rhona nodded, she held up her left hand, extended her left index finger and used her right index finger to tick off her points. "You left Ottawa because you didn't like the old boy network. Don't you have a First Nations grandmother who lives on a reserve somewhere in Ontario? You filed a complaint about references to squaws."

"It didn't do any good."

"You never know—won't whoever made the remark be more careful in the future? Anyway, to continue, you solved your last homicide case. You wear cowboy boots because you're short." She cocked her head to one side. "I have a thought. Do you think it's because you watched too many cowboy and Indian movies where the good guys, the cowboys, got to wear the boots?"

Rhona laughed. "No doubt you have a psychology degree?"

"To continue—you followed your boyfriend, who's with the Ontario Provincial Police, to Toronto. You've broken up with him. And you had luck and connections to get moved to Homicide."

Did she have no secrets? "Where did you find out all that information?"

"A constable's brother is with the Ottawa police."

"My turn," Rhona said.

"You want to hear why I'm a police officer—that's always the question," Zee Zee said. "I've told the story so often, I could recite it in my sleep. As a six-year-old Somalian refugee, didn't I come to Canada from one of the most lawless countries in the world? Although I was young, I've never forgotten what it was like to live without law and order." Her dark eyes clouded, and she seemed to be picturing something horrible. "I studied business at York University—I wanted to be a successful businesswoman. I opened a gallery to showcase African artists. The arts community and the buying public loved it, and I made money." She shook her head. "It wasn't very fulfilling." She clasped her hands together. "I thought that if I became a police officer, I could make a difference. In our community, women are not equal. I'm not ashamed to say I'm a role model—our women need them." She laughed. "Talk about touching speeches. Why aren't you mopping your eyes? Enough. Time to get back. Did I say that Frank's a stickler for promptness?"

Back at her desk, Rhona evaluated what she'd heard. Good to know about her boss. His aversion to Tim Hortons disturbed her—she depended on coffee and doughnut fixes. But she recognized that this was her big chance. Misogynist or not, she intended to prove she could do the job.

She surveyed her overflowing in-basket. Since her move to Homicide, she'd been assigned routine tasks. Many required filling out paper work. Although only thirty detectives worked Homicide, their case documentation in quadruplicate required one woman to do nothing but run the copying machine. The paperless society had not arrived.

Although she hated completing documentation, she knew it was necessary to do it and do it well. Years before, one bad experience in court had taught her the importance of record keeping. A defense lawyer had not only twisted her words but also suggested she might have had a questionable motive for not including all relevant information. She'd kept meticulous notes ever since.

"Got something for you." Frank Braithwaite dropped a file on her desk. "Your first case. Someone tampered with a young guy's motorcycle brakes and killed him. Hate to think what the poor bugger thought when he pumped the brakes and nothing happened. Must have been quick—he hit a loaded dump truck. Happened on Parliament Street. We're lucky the traffic guys saw that the brakes had been cut. Probably took a careful look when witnesses told them the guy didn't slow down. No skid marks either. After they saw the cuts, they called Homicide."

She hoped this would be a relatively uncomplicated case. The master board detailing each officer's cases recorded ongoing and solved crimes in different coloured marker. She didn't want her first case to remain unsolved for all to see. As if she had spoken aloud, Frank cocked his head to one side and regarded her quizzically.

"I'm pairing you with Zee Zee." Frank frowned. "Be interesting to find out how two *women* go about solving a crime—they don't often get a chance. But then, unless they have something special going for them, not many women are appointed homicide detectives. Certainly it will give you two the opportunity to show us what you can do."

She couldn't accuse him of hostility or prejudice but, although he stated facts, there was no mistaking his meaning. And what about this *you* and *us* stuff. They'd better do well, or he'd use their failure as an excuse to turf her out, special status or not.

Rhona reached for the file, although there wouldn't yet be much to read. She'd skim it before she dropped it in her large bag's side pocket. The bag did double and even triple duty as a briefcase, purse and a place to stash the tools of the trade. She made sure she had her notebook, tape recorder and cell phone.

Frank's gaze focused on the bag. "That has to be a weapon in itself. Better than a billy stick." His eyebrows rose. "Maybe it's something all our officers should have."

Was he joking, criticizing or merely commenting? From Zee Zee's rundown, she guessed his remark was designed to knock her slightly off base. She wouldn't play his game—she'd go for humour. "Definitely. It should be standard issue. I've used it to knock out more perps than you'd ever believe. It deserves its own citation."

Zee Zee, carrying her teapot, emerged from the duplicating room which doubled as the department's food and coffee preparation centre. Frank beckoned her to join them. He related the case's details without innuendo or underlying messages.

Interesting. Why had he directed his snide comments at her? Maybe because there hadn't been a witness. Or perhaps he'd had previous run-ins with Zee Zee and knew enough to leave her alone. After he left, she repeated his remark to Zee Zee.

"He's thrown down the gauntlet." Zee Zee offered tea before she filled her own mug. "Can we solve this one brilliantly and in a hurry?" She raised an eyebrow. "Shouldn't be a problem. Aren't we twice as smart?"

"Undoubtedly."

Zee Zee parked her tea pot, checked to make sure she had everything she needed and nodded toward the door. "First things first. We'll interview the family."

On Winchester, they parked and walked to the Hartmans' house. Before they entered, they stopped and looked at the front yard.

"Two more Harleys?" Zee Zee said, although the evidence sat on the front yard parking pad.

"They look the same to me," Hollis said.

"They're probably different years, but it would be hard to tell them apart. I wonder if Ivan's was the same? And check out the parking spot—looks like it's had a new coat of asphalt recently?" Zee Zee reached for her cell. "Time to get the techies here. We'll cordon it off and check for fingerprints on the pad and the other bikes."

Three

Murdered—the word expanded to fill the Hartmans' kitchen.

Hollis knew her face must look as blank-faced and wide-eyed, as the others did.

Tomas shuddered and crushed his empty beer can. "Murdered! Ivan. Why? Who would kill Ivan?"

The metallic crunch. Magnified a thousand times. Spilled oil and gas and blood. She hoped it had been quick, that he hadn't suffered.

"The police will figure it out," Manon said.

"Never mind the police. *I* want to know. What was going on in my brother's life? What was he doing? What had he done? Why? Why would someone kill him?" Tomas stabbed his finger at Curt. "You must know."

Curt, grey-faced, gulped his rum and plunked the empty glass down. He ran both his hands through his hair and shook his head. "You're right. I should, but I don't. Ivan and I haven't talked much lately. He was aware of what I thought of his dead end job and lack of ambition. He avoided me." His dark eyes narrowed. "But don't blame me. You're his brother—what did *you* talk about?"

Etienne leaned against his mother. He sniffled. "*I* was his brother too. I loved him. He played cards with me and made terrific chocolate chip cookies."

Manon tightened her grip. "And he loved *you.*"She released one hand to stroke his dark hair.

"Give me a break—I just got home this week—how would I know? Even when I lived here, he never hung out with me." Tomas's shoulders rose, and his chin lifted. "I asked him sometimes. I did. But he turned me down." His shoulders slumped. "Jesus, I probably didn't know him as well as Etienne. What did he do for fun? Who were his friends? I don't know." Tomas's lean, hawk-like face twisted. He collapsed on a chair with his head in his hands. "And I feel really bad about it," he said in a thick voice.

Nadine, crying softly, brought the teapot, sugar, milk and cups to the kitchen table. "Tea?" she asked.

Manon, Etienne and Tomas nodded.

"Two spoonfuls of sugar for everyone," Hollis directed.

Several moments of silence broken by clinking spoons and Etienne's muffled sobs

Manon encircled Etienne with an arm as they drank their tea. Clearly her priority was *her* son.

Hollis wasn't family. Should she leave? At least make herself scarce while they digested the news. She shifted and rose.

"Hollis, don't go. We need you. You've experienced this. What happens now?" Manon said.

Hollis sank back. "Police officers will come and talk to everyone. They'll go through Ivan's things searching for evidence."

Tomas lifted his head. "Dad, if the police haven't told Mom, you *have* to do it. I could, but it should be you. And you should go *now,* right now, before there's anything on radio or TV."

Curt, who'd refilled his glass, took a long swallow. "You're right. I told the officers at Sunnybrook that I would." He grimaced. "False courage. Lena will blame me." His lips set in a straight line. "Maybe she should blame ambulance dispatch.

Why in God's name did they take him to Sunnybrook? Downtown hospitals have trauma units. Anyway, no matter what the police say, Lena will blame me."

As if on cue, the doorbell rang. Nadine answered and brought two police officers into the kitchen.

Impossible.

Hollis recognized Rhona Simpson, the Ottawa detective who'd been in charge of her husband's murder case. Rhona looked equally surprised.

Hollis recovered first. "Detective Simpson, you've transferred to Toronto?"

Rhona introduced Zee Zee and added, "I investigated Ms Grant's husband's murder a year ago. It was my last Ottawa case." She nodded to Hollis. "The world grows smaller and smaller." She directed her next remark to Curt. "You're Ivan Hartman's father."

"I am." Curt introduced everyone else.

"Sorry to intrude on your grief. If you can manage it, we'd like to ask questions. Time is important," Zee Zee said.

"Perhaps we should move to the living room," Manon said. Propelling Etienne ahead of her, she led the way.

Zee Zee took notes while Rhona conducted the interview. "I understand your son didn't live with you all the time? Any idea where he was going?" Rhona asked Curt.

"None. Not to work. He works..." Curt's eyes widened. He swallowed as if a large foreign object were stuck in his throat, "Worked, at the Buy Right Superstore on St. Clair. If he was going south on Parliament Street, he wasn't going there."

"He also worked for Catering Plus. I have their phone number but not their address," Manon said.

"Did he have alcohol or drug problems?"

"Of course not," Curt said. His gaze and Manon's flicked to Tomas and away again.

Zee Zee made a note.

"Was he worried about anything? Depressed?"

"Are you implying he cut his own brakes?" Curt bristled.

Rhona held up her hand. "I'm not implying anything— these are routine questions. Did he belong to a gang?"

"Not Hell's Angels, if that's what you're suggesting. No, not a member of any gang."

"Any trouble with the police?"

Curt shook his head.

"We found a current student card from George Brown College in his wallet. Which campus was he at, and what was he studying?"

"George Brown," Curt repeated. He frowned. "I didn't know he was studying anything." He addressed Manon and Tomas. "Do you know?"

They shook their heads.

"I do," Etienne said.

He had everyone's attention.

Etienne managed a smile, although his eyes were swollen and his nose was running. "He was taking cooking. He was going to be a chef. He had a big white hat and everything."

"We might have guessed," Manon said. "But why didn't he tell us? Why is Etienne the only one who knows this?"

Rhona addressed Etienne. "George Brown has several locations around Toronto. Do you know which campus he was at?"

Etienne thought for a moment. "You know the big castle on the hill? He told me that every time he passed it, he thought of me. He promised to take me there in my summer holidays."

"Good work. The Casa Loma campus." She turned to Curt. "Was Ivan's bike the same as the other two parked outside?"

Curt nodded. "Different years."

"Please don't use either bike. We'll test them and the pad for prints. We'll have more questions later. What about Ivan's room—we'd like to check it out."

"My room is there too. We share the third floor," Tomas said.

"Please come up and remove whatever you'll need for a few days. We'll secure the site until we finish our investigation. After we've spoken to Ivan's mother, we'll be back to make a thorough room check and ask follow-up questions," Rhona said.

"I told the police at the hospital I'd tell Ivan's mother, my ex-wife, Lena Kalma. If you're finished with the questions, I'll go and get it over with," Curt said.

"We'll give you time before we call on her. Please tell her not to touch anything in his room until we've checked it out."

Curt headed towards the front door.

"Papa, they said that you aren't supposed to ride your bike. Even if you could, I don't think you should," Etienne said.

"What?"

"You have a bike like Ivan's—I don't want anything to happen to you."

"My God, out of the mouths of babes." Manon's hand rose and briefly covered her lips. Her eyes wide she said, "It's true. Maybe whoever did this terrible thing didn't intend to kill Ivan. Maybe it's a serial killer, and he plans to kill all of us." She looked like she'd like to ratchet each word back into her mouth.

Rhona sighed. Too much television. Serial killers were rare, although to watch crime shows you'd think one lurked around every corner. The killer *might* have got the wrong victim, but there'd be time to talk about that later. "Serial killings are rare. This certainly doesn't look like one. I think you can put the thought right out of your mind," Rhona said reassuringly.

* * *

"They didn't know much about him, did they?" Zee Zee said while Rhona navigated across the city. "I wonder if it's because they're Anglo-Saxon?"

"Would your family be different?"

"I'll say. Family and clan are important for us. Are they too important? A good question. Family is one reason Somalia is such a mess. Everyone belongs to a clan and defines himself that way." She sighed. "Clans are forever at war with each other. It's feudal, never ending and may never improve. Are strong family attachments bad? Is Anglo Saxon reserve and refusal to get involved in other's lives a good thing? Are there definitive answers? I don't think so."

"Did feuding force you to leave?"

A long silence. Rhona glanced at Zee Zee.

"Sorry. It's a painful subject. My father was an Ethiopian Christian physician. The rebels killed him and my brothers because of their beliefs. My mother and I escaped and lived in a refugee camp for two years. Finally one of my mother's brothers sponsored us to emigrate here. We do have tightly knit families. For example, our single women, no matter how old they are, do not live alone. I'm thirty-five, but because I'm unmarried, I live with my mother. I can tell you she knows a thousand times more about me and everyone in our extended family than Ivan Hartman's family knew about him. There's no way I'd be studying at George Brown without her knowing all about it. And my mother isn't particularly inquisitive—it's the way we are."

"I'm sorry to hear what happened to you. It's hard to imagine." She meant the murder, not the extended family. Rhona's own clan played a large part in her life.

"Even harder to live," Zee Zee said. "Maybe Ivan's mother will have more to tell us?"

She clearly wanted to change the subject. And who

wouldn't? They agreed it was Zee Zee's turn to interview.

Rhona drove south then west to the far reaches of Queen Street. In her first months in the city, she'd read dozens of books about Toronto and memorized the gazetteer. She sometimes amused herself by thinking about passing the cabbies' test if police work didn't pan out. She not only knew streets but also had familiarized herself with the characteristics of neighbourhoods.

Lena lived in South Parkdale, a run-down district with few trendy bars and boutiques. Investors and home buyers considered it an iffy neighbourhood for two reasons. First, because of its proximity to 999 Queen Street, the mental hospital. Secondly, because the conversion of many large homes into warehousing rooming houses for the mentally ill and down-and-out had populated the streets with frightening people.

Lena Kalma lived in a former store on Queen Street. Two display windows flanked a glass-fronted door from which she'd removed all hardware. She'd painted almost everything vermillion, wood and glass alike. The exception—each window and the door had a shoebox-sized unpainted glass rectangle located at the average person's eye level. Underneath she'd stencilled the word "LOOK" in white.

Naturally, they did.

She'd affixed boxes to the other side of the unpainted glass rectangles. A colour diorama filled the first one. Somehow, inside the small space, she'd created an illusion of great depth. Far in the distance, an ambiguous tiny figure, arms uplifted, screamed in terror or ecstasy. The second box contained a foreground unisex face pressing against the glass. A viewer could read its enigmatic expression as horror or jubilation. The third box's black interior held the white floating word "oh". Nothing made immediate sense but challenged a viewer to provide her own explanation.

Rhona stepped back. "As if this neighbourhood's residents don't have enough problems. Now they have peepholes in blood red windows to make them question their sanity." She grinned at her partner. "If I had to, I'd make a wild guess that an artist lives here."

Since the centre door lacked a doorknob, they moved to the bright red door next to the storefront. Zee Zee lifted her hand to press the bell. Before she touched it, the door opened a crack and a tall woman peered at them.

"I've been waiting," she said, hovering behind the partially open door. She wore a white coverall and head scarf. A surgical mask dangled on her chest. Her red-rimmed eyes stared at them balefully.

After Rhona and Zee Zee identified themselves, Zee Zee said, "You're Lena Kalma?"

"Yes," the woman said, widening the opening and allowing them inside. Stairs climbed from the small hall.

"Follow me," she ordered and passed through a doorway into the storefront's front room. Here the opaque paint on windows and door allowed no natural light inside. Overhead fluorescents illuminated chaos. Tiers of stacked containers teetered and threatened to topple. Rusty buckets, feather boas, old clothes from a dozen ethnic groups—an eclectic mix—swung from ceiling racks. A stew of smells defied cataloguing—old leather, dust, sweat and stale air. Lena tacked through the room and wove down the hall through the labyrinth of cartons. One or two stacks climbed upward and scraped the ceiling.

"Wouldn't the fire department be unhappy?" Zee Zee murmured. "Isn't this house a four alarm waiting to happen?"

Low wattage wall sconces lit their way. Finally they emerged into a large room. Dazzling late afternoon June light flooded through floor to ceiling windows. Although not as crowded as the front room or the hall, a host of unrelated objects hung on the white walls. Magenta, ochre, indigo, fluorescent orange—Rhona's eyes flitted from object to object. Possibly the room contained something made from every natural and unnatural colour. It pulsed with energy. Hundreds of photos littered three tables ranged along one side. Lena indicated that they should sit on one of the four straight chairs lined up as if they'd entered a doctor's waiting room.

Rhona chose the one burdened with the smallest pile. She carefully lifted off a tricorn hat, three art books and a Mexican *serape* before she lowered herself to the lime green and orange-striped chair. Zee Zee gingerly removed a nest of fifties style Pyrex mixing bowls topped with an actual bird's nest before she sat down. While the detectives cleared space for themselves, Lena tipped miscellaneous items from a short antique wooden bench and pulled it over to face them. Before she sat down, she pointed to the tables.

"I can't stand doing nothing. I feel so helpless." She frowned, "I'd like to run out and kill Ivan's murderer." She sniffed. "Don't worry. Since I can't do that, I'm going back through all my photos and making a photo collage of Ivan's life."

"I'm sorry for your loss and apologize for intruding on your grief, but we need to talk to you about Ivan. Tell us about his life, his friends, his enemies, that kind of thing," Zee Zee said.

"Enemies." Lena thrust her head forward. "He didn't have enemies. You have to piss people off to have enemies. Ivan specialized in niceness. He should have told his father to go to hell. Should have lived with me. I loved him. His father didn't." Her voice shook, and her lower lip trembled.

"He did live here sometimes, didn't he?"

Lena bit her lip to regain control. "Not recently."

"When did he leave?"

Lena straightened and contemplated them like a predator considering tasty prey. "If you can imagine, he accused *me*, his mother, of prying. He said he wasn't going to live where his personal life wasn't private." She crossed her arms on her chest. "Private!" Her voice skidded up the scale to high C. "I *am* his mother."

"Did he move out because of something specific?"

"That's none of your business. It has *nothing* to do with his murder."

"We decide information's relevancy. Please tell us."

"He *said* I read his emails."

"Did you?"

Her eyes didn't quite meet theirs. "I might have happened to touch some key or other and seen it."

Zee Zee said nothing. The silence stretched and expanded.

Finally, Lena said, "I wanted to find out why he spent so much time in his room."

"And, what did you discover?"

"He didn't save many emails," she said defensively.

Rhona didn't buy this. More likely Lena had erased ones she didn't like, and that's how Ivan had found out what she was doing.

"We'll have a look at his computer."

"Good luck. He took it. Maybe it's at his father's house."

They hadn't seen a computer or a laptop in his apartment. They'd have to follow up on this lead. "Show us his room, but first tell us about his problems with his father?"

"His father was the be-all and end-all for Ivan. He craved Curt's love and approval."

"Did he tell you he was going to George Brown College?"

"I knew *nothing*, and I was his mother. He told me nothing, shut me out of his life. I only wanted the best for him. Why do sons do that? Tomas doesn't tell me anything either." Lena jerked to her feet, sending the bench crashing. She didn't pick it up. Instead, she motioned to them to follow her. "Come upstairs. I guarantee that his room will tell you nothing." She pointed at them. "Nothing. I keep using that word. My son was a mystery—a big zero—a nothing." She strode from the room.

They followed her upstairs and along a hall to the only door that sported an unlocked padlock dangling from a latch.

"Is the lock new?"

"He installed it a week before he left." She straightened. "Of course I had to intervene. In case of fire, I *insisted* on having a key."

Which rather defeated the purpose. No wonder he'd moved out.

The room resembled a monk's cell.

"Please don't come in here or allow anyone else to do so until we've checked everything out." Rhona said.

"Help yourself. If you find anything that tells you about my son, it will surprise me." Lena nodded dismissively. "Poor Ivan. Whoever killed him deserves to suffer pain like he did. Can you imagine his panic, his horror when he realized his brakes wouldn't work? We don't execute killers any more—maybe we should. Or maybe we should mete out justice ourselves." Her eyes narrowed. "I'm capable of doing that. I would enjoy watching his killer suffer like my poor boy did. You'd better find him before I do, or don't hold me responsible for what I'll do."

Four

After they'd spoken to Lena, Rhona and Zee Zee returned to the Hartmans' to interview each family member individually. They began with Curt. He escorted them to the family room, casually furnished in yellow and cream. A bowl of red apples on the glass and brass coffee table added a splash of colour. Inside, he positioned himself beside a wing chair upholstered in mustard yellow corduroy and waved them to the sofa.

Rhona knew better. She was too short. The sofa would suck her down like quicksand or leave her perched uncertainly, unable to lean back because of the seat's depth. A leather desk chair on casters provided an alternative. She rolled it to face Curt. Zee Zee, close to six feet tall and in no danger of being mired in the sofa, relaxed against the cushions and prepared to make notes.

"Have you identified any of Ivan's enemies?" Rhona said.

"No. Or friends either. He was a lone wolf." He shrugged. "Not a true wolf—that implies strength and fierceness. He had neither—he was a loner." He extended his legs and examined his shoes before he said, "I like my house shipshape. Like it to run well. No upsets. On an even keel." He smiled faintly. "I'm a sailor. Nautical terms explain things. Until now, Ivan never rocked the boat."

Sounded like navy or army boot camp. The house revolved around Curt and his needs, and he resented the rough water stirred up by his son's murder. Talk about egocentric.

"We're covering all bases. Because you had similar motorcycles, you or your son Tomas may have been the intended victim. Can you name anyone with a motive to kill you?"

"Me?" His mouth curved into a sardonic smile. "I expect many people would like me dead. Whether anyone would do it—that's an interesting question."

"Mr. Hartman, this isn't a game. Someone killed your son in a horrible, premeditated way. If you were the intended victim, he or she may try again. We need to work quickly. Give me names."

"My ex-partner, Arthur White, and my ex-wife, Lena Kalma, both hate me. Sometimes Arthur hangs around, muttering threats."

"Have you reported him?" Zee Zee said, looking up from her notebook.

"I don't take him seriously. Arthur's a zealot. Once he clamps onto a subject, he hangs on like a pit bull until something else comes along. I figure he'll eventually move on."

Zee Zee shook her head but said nothing. Stalking was a crime, and stalkers were to be taken seriously. They seldom shed their obsessions.

"I'll add the SOHD opponents to the hate list. They harass me with abusive phone calls." His eyebrows rose. "On occasion, the caller has threatened to do more. They never say kill, they say *remove, destroy*—words like that."

"SOHD?"

"Stamp Out Hereditary Diseases. I'm local chapter president." He moved into lecture mode. "We want to reduce numbers in hospital by eliminating hereditary diseases. We lobby for government money to educate people to voluntarily take genetic testing and not have babies if they carry hereditary

34

disease genes. Our opponents, the same people who oppose abortion, think it's like playing God." He ran his hand through his silvery hair and turned slightly as if displaying his best side to the camera. "Because I'm known to be good with media, I've become their spokesperson."

"Thank you—we'll follow up on those leads, and we'll have more questions." Despite his speech, he looked exhausted. "But that's enough for tonight. We'll talk to Tomas now."

Tomas knocked before he came in. He was taller than his father. His red-rimmed eyes and clenched jaw reflected his stress.

"I'm sorry about your brother. What can you tell me about him and about you?" Rhona said.

"Not enough. I feel awful." He pulled a wad of soggy tissue from his pocket, blew his nose and apologized as he sat down. "Dad says you want information about me in case the killer tampered with the wrong bike."

"It is a possibility."

His features relaxed. Maybe it felt better to hear suspicions validated.

"You want to hear if I have enemies—if I belong to Hell's Angels or deal dope." He shrugged. "I did do drugs at thirteen. They busted me." His eyebrows rose. "You can imagine my father's reaction—major league anger. Not about me. About *him* and *his* reputation. Everything's always about *him*. I ended up with a warning. The old man—ever since I saw *Cat on a Hot Tin Roof,* I think of him as Big Daddy—wanted me in detox." His eyes brightened. "Thank God for my stepmother. She intervened. Told him she'd handle everything." He stopped and frowned. "It isn't a secret, but I don't know if she's told you that she has problems with depression."

"Not yet," Zee Zee said.

"Well, it's true. She'd learned from firsthand experience

how much better you feel if you exercise hard. I was a good swimmer—she encouraged me to become a competitive swimmer." He leaned forward and spoke with intensity, "For years, years, she drove me to swimming practice at five a.m., even though she had Etienne and a full-time job." He smiled. "I suppose you don't hear much praise for stepmoms, but Manon has always cared about me and Ivan."

His smile disappeared. "My dad is great if you're doing fine. We sail and bike and have fun. He's no use if you have problems. But you want names of anyone who might have it in for me." He shrugged. "I came home from the University of New Brunswick last week. I don't have a girlfriend right now. I don't think I've seriously pissed anyone off. When I asked myself if anyone wanted me dead, I didn't come up with a name, but I'll keep thinking." He met her gaze. "It's not a happy thought that whoever did it made a mistake and still wants to murder me or my dad. I promise I *will* think about every single person I've ever met. If I hit on a name, I'll call you. Believe me I will."

"Now tell us about Ivan. Who did he hang around with?" Rhona didn't expect Tomas to know but had to cover the ground.

"In high school, no one special. He wasn't victimized, bullied, nothing like that, but he didn't have close friends. He liked girls, but he was shy—he had bad acne in high school. At Christmas when I came home, I saw a big difference in him—he smiled a lot and whistled. When I commented he shrugged and gave me a platitude."

"You have no idea what brought about this character change?"

"None."

"Did he always like cooking?"

"Forever. He was really good."

"Do you know where his computer is?"

"His computer? No."

Rhona thanked Tomas and asked to see Ivan and Tomas's apartment. Upstairs, they slipped on gloves before they opened drawers and examined cupboards and book shelves. In case they needed anything fingerprinted, they made sure not to contaminate the scene. Ivan didn't have many personal mementos. The one photo in his room pictured Etienne as a toddler splashing in the bathtub.

Zee Zee plucked it from the shelf. "Is this the room's single photo because he loved his brother, or because it was the only child's photograph he could legitimately display?"

"It's horrible when you have to ask questions like that. It's a wonder all cops aren't total cynics," Rhona said.

Heavy cookbooks and photo albums crammed particle board bookshelves that sagged under their weight. Ivan had filed hundreds of recipes in photo album pockets intended for 4x6 pictures. This storage system was new to Rhona. If she ever found time to cook in a serious way, she'd remember.

In one album, she found a card with fellow students' names and phone numbers. She'd faxed George Brown earlier for class lists. "We need his cell phone number to check his calls," Rhona said, showing the card to Zee Zee, who stood at Ivan's desk sorting through the papers in the file drawer.

"He designated one for bills." Zee Zee extracted a red folder and thumbed through it. "Here they are. We'll go back a couple of months and track them. Wasn't he a tidy young man? I wish I kept my records in such good order." She straightened up and allowed her glance to sweep the room. "If his computer isn't here and isn't at his mother's, where is it?"

"At his mother's, I wondered about child pornography.

Maybe that's why he locked the door. Maybe when he figured she was reading his email, he took his computer and left home?"

"I had the same thought. It might provide motivation for his murder. We'll run his name through the records in the sex crimes unit."

"We have to find the computer. Before we leave here, we'll see if anyone can tell us."

Rhona waved the card listing students' names. "Some students may come to the visitations or attend the funeral—we'll talk to them." She considered the card. "In the meantime, we'll match names with phone numbers and call the ones he spoke to most frequently."

*   *   *

"Absolutely no idea," Curt said when asked about the computer's whereabouts as they were leaving.

They talked outside as they headed for the car. "We have a lot to check—Ivan's mystery life, Curt's enemies—the list grows ever longer," Rhona said.

"Not much we can do about Ivan's life tonight. If SOHD's opponents are the same people as the anti-abortionists, I've run into them before. They allegedly murdered an abortion clinic doctor. I say *allegedly,* because the police never pinned it on them—the killing remains unsolved. If it's the same lot, we shouldn't underestimate them—those men and women are dangerous. As for Arthur White..." Zee Zee's voice trailed off.

"Should we talk to him tonight?"

"Why not? It's not late. Our appearance on his doorstep may unsettle him enough that he unintentionally reveals something. I'll interview. I knew him years ago in my other life."

Rhona found a parking spot close to Arthur White's

apartment, a low rise near the intersection of St. Clair Avenue and Yonge Street. Ten thirty. It took a second and then a third push on the bell before a squeaky voice responded and buzzed them inside.

The elevator, shabby but clean, smelled like dogs, incontinent dogs. On the fifth floor, dim light and threadbare stained carpeting left an impression of genteel poverty. Halfway down the hall, a diminutive man with a halo of white curls awaited them. They followed him into a half-furnished apartment. Lighter coloured spaces on the wallpaper indicated where paintings had hung. In the living room, two upholstered chairs huddled on the bare floor. A darker wood rectangle in the room's centre acted like the carpet that must once have been there.

"She took everything that belonged to her family, and half the things we'd bought together," Arthur explained and grimaced. "She insisted on scrupulous fairness—I'll give her that." He nodded at the two chairs and collected a metal kitchen stool for himself. Perched on it, he hooked his feet around the rungs.

"We're here to talk to you about Ivan and Curt Hartman." Zee Zee indicated the recorder. "We'll have to tape what you say."

Curt peered at her. "Don't I know you?" He considered. "I do. You ran the Horn of Plenty Gallery—wonderful African art and textiles—wonderful things." He frowned. "And I heard you did well. Why would you give that up for a police career?"

"You have a good memory. It doesn't have any bearing on why we're here, but I'll tell you that although I succeeded, I wanted to do more with my life. But this isn't about me. Tell us about Curt Hartman?"

"Curt—that bastard." The little man's face folded in on itself, and he scowled.

"What happened between you and Mr. Hartman?"

"It's not complicated. I represented him, sold his work everywhere." He shifted on his uncomfortable-looking seat. "I considered him my friend. We owned a sailboat together. When he was married to Lena Kalma, the four of us went sailing in the Caribbean." He paused, as if remembering a pleasant holiday.

Zee Zee didn't interrupt.

"A few years ago, he left me for a bigger, more prestigious gallery in Yorkville." Arthur crossed to a half-empty bookcase, plucked a well-thumbed volume from the bottom shelf and waved it at Zee Zee. "Curt's biography—have you read it?"

"Not yet."

"He *says* I ripped him off." Arthur exhaled dismissively. "Can you imagine he'd make a charge like that after the years we worked together?" His shoulders sagged. "My gallery went bankrupt last year after this book came out. Artists removed their paintings." He shrugged. "You can't run a gallery without work to sell. I'm suing him for defamation. Even if I win, it won't restore my gallery or bring my wife back." His voice thickened and tears threatened. "They were my life," he quavered.

"Your wife left at the same time?"

He pulled a large, none-too-clean handkerchief from his pocket and wiped his eyes. "And took half my assets and..." he waved at the apartment, "half of everything." He sniffed. "I can't offer you a decent cup of coffee, not that anyone drinks coffee at this hour. She grabbed the coffee maker. Now I'm reduced to drinking instant; I won't offer that vile beverage to anyone."

"Did you know Ivan?"

"Not as well as Tomas, who loved sailing with us, even as a very little boy. Ivan never came. Apparently he threw up even if the water was mirror-calm, not that you sail if it is. But you get my drift. He wasn't comfortable on Lake Ontario. A big wading pool probably makes him nauseous. A nice young man. Too bad about him."

There was no sorrow in his voice; it was a perfunctory thing to say.

Zee Zee pulled one of her cards from her black book and scribbled something on it. "We may be back. In the interim, go to the nearest police station and have your fingerprints taken."

"You have to be kidding?"

"We're not. It's routine in a murder investigation for those who might be involved. And we'll want proof of your whereabouts in the hours before the murder."

"Well, you won't get any, because I don't have any. I was alone. I'm always alone."

He walked them to the door, shaking his head and muttering under his breath.

Back in the car, Rhona pulled away from the curb. "Arthur certainly has reason to hate Curt. Could he kill him? It's a good question. He definitely warrants a second interview." Rhona drove them back to headquarters, where they split up, picked up their own cars and headed home. Cruising up Yonge Street toward her apartment, Rhona considered Toronto air. Almost midnight, and it remained chokingly thick and oppressive. Why hadn't someone warned her about summer air pollution?

Back in her shabby apartment, she stripped off her working outfit, her tailored and now crushed black linen pantsuit, perspiration-stained silk blouse and black cowboy boots and tossed them toward her unmade bed.

Opie, her oversize tortoiseshell cat, vocalizing his

displeasure at his long, boring day, stalked around her legs. Then he batted at her without sheathing his claws. He didn't like the new apartment either, and she didn't blame him. For the same price she'd paid for her spacious Ottawa townhouse, they rented a cramped one-bedroom apartment. Probably built on the cheap right after World War Two, it had concrete walls, window air-conditioners unequal to their task and mold in the bathroom fan outlet.

Right now, mold or not, a shower was the answer. Then she'd treat herself to a vodka martini. She couldn't solve the crime tonight, unless her unconscious worked overtime and woke her at dawn with a brilliant insight.

Rhona, after a night of broken sleep, woke at first light, shortly after five, found the Advil and gulped two. Once the pills began working, she attended to the one domestic chore she could no longer postpone—she cleaned the cat's litter box. That task completed, she offered Opie an extra-special breakfast of tinned tuna, filled his water bowl and topped up his cat kibble, knowing how much he'd resent it. He condescended to eat dry food only if he believed starvation threatened.

Domestic duties done, she luxuriated under the shower. Two good things about her apartment were strong water pressure and a large shower head. By six thirty, she'd dressed in a blue seersucker pantsuit, navy blouse and black cowboy boots, eaten a bagel and made coffee. She poured herself a rejuvenating mug before she filled a thermos. Since Frank disapproved of coffee shop stops, she'd brew her own and haul it to work.

*   *   *

"I thought you'd arrive early." Zee Zee greeted her at seven and pointed to Frank's office. "We didn't beat him, but we're here and ready to roll. Let's dig into the data bank and identify SOHD's opponents? If they're the same anti-abortionists I know, we'll find two names I've dealt with before—Barney Evans and Allie Jones."

Minutes later, she reported to Rhona. "Barney's out on parole after serving time for assaulting a police officer. I'm still steamed because we couldn't convict him in the Oshawa doctor's murder." She clenched her jaw. "I'd love to put him away."

"What about the woman?"

"Allie's got a sheet as well. Mostly from protests and demonstrations where she attacked police officers or resisted arrest. She presents herself as a sweet, neatly-groomed woman who stays at home baking apple pies. But if you've ever seen her face when she's picketing an abortion clinic, you realize what a front that is. She's vicious and single-minded—she says she'll do anything to stop abortions. Don't underestimate her."

"Lovely. Which one do you want to interview?"

"Barney. We'll go now."

The parole office provided Barney's current Port Credit address. While she drove, Rhona reviewed what she'd read about the community. Port Credit had once been a working class suburban district where small houses crowded around now-deserted factories, mute reminders of Canada's past manufacturing history. Rail lines ran through the area, and Lake Ontario wasn't far away. They pulled up in front of a tiny clapboard house. A mowed lawn and unadorned front porch neither repelled nor invited.

"Barney Evans?" Zee Zee said to the woman who peered at them through the screen.

"Not again," she grumbled and shouted, "It's them again, Barney." Her lips turned down. "You might as well come in—you will anyway. He'll be along. Don't think he's up. He may

43

brush his teeth." She shrugged. "Or not. I'm making strawberry jam. Went to the pick-it-yourself place yesterday." She disappeared into the back.

"I didn't think we wore signs on our foreheads," Rhona murmured.

"Not for most people—but don't you think that if you've had a number of brushes with police, you develop a sixth sense?" Zee Zee answered quietly.

In the small hall, wallpapered in a grey, narrow stripe, an overhead light with a smoked glass shade cast little light. Rhona untangled the odours assaulting her nose. Boiling jam almost, but not quite, cancelled stale cigarette smoke, cat pee, rotting wood and rancid fat.

"She could have moved us to the front room or the kitchen," Rhona complained, concentrating on breathing shallowly.

As if she'd heard her comment, Mrs. Evans, if that's who she was, poked her head out of the kitchen. "Sit in the living room," she ordered and returned to her jam.

They did and set up the tape recorder alongside a flickering soundless TV.

"Maybe he's having a shower?" Rhona said as minutes passed. She leaned toward Zee Zee and away from an overflowing brown glass ashtray sitting on a chrome stand. "Could we do this outside? I may throw up."

"Poor little cop," a voice said.

The man in the doorway would not have drawn attention in a crowd. He had a small quantity of sandy hair pulled across his forehead, pale, pasty freckled skin and a slightly overweight, paunchy body. If you disliked pigs, you would describe him as porcine.

"You again," he said to Zee Zee. "What is it this time? Seems to me you didn't do too well last time," he smirked.

44

"We're recording this interview," Zee Zee said. "We're here to talk to you about Curt Hartman."

"That asshole."

"Do you belong to the anti-SOHD group?"

"It's not an organized group."

"What does that mean?"

"We don't have meetings."

"How do you decide when to picket, protest, whatever you do?"

The man's small eyes squinched. "Where you guys been—email, of course."

"And why do you oppose SOHD?"

"Give me a break. Genetic testing. Killing those who aren't acceptable. SOHD—it's another justification for abortion. I'm not giving you the spiel—you know what we think." His pudgy hands clenched. "We're prepared to wipe them off the face of the earth." He nodded at the tape recorder. "You can record that—wipe them and their people from the face of the earth."

Zee Zee shook her head. "What happened to allowing individual expression of opinion? Freedom of speech. Is that only for those who agree with you?"

"I'm not arguing with cops." Barney folded his arms over his stomach.

"Where were you on Sunday night?"

"You're crying in the dark, lady. Right here." He slapped the stained velour sofa, releasing a dusty cloud. "Right here with the old lady, sippin' a few brews and watchin' TV until we sacked out. I never went out."

"And your wife will confirm that?"

Barney smirked. "Of course."

"We'd like to see your computer. Your emails sound interesting."

"My computer. What the fuck?" Whatever he'd expected them to say, it clearly hadn't been this. His eyes darted to the next room, where a laptop sat on a table amid a drift of paper.

"A laptop—that makes our job easier. We can take it with your permission or wait here until the warrant arrives. Up to you." Zee Zee stared into his tiny little eyes.

Barney sucked his teeth, a revolting sound. He appeared to be mentally reviewing his files. "Take it."

"Password?"

Forms filled out, Rhona tucked the computer under her arm.

"We'll copy anything we need," Zee Zee said.

"I'm sure. Don't forget how well you did last time," he said mockingly.

"Charming fellow. I assume we have his fingerprints," Rhona said when they were back in the car.

"Isn't he? Yes, we do. You'll enjoy Allie even more," Zee Zee promised. "She lives downtown in a very nice apartment on King Street. There's a psychiatric term for people like her, but I can't remember exactly what it is. They're perfectly normal unless you mention the one subject they're fanatical about."

The complex on King combined townhouses with two apartment towers. They parked and walked toward the second tower. Young people in their twenties flowed in and out.

"Isn't this a funny place for a middle-aged woman to live?"

"Not really. She proselytizes whenever possible. Many single young women live here."

Once buzzed inside, they shot up to the tenth floor and walked along the hall toward the woman who stood outside her door waiting for them.

At nine o'clock on a hot Tuesday morning in June, Allie wore stockings, Cuban heeled sandals and a shirtwaist dress with pearls around her neck. She might have been setting out for a tea party or, had she worn a hat, to one of Queen Elizabeth's garden parties. Over-lavish and dated makeup along with blonde hair teased and sprayed to encase her head like a helmet completed the picture. Her face revealed her age. Pouches under her eyes, drooping jaw and deep lines bracketing her mouth told their tale.

"Two women detectives, how nice. Do come in?" she invited. She didn't seem surprised. Barney must have phoned and warned her to expect a visit.

Chintz enveloped the living room from top to bottom and end to end. Every mahogany tabletop sported Royal Doulton figurines of women with blowing skirts. An overpowering scent of air freshener with an underlying suggestion of bleach identified a passion for cleanliness.

"Let me bring you tea," she said in a light, trilling voice.

She must have had everything prepared. It wasn't more than a minute before she returned, carrying a silver tray with almost translucent china tea cups, a highly polished silver pot, hot water jug, cream, sugar, a plate of lemon slices and another of cookies.

They waited while she fussed, chattered about the weather and poured tea. Once she'd completed her task, she sat back. "Well, ladies, what can I do for you on this lovely summer morning?"

"We're here to talk to you about Ivan Hartman," Rhona said.

"Ivan Hartman." Allie frowned. "I don't know any Ivan Hartman."

"What about his father—Curt?"

Allie Jones morphed into a hissing, spitting venomous snake. "That murderer. Don't speak his name when you're guests in my home."

No point asking her opinion of SOHD or Curt. Might as well get to the point. "We're not guests—we're police officers, right? Where were you on Sunday evening and overnight?"

"I won't answer—*you* find out where I was." She rose. "That's all I'm saying. If you want to ask me anything else, I'll call my lawyer."

"We want you to go to the nearest police station to be fingerprinted," Rhona said, handing Allie her card.

"You have my fingerprints on file," Allie said while she swung her arms in a repetitive sweeping motion intended to move them out of her apartment. Rhona felt like a recalcitrant chicken.

The door slammed behind them. In the hall, Zee Zee turned to Rhona. "What a waste—I didn't have time to take a sip," she said. "But on second thought, it could have been poisoned."

"What a transformation!"

"We'll post those two high on our suspect list."

Five

Hollis excused herself after breakfast on Tuesday to make arrangements in Ottawa for her prolonged Toronto visit. She extended MacTee's stay at the kennel, cancelled the paper, and asked a neighbour to clear her mailbox. A knock at her bedroom door startled her. Manon hovered.

"I hope Ivan's death won't change your mind—that you and MacTee still plan to stay with us when you come back for Curt's course."

She knew they'd draw her into the family's recovery from sorrow. She and Manon wouldn't have the carefree fun Manon had planned when she'd heard Hollis's news. And she'd be distracted from painting and decision making. Furthermore, she'd coped with her husband's murder the summer before. Did she have enough emotional reserves to help Manon and the family? She gave herself a mental shake. Time to bury her doubts—she must say yes—she loved Manon like a sister and owed her a huge debt. She'd just have to do the best she could.

Manon's raised shoulders, pinched features and clasped hands revealed her stress. "There's something else," she said in a small, apologetic voice.

Hollis waited.

"I feel guilty about Ivan—about not paying enough attention to him. Since he died, I can hardly think about anything but finding out who he really was." She wrung her hands. "You know I'm obsessive. I fixate on something and can't leave it alone. I won't rest until I learn *every* detail of Ivan's life." She tightened her grip, pressed her elbows against her sides and hunched forward as if to protect herself from a blow. "I can't do it myself." Her voice broke. She gulped, straightened a little and expelled a shaky breath. "Even when the police do say it's okay, I won't be able go through his belongings. Or contact his friends—or anything else I'd need to do to uncover his real identity." She leaned toward Hollis. "Could you do it?"

Hollis had felt like this after Paul's murder, when she'd realized how little she knew about his life. An obsessive-compulsive need to investigate—to find out who he'd really been—had taken over her life.

"I can try." She hugged Manon. "I can start, I suppose, by talking to people at the visitation and funeral."

*　　*　　*

Tuesday and Wednesday passed in a blur. On Thursday, the Hartmans and Hollis prepared to accept condolences at the funeral home. When they entered the building, Hollis decided funeral home designers, if there was such a breed of cat, must conspire to create look-alike establishments with muted light, music, colours and tasteful semi-inspirational paintings. Like every other one she'd ever been in, it looked, sounded, smelled and felt beige. The family, sombrely dressed, lined up inside Salon C.

It was good to feel appropriately dressed. She'd unearthed a black linen dress with a white shawl collar in a high-end secondhand clothing store. She hadn't been able to resist a large enamelled flower brooch and a belt of multi-coloured beads, but she'd refrained from wearing them.

Rhona and Zee Zee arrived and spoke to the family. Then

Zee Zee stationed herself beside the condolence book, where she encouraged visitors to sign—having a record of attendees could prove helpful. Rhona worked the room.

Hollis stopped at a large photo of Ivan set on an easel above two floral arrangements. She bent to read the cards. One was inscribed, "Your loving family". The other, a beautiful arrangement of white roses, lilies and greenery bore an unsigned message, "With all our love, we will remember you forever". Wow, someone, no, more than one person, it said "we"—had really cared but hadn't felt comfortable signing the card. Another mystery. Who had been in Ivan's life who felt like this?

Mulling over the words and their significance, she wandered to one of four photo boards. Lena had arranged collages emphasizing happy moments in Ivan's life. These displays gave visitors focal points for conversation.

A crowd of young people fluttered in on the dot of two. First they clustered together as if to gain strength from one another. Then, en masse, they rushed through the receiving line. Once they'd accomplished this daunting task, they swarmed inside, where they regrouped beside the first photo collection. A tall, lean young man hovered on the fringe. Hollis moved closer and caught her breath as an overwhelming mix of after-shave and perfume—a perfect example of why hospitals asked you not to wear anything scented—assaulted her nostrils. She maneuvered to separate him from his fragrant flock.

"Hi there," she said.

He narrowed his eyes and peered at her. As if he couldn't quite believe she was speaking to him, he swung around and peered behind him. "Hi," he finally responded, cocking his head to one side and waiting.

She held out her hand. "Hollis Grant, I'm a friend of Ivan's family. Were you Ivan's friend?"

He accepted her hand, shook it briefly and said, "Willie. Yeah, we took classes together."

"At George Brown?"

He nodded.

Not exactly forthcoming. She'd try another tack. "What made *you* choose cooking?"

His angular face brightened. "My mom died when I was a kid. After that, my dad and I kinda of did a lot of cooking. Our career counsellor in high school said good chefs made a lot of money and could take their pick of jobs, so..."

"Is that why Ivan was there?"

Willie's eyebrows drew together. He shook his head. "Not for money. Ivan never had any doubts—he said he'd always wanted to be a chef. Like wow, the things he knew. Pretty cool."

"Willie, are you coming?" A pretty girl in a sleeveless pink dress that showed off a tan tucked her hand under his arm. "We're going to raise a few for Ivan," she said over her shoulder as she propelled the unresisting Willie away.

More young people, along with a smattering of older visitors, shuffled through the line before collecting in shifting knots in the reception room. Two middle-aged men stepped to one side away from the crowd. The taller one, in blue blazer and grey flannels, glanced quickly around as if to assure himself no one was within earshot. He bent his head and spoke to his companion.

An interesting place for a private conversation. Hollis slid closer. Rhona did the same—they'd both caught the vibes.

"Olivero, I'm surprised you're here," the tall one said. I wouldn't have thought you'd go anywhere near Curt after what he did to you." He fingered the white handkerchief in his breast pocket. "Talk about an egotistical, self-serving thing to do. He didn't want it—he did it to screw you."

Olivero, portly in a well-tailored grey, pin-stripe suit, shoved his hands in his pockets and sighed. "Wouldn't it have looked great if I'd stayed away? Can't you hear them? Olivero couldn't take it. He's licking his wounds."

"No one would have blamed you. In fact, I'll bet people are as surprised to see you here as I was."

"It doesn't matter. That isn't why I came. My being here has nothing to do with Curt—I'm here for Manon—she's my friend." When he mentioned Manon, he smiled.

"Friend?" The man's tone implied this was a euphemism for a more intimate relationship.

"Get stuffed," Olivero muttered and moved away.

Interesting. What had Curt done to Olivero? Had Manon and Olivero had an affair? Was it ongoing? But back to business. Surely, whatever the complexities of their lives, they had nothing to do with Ivan's murder.

At the visitation after dinner, the nature of the visitors changed. A great many artists, friends of Lena and Curt, swirled through the line. Manon's colleagues, Tomas's contemporaries and Etienne's friends' parents visited. Hollis drifted from group to group.

A young Oriental woman attracted her attention. Her round, black-framed glasses, short spiky, hair, nose studs, multiple earrings and flamboyant clothes shouted "artiste". Hollis sauntered over and smiled. "Hi, I'm Hollis Grant, a family friend. Are you Ivan's friend or Curt's student?"

Intelligent eyes assessed her. "Technically, I'm not a student until Tuesday—I'm taking his Great Masters course."

Surprise. Hollis would have pegged her as an avant garde artist, someone bent on shocking the world with installations or videos. "Me too," she said.

The girl's eyes widened. Apparently Hollis didn't fit the

profile either. "I'm Kate Wong." She immediately motioned for two men chatting nearby to join them. One was a compact, muscular East Indian man, and the other a man whose skin colour and sharply chiselled features also indicated exotic ancestry. "Those two are Patel and David. The three of us took Curt's second semester course. Patel is terrific." She eyed Hollis. "You do know Curt had a heart attack?"

Hollis nodded.

"The college appointed a substitute, but I decided that wasn't good enough. It was Curt I wanted, so I applied for the summer course."

Kate performed the introductions and added, "Hollis is a Hartman family friend who's taking Curt's course."

"I've enrolled, and David's just told me he has too," Patel said.

"You're kidding. Old home week," Kate said.

Hollis had worried that everyone in the course would be decades younger and she'd feel out of place. Probably her concern came from watching older students who had taken her courses at the community college. They'd almost all been anxious, afraid they wouldn't be able to compete, to keep up with her course demands. Kate certainly was much younger, but Hollis pegged David's age as late twenties or early thirties and Patel as more than forty. How could they take day courses? They must have jobs. When she knew them better, she'd ask.

"Welcome," Patel said and shook her hand. His firm grip and warm brown eyes made her feel his words were sincere. This was a man she knew she'd like.

David, tall and arrow thin, eyed her with dark eyes filled with curiosity. He cocked his head to one side, flicking back his black hair. "A family friend?" he said.

"Curt's wife, Manon, and I go back to university undergraduate days. Because I live in Ottawa, they invited me to be their guest." Hollis said.

"You're already here for the course?" Kate asked.

"No. I was visiting when Ivan was killed, and they asked me to stay and help with all the things that had to be done. It's still hard to believe he's dead. Anyway, tomorrow afternoon I'm going home on the train. My dog and I will drive back on Tuesday."

"Have you ever taken a course from Curt?" Patel said.

"Years ago, when I was at OCAD as an undergraduate."

"It will be interesting to see if you think he's changed," Kate said. "He has a tough guy reputation, and he demands a lot, but I think he's fair and he wants us to succeed." She turned to the two men. "Would you agree?"

"I find him helpful. He doesn't tolerate foolish remarks or students who don't work. He says it is a sin not to use your talents. I agree. If I didn't think so, I would have remained in Madras and been the accountant my family intended me to be." Patel's lips twitched. "That would have been calamitous for me and for my family's reputation. My grasp of mathematics is rudimentary. To address Kate's point, I think he must have mellowed. Maybe being sick does that to you." He frowned. "I can't imagine what his son's death will do."

"We need to be kind. Not give him any trouble. Not that we would, but he's going to need our sympathy,"

"Little Miss Goody Two Shoes, now you've taken on Curt. Last term you spent your time nosing into people's business, making suggestions about how they could improve their lives. You should give up painting and become a social worker. Interfering in a person's life without a second's hesitation and with perfect confidence that you're right—that's a major criteria for admission into the field," David said.

"Kiss my ass," Kate said.

"Take it easy, you two. This is a funeral home, and we didn't come to fight. It's inappropriate behaviour," Patel said.

David glowered at him but didn't say anything else. His anger had been sudden, but who knew what had happened between Kate and David in the past. Whatever it was, they clearly didn't like each other. Time to change the subject. "Are all three of you traditional painters?" Hollis said.

Kate shook her head. "Anything but. I do constructions, assembled pieces of found materials, but the focus of each is a miniature of a classic. The subject relates to the assembly. I want the tiny paintings to be as nearly perfect as I can make them, because that heightens the impact."

"I hope you brought slides. They sound interesting," Hollis said.

"I've heard that in the first class Curt shows the three slides we submitted to be accepted for the course. We'll see what stage each of us is at," David said. "My pieces don't photograph well. They're three dimensional. I paint a huge copy of a famous painting on a wooden panel. Then I shatter and reassemble it in a meaningful way. Synopsizing my work, I'd say I'm interested in remnants after a cataclysmic event has occurred."

He sounded as if he should be writing the gobbledygook that passed for artistic criticism in some art journals. Hollis got nervous when someone used words like "meaningful". But given his attack on Kate, she certainly wasn't going to say so. She had to admit she also felt defensive about her own huge, happy paintings of domestic icons.

Whatever they were, "meaningful" wasn't a word that came to mind.

"I'm into semi-abstraction of cityscapes. I've always admired

Richard Diebenkorn and his California landscapes. But I admire the masters' techniques and want to learn as much about them as I can," Patel said. He didn't sound apologetic.

"What about you?" Kate asked Hollis.

"Conventional," Hollis said.

"Curt invited us for drinks the first evening of the course. I wonder if he'll still do it," Patel said.

Hollis hadn't thought much about the invitation when she'd received her registration package. Curt always invited his students to his house. But Ivan's murder and his heart problems could change that.

"You're staying with them. Do you think he'll have us over?" David said.

Over lunch the day that Ivan had died, Manon had insisted he would carry on as usual. Probably he'd feel an obligation to host the class get-together. Or that it would be a sign of weakness not to do so. "It'll be hard, but I'm sure he will," Hollis said.

"We had a great time at the one last semester. Ivan made fabulous canapés—really different. Curt's cute little boy, I forget his name, passed them around." Kate winced. "That sounded callous—sorry."

"Hey, it was only a comment. I thought the same thing," Patel said.

Silence for a second, then everyone spoke at once. They laughed self-consciously.

Patel checked his watch "Time for me to go. It's my night to be the maitre d' at Toronto's finest curry palace. See you next week," he said. He put his hand on Hollis's arm. "And you drive carefully. The 401 can be stressful." He turned away, and David limped after him.

"Was David in an accident?" Hollis asked Kate.

"Don't think so. It's not new. But I've never heard him talk about it." Kate frowned. "Actually, he doesn't talk much about himself. He's a prickly guy, but you just saw that." She hovered close to Hollis and whispered, "See the man with the bushy grey beard?"

"Hard to miss. He looks like he dressed in the dark in whatever he found in a Goodwill bag."

"Do you know who he is?"

"I haven't a clue."

"Sebastien Lefevbre," Kate whispered. She watched Hollis's face, waiting for her to recognize the name.

It seemed familiar, but when she ran it through her mental data bank, she didn't make a connection.

Kate shook her head. "You *must* recognize him. He's our most famous portrait artist. He's painted everybody who's anybody. Remember Prince Philip's portrait and the furor it caused?"

"Of course. I don't know why I drew a blank. Trudeau sliding down the bannister is my favourite—it perfectly captures his bad-boy charm."

Hollis felt the atmosphere change. A palpable feeling of unease swept the room. She scanned the room to see the cause.

"You are such a hypocrite."

An abrasive voice ripped through the room's subdued murmur like a chainsaw. Lena had reared back and grabbed Curt by his suit lapels. "You pretend to care, but you don't. As far as I'm concerned..."

Curt pushed her away.

"As far as I'm concerned, *you* killed him. You gave him that bloody motorcycle." She'd planted her hands on her hips. Her voice rose higher. "What loving father presents his teenage son with a lethal weapon?" She jabbed a magenta claw. "A narcissistic man who wishes to kill his children."

Curt blanched and clenched his jaw. Before he could respond, Manon took his arm and said something in a low voice.

Lena turned on her. "And you. The home-wrecker. What responsibility do you have for my son's death?"

Six

"I identified another possible perp," Rhona said to Zee Zee after the visitation. "Olivero Ciccio is an artist and teaches at the Ontario College of Art and Design. Curt screwed him in some way, and he has a thing for Curt's wife. Let's see if we can meet with him before tonight's reception."

Back at the shop, Rhona googled Olivero. According to his website, he did three dimensional whimsical constructions as well as conventional paintings. The examples on the website made her smile. Was humorous artwork as underrated as comic or satirical writing? Probably seriousness counted in the art world. She made an appointment to speak to Olivero and his wife.

The Ciccios lived in Riverdale. South and east of Cabbagetown, this neighbourhood hovered on the cusp of gentility. One half of a semi-detached house would be clad in insul-brick with old chrome and plastic kitchen chairs lined up on the porch and a weed-filled yard. Its other half would exhibit all the hallmarks of an expensive gentrified upgrade. New high R-value windows, an enamelled front door and a front garden with periwinkle ground cover and a manicured privet hedge would create an appealing image. Half the neighbourhood belonged to old-time residents and half to the upwardly mobile who renovated or paid hefty prices for the already renovated. These trendy young things harboured long term plans to improve Riverdale and raise their houses' values so they could sell for a huge profit and move on to more expensive neighbourhoods like the Beach or the Annex.

The Ciccios' detached brick house stood back from the street. Conservatively painted, with a neat perennial garden and a manicured lawn to set it off, it wouldn't have drawn a second glance except for an arresting garden sculpture. Close to the house, an eight foot high wooden angel with a pair of garden shears in one hand turned to stare at her neatly clipped wing. She wore a silver metal halo with the word "oops" in brass letters fastened to it. Rhona smiled—whimsical and charming described it perfectly.

A small woman in jeans and a navy blue sweater answered their ring. Regular features, brown eyes, short, dark hair sprinkled with grey—an unremarkable appearance. Her neighbours or people who'd met her would refer to her as "very nice" or a "good neighbour" but only be able to describe her in general terms. A polite golden retriever accompanied her. Navy blue had been an unfortunate choice, given that she lived with a breed noted for the quantities of blonde hair it shed.

Inside, Anna Ciccio led them into a tiny living room. While she fetched Olivero, they surveyed their surroundings. Heavy drapes, maroon and gold-patterned wallpaper and overstuffed dark green plush furniture made the room seem smaller. An amusing painting of flying cows by Olivero provided one bright spot of colour. Rhona guessed Anna had decreed that Olivero could do what he liked in his studio, but she would decorate everything else.

When the couple returned, Olivero, who looked exhausted, sank down and arranged sofa cushions behind him to support his back. Anna chose a chair opposite the sofa.

"We're here to talk about Ivan Hartman and his family," Rhona said and noted a puzzled expression on Anna's face. "We're broadening our investigation to include all the

Hartmans' acquaintances," she added.

Anna, feet and ankles together, clasped her elbows with her hands and pulled them tight to her body. Her features closed in on themselves—she reminded Rhona of a clam or an oyster retreating into its shell.

Olivero leaned forward with his hands on his knees. "Curt and I work together at OCAD. We've known each other for years." He lifted his head and directed a level gaze at Rhona. "Not friends. I don't think Curt has *any* art world friends. He's far too competitive and critical. But we manage."

"Someone said you'd had a disagreement recently," Rhona said.

Anna half-closed her eyes and stared downward.

Olivero shrugged. "I was nominated for department chair. Curt voted against me. He's entitled to his opinion."

"He was jealous." Anna's voice was low and bitter. "Everyone likes Olivero."

"And how do you feel about Curt?" Rhona asked.

"Curt is a fool, an egotistical fool, but not as bad as his wife. Always playing the sensitive, misunderstood, hard-done-by woman. Now I ask you, how that can be? She has a terrific career, a beautiful house and children. How can she even suggest such things?"

Olivero raised his arm as if to stop her. "Anna, take it easy. Manon has psychological problems. That can happen to people, no matter what material things or education they have."

"So she says and so you believe. You are such a silly man. She managed to make you her champion. Fools, she makes fools of men."

Jealousy, dislike, hatred—Anna could have murdered *Manon,* but did she have reason to kill Ivan? Rhona thought.

"And Ivan and Tomas Hartman, what about them?"

"Nice young men. I only knew them to say hello. Because

we don't have children, we never socialized with other families like some of my colleagues did," Olivero explained.

"Did you know the sons?" Rhona asked Anna.

"To say hello," she mumbled.

Rhona addressed her next remark to Olivero. "Your sculpture outside is delightful. So are the ones on your website. I take it you're very comfortable with tools."

Olivero shifted and considered her silently for a moment. "Are you asking if I'm knowledgeable enough to sabotage a motorcycle?"

"Are you?"

"Of course. Like ninety per cent of Torontonians. It isn't hard to cut holes in something."

"And where were you on Sunday evening, June 26th?" asked Zee Zee.

"Right here. We both were."

"Thank you." Again Rhona produced a card and handed it to him. "At your convenience, would you both go to 51 Division for fingerprinting."

Their eyes widened as they absorbed the implications of Rhona's request.

"My wife may hate Manon, but neither of us would do anything violent," he said in a low voice as he escorted them to the door.

"What do you think—could either one have done it?" Rhona asked later as they drove north.

"Keep them on the list. Although Anna hates Manon at the moment, I can't see what she'd gain by killing Ivan or Curt?"

*   *   *

On Friday, Rhona and Zee Zee brainstormed while they ate two take-out lunches Hollis had collected from a nearby Tim Hortons.

"Initially, Frank thought it might be a simple open and shut case—a gang vendetta, a lover's quarrel, a drug deal gone bad..." Rhona said with a sigh.

"So far it's none of the above." Zee Zee had cleared a space on her desktop and was fastidiously arranging her lunch as if she were dining in an expensive restaurant. She shook her head. "Who leaves three Harleys parked outside? I may be a super-cautious cop, but isn't that asking for trouble?"

"Ego trip," Rhona mumbled. She washed a morsel of whole wheat roll down with a swig of coffee. "Curt Hartman strikes me as a guy with a giant ego, capital G, capital E. I understand why Tomas Hartman calls him Big Daddy. Did you ever see the movie, *Cat on a Hot Tin Roof,* with Elizabeth Taylor, Paul Newman? Orson Welles was Big Daddy?"

"No. But doesn't the name fit Curt? Motorcycles aside, an artist might be hated for many reasons." She stirred her chili. "Envy—there's a reason it's a deadly sin—it's a corrosive, destructive force. Wasn't a jealous contemporary accused of murdering Mozart? There must be students or other artists Curt destroyed with private or public criticism. It's an unstable community. No matter how high your reputation is at any given moment, you're only as good as your most recent work."

"Tell me about his work."

"It's valued internationally. He's admired because he teaches. Not loved or revered or even liked."

Frank Braithwaite walked in. Rhona twitched a napkin over her doughnut.

He waved and marched over. "I assume you two are tying up loose ends in the Hartman case." His tone was jocular, but his eyes were not.

"Afraid not. It's getting more complicated every day. Not open and shut, as you'd hoped," Rhona said. God, why couldn't she just have said no? She was such a wimp sometimes. "Let me tell you what we've done." She itemized who'd been interviewed and the leads they were following.

"I've heard from the mayor. Curt Hartman has complained about our inability to solve the murder." He sighed. "This isn't a TV show where they neatly wrap up in half an hour. I can't provide any more people. Have you used the profiler?"

"I checked for similar crimes, but this is a stand-alone. Profiling would only help if there was more than one similar crime," Zee Zee said.

Frank flipped the napkin off Rhona's doughnut. He shook his head and clicked his tongue against his teeth. "Shame on you—you're confirming people's worst suspicions."

After he left, Rhona fumed. "It's a goddamn doughnut. You'd think he'd caught me snorting cocaine or taking payola or worse. And how come he didn't comment on yours? It's discrimination."

"How do you figure that?"

"You're thin and elegant. I'm not, so he focuses on me—definitely discrimination."

Zee Zee laughed. "I can give you chapter and verse about discrimination, because I'm black, not because I'm thin. I'm not apologizing. I was born this way."

"Lucky you. Back to the Hartmans. The perp will try again if he killed the wrong man."

"Did you warn them to be careful?"

"Not when we thought it would be a straightforward case." Rhona collected their dishes. "I'll drop around after the funeral and talk to them."

"Back to the grind. Now that we've broadened the scope, we'll press father and son to tell us what they have to hide—everyone has something."

Seven

On Friday morning, pelting rain discouraged all but a few morbidly curious onlookers from waiting outside the funeral home while the ceremony took place. Later, when everything was over, the family, sheltered by umbrellas, headed for two waiting cars. Manon, Lena, Curt and Etienne went first, followed by Manon's mother, Tomas, Etienne and Nadine.

As she bent to slide into the second car, Hollis looked ahead. A young dark-haired woman wrapped in a shiny black rain cape with its hood pulled up to shield her from the rain had run forward and touched Curt's arm. Hollis heard her say, "You're Ivan's father, and I..." Curt made a dismissive gesture and followed Manon into the lead car. Hollis caught the briefest glance before the girl turned away and stepped back. She considered rushing after her but felt it would be inappropriate. But who was she? What had she wanted?

"Was that girl Ivan's girlfriend?" Hollis murmured to Tomas.

"Search me. He never talked about a girl," Tomas said.

"I wonder what she intended to say to your father."

*   *   *

Back in Ottawa late on Friday evening, Hollis opened her door, scooped up her mail and ran to answer the ringing phone.

"Detective Simpson came by an hour or so ago," Manon said. "She told us to be careful—said that Curt or Tomas might be targeted. She warned us to watch for suspicious parcels, avoid isolated places and keep an eye on Etienne."

This was bad news. There was no point in adding to Manon's fear by expressing her shock. She made a conscious effort to suppress her alarm. "They're probably just covering their bases until they get a handle on who killed Ivan." She hoped her voice sounded normal and reasonable.

"I requested protection, a police officer inside or a police car outside. She claimed they lacked the manpower. Then I asked her what progress they'd made."

"What did she say?"

"That she wasn't at liberty to discuss details. She reassured me they were doing everything possible. She churned out the sort of polite remarks people make when they haven't a clue and don't want to talk about something. It felt like I was speaking in a huge empty void that sucked up everything I said and didn't give anything back. And there's something else..."

The low, defeated monotone alarmed Hollis. She imagined Manon's slumped shoulders and downturned mouth. How unfair it was for Manon to have to cope with this. Manon appeared to be an efficient banker, a woman in charge of her life and herself, although those close to her knew she fought an ongoing battle with depression and panic attacks. She constantly struggled to deny her urge to convert relatively ordinary events into crises. Hollis hoped this was the case; hoped Manon's molehills had grown into mountains. But the warning sounded serious. Was she strong enough to help Manon deal with her anxieties?

"What? What else has happened? I hope Tomas and Curt aren't riding their bikes until the killer is caught."

"Tomas suggested that maybe they shouldn't. Curt blew up and ordered Tomas not to be a coward."

"Sounds like Tomas was being sensible."

"Exactly. Then Curt sneered that Tomas should paint his yellow if he was afraid the killer would confuse their bikes. Maybe it was an attempt at humour, but it wasn't funny. Curt said only serial killers used the same *modus operandi* repeatedly. He said a run-of-the-mill killer wouldn't tamper with either bike. He's probably right, unless it *is* a serial killer."

"Why would Curt or Tomas be targets?"

"I can't imagine that Tomas is. As far as I know, he leads a relatively blameless life. On the other hand, Curt's enemies are legion. However, I have a terrible feeling it *is* a serial killer who's after all of us. A deranged murderer will pick us off one by one." A long, indrawn breath. A shaky voice. "I'm terrified for Etienne."

Why would a killer want the whole family dead? Particularly eleven-year-old Etienne. Not a rational idea but, when it came to Etienne, Manon had never been totally rational. Etienne was the child her physician had counselled her not to carry to term. She'd rejected his advice and suffered through a difficult pregnancy made more stressful by a severe bout of depression. Hollis remembered how hard it had been for her.

"I'm up at night again. I didn't tell you when you were here, because I thought it would stop," Manon said.

Hollis searched her memory. "You think you've lost Etienne. You're sleepwalking, searching for him."

"I did it for a whole year after his birth."

"You had a reason. He nearly died when he arrived prematurely. Right now, uncertainty about Ivan is taking its toll on your mental equilibrium. You must be exhausted if you're wandering around every night."

"I'd fall asleep again if Curt woke me up and shepherded me back to bed. But my sleepwalking upsets him. I think he's afraid it means I'm having a total breakdown. He reacts badly."

"How?" Hollis wished her bedroom had been on the same floor—she might have heard this nocturnal problem and been able to help.

Manon took a quick breath to steady her voice. "It's three a.m., and he lectures me. Tells me to get a grip. Says I'm neurotic and revelling in my craziness." She sobbed. "I'm not. I'm doing everything I can to stay on an even keel. He upsets me so much, I can't go back to sleep. Next morning, I'm a basket case."

"Hang on. I'll be there on Tuesday. Are you..." Should she ask if Manon was keeping to her medication schedule?

"Taking my meds and seeing my psychiatrist? Yes to both questions. I'm not about to go off the deep end. Mostly I do okay. But I'm terrified my sleepwalking means that subconsciously I know something. I'm afraid my body is warning me Etienne's in danger. Warning me to keep him from being the next victim."

Useless to argue. Nothing she said would change Manon's mind. "You should have sent him back to Quebec with your mother."

"I thought about it, but I can't bear to have him out of my sight for more than a few hours. I also considered resigning and staying home with him. Curt blew up when I suggested it. He said it would be the very worst thing to do, that I'd make Etienne into a nervous wreck like me. He ordered me to 'pull myself together'. I hate that phrase. As if you wouldn't do it if you could." She laughed shakily. "Even to me, my theory that the killer has his sights set on the whole family sounds crazy when I say it out loud." She paused. "There's something else. Curt says they've implied he may have had something to do with Ivan's murder."

Why hadn't Manon told her these things while she was still in Toronto?

"How strange. Why would they suspect Curt? I can hear him saying 'Next they'll be accusing me' when he criticizes them for their inability to arrest the killer. I can't believe he means it, or that the police believe it. Curt seemed okay at the funeral. How do you think he's bearing up?"

"Not well. He's in denial." A whisper. "I think he's gone a little crazy."

"Crazy? You can't mean that?"

"Not crazy, crazy—but weird—weirder than me. Other things are happening...I'm desperate."

Hollis reviewed what she had to do before she drove back to Toronto. There was no way she could get there any earlier. But she had to allay Manon's fears.

"This is easy to say, but not to do—try to relax. Take each hour as it comes. Don't think of all the bad things that could happen. And I'll call Rhona to see if I can get any more information."

Hollis hung up and punched in the cell phone number on the business card Rhona had given her.

"We *are* making progress," Rhona assured her.

"Warning the Hartmans to take care. Implying Curt had something to do with Ivan's death—that's progress?"

"This isn't television. All relevant information doesn't drop into our laps like manna from heaven. People lie or don't cooperate. For one reason or another, they don't come forward when they have information. Motive helps. In Ivan's case, we don't have one. Anyway, what business is it of yours?"

"Sorry. I did come on strong. I just talked to Manon. She's

so spaced out and worried she's barely functioning. I owe her big time, and I want to help her get her life back on track."

"It's a tough situation for anyone."

"I'll be in Toronto on Tuesday for a three week course at the Ontario College of Art and Design. Can I tell Manon I'm buying you lunch on Tuesday? It will give her something to focus on. Even in a murder investigation, you must take time for lunch. Also I have something to tell you that may be news."

Rhona heard the conciliatory, almost pleading note in Hollis's voice. What harm would it do? She might even learn something useful. Lunch. There was a Tim Hortons two blocks from OCAD and not too far from her office at College and Bay. She'd order their chili and doughnut special without worrying that her boss, with his anti-Tim Hortons attitude and doughnut phobia, would appear.

*　　*　　*

Hollis arrived in Toronto on Tuesday morning with MacTee and assorted bags and bundles. Curt and Manon lived in Cabbagetown, a densely populated older neighbourhood. She wrestled her truck into a tiny space and wished she drove a Smart Car or a Mini. Before she entered the Hartmans', she again admired the restored Victorian with its wraparound porch. The asphalted motorcycle parking pad on the front lawn definitely detracted from its period charm.

After she'd delivered MacTee into Nadine's custody, she hurried to Carlton Street and boarded a streetcar. At Yonge Street, she transferred to the subway and emerged on University Avenue minutes later. She raced along Dundas Street, regretting that she was late for her twelve thirty lunch. It was twenty to one, and she hated being late. She hoped

Rhona had waited. Perspiration soaked the back of her T-shirt. She wished she'd thought about July's noon heat at five in the morning, when blue jeans and a navy T-shirt had seemed right. And she should have sorted through and left behind whatever weighed down her navy polka dot handbag. She exhaled noisily when she spied Rhona sitting at a window table in Tim Hortons.

Inside, Hollis removed her aviator sunglasses, replacing them with her usual red-framed pair, blinked and waved. She marched over. "Sorry, the traffic on the 401 was brutal. It took me forever to get here." She dropped her bags on an empty chair and sat down. They contemplated each other while they swung slightly on the swivel chairs attached to the Formica-topped table.

"I started." Rhona gestured at her plate. "Better buy your food."

Hollis went to get a sandwich before rejoining Rhona.

Rhona picked up her fork. "Tell me again why you're involved?"

Hollis steepled her fingers and pressed the tips against her chin. "In first year university, Manon saved my life—I'll always owe her."

Rhona's eyebrows rose.

"I won't give you the gory details, but believe me, she did. And now her life is chaotic, and I'm helping her sort it out. Manon feels guilty because she attributed Ivan's withdrawal to growing up and didn't make an effort to win his confidence. For her peace of mind, she needs to learn more about his life, but she can't bring herself to act. She's fragile emotionally— this isn't a new development—she always has been. I'm prepared to research Ivan's life, if knowing more will help her regain her stability." She looked quizzically at Rhona. "Is

Manon right when she says you think the killer may target other family members?"

"The father or the older brother may have been and may still be the target. You said you had something to tell me."

"I noticed two things at the visitation and funeral that may be significant."

"Go ahead."

"I'm sure you probably saw that there were only two floral arrangements because the family asked for charitable donations instead of flowers. One bouquet came from the family. The second had an unsigned card. Whoever sent it wrote, "With all our love, we will remember you forever." No one in the family has a clue who might have sent it. Those are strong words. Someone cared a great deal. Do you know who it was from?"

Rhona nodded. "We're way ahead of you, but no closer to an answer. According to the florist, a young woman who didn't give her name paid cash. The florist had never seen her before. What's the second thing?"

"A young woman..." Hollis reflected. "Maybe it was the same woman who rushed forward when the family left the reception. She wanted to speak to Curt, but he brushed her off. I almost got out and talked to her—I wish I had."

"We missed that," Rhona admitted. "I wonder who she was."

Eight

Hollis felt an inane smile spread across her face when she entered studio 23 at OCAD. She inhaled the evocative odours of oil paint, linseed oil and turpentine. Students perched on grey metal stools behind three trestle tables loaded with wood panels, jars, bottles, sticks and bundles of fur. She took the last empty stool, nodded to Patel, Kate and David and surveyed the class.

Sebastien Lefebvre sat with the students.

Why was he here? Surely not to learn anything? Perhaps he'd been invited to share his expertise. But that wouldn't happen in the first class. Very odd, but perhaps there was a simple explanation.

A cluster of easels, a slide projector on a metal cart and a dais plunked in the middle of the room indicated that Curt planned a variety of activities for his intensive three-week course.

Curt strode in, swinging a battered leather briefcase with a tooled Haida Indian motif. He'd owned this distinctive bag for years; she'd admired it when she'd been a student. Tall and elegant in polished tassel loafers, black socks, pressed chinos, black snakeskin belt and a black polo shirt, Curt didn't introduce himself but did smile.

But only for a minute. When he saw Lefevbre, his eyes widened. An open-mouthed expression of astonishment replaced his smile. He took a deep breath as if to give himself time to decide on a course of action. He set the brief case on the floor and took a second deep breath. "Welcome to the course."

Apparently he planned to give his regular spiel. But whatever Lefebvre was doing here, he had not consulted Curt before he appeared.

"Before I discuss what we can expect from one another, I want to apologize. I know you all received an invitation to a drinks party at my house this evening." He paused as if considering what he would say next. "Because of..." he paused, "the circumstances, I'm postponing the evening until the end of the course."

That was a surprise. Hollis had expected him to soldier on, but maybe he'd realized that the family couldn't cope with a party.

"I think of myself as a mentor, a man who encourages and nurtures talent," Curt continued.

The flip side of the coin—she'd heard him mercilessly mock and discourage aspiring artists he judged to lack promise. Never a kind man, he'd justified his behaviour as a dash of cold water designed to save mediocre artists years of frustration. She remembered Kate's comments. Perhaps he'd changed since she'd been a student.

He glanced from student to student as if one look at each face would reveal the degree of talent this summer's class possessed. "I don't conduct this session in a Toronto July because I need the money. In fact, giving a course is a tremendous financial and creative sacrifice." He allowed the impact of his words to sink in, smoothed back his unruly silver hair with long, bony fingers and leaned slightly forward. "Because galleries compete for my paintings, any time away from my easel costs me a great deal of money." His silver eyebrows rose and his nostrils flared. "If you're up on art news, you've read about Dallas and San Francisco competitively bidding for one of my paintings." He brushed his hand through his hair again. "All this is a preamble to underline what I have to say." He pointed to himself with his right index finger. "Since *I've* sacrificed time and money, I expect you..." he directed his finger at each student in turn, "to work to capacity to learn everything possible during the course. Now I know some of you, and some of you know each other, but we will proceed with introductions as if none of you knows me or anyone else. Please introduce yourself and give us background information about your art training and experience. I will project your slides as you speak." He consulted a list next to the slide projector. "Kate Wong." He flicked the switch.

A slide of a multicoloured assemblage of sticks that resembled oversize Tinker toys wired with a light focused into the interior on a tiny reproduction of a Botticelli painting.

"This is the second course I've taken with Professor Hartman. Right now I work as a commercial artist here in Toronto, but I *will* make a living and reputation as a professional artist."

Curt clicked to a second then to a third slide. "Any comments, Kate?" he said.

"No. They *should* speak for themselves."

Kate's eyes, body and voice expressed focus and intensity. This woman had set her sights on a goal she intended to reach. There was nothing derivative about her work. Kate's talent appeared to match her ambition.

"Where did you study?" Curt asked.

"McGill."

Curt nodded approvingly and flashed a slide of a fog-shrouded coast featuring menacing androgynous figures moving toward a beached boat.

"Tessa Steeves. I graduated from the Nova Scotia College of

Art and Design three years ago. I live on Grand Manan Island in New Brunswick and supplement my painting income with year-round waitress work. Grand Manan is an artist's paradise filled with kindred spirits. But it's a long way from Toronto or Montreal. It's even further from New York. I thought I'd better make myself known in Upper Canada."

Her contented smile and tone of voice belied her words. Tessa might be taking the course, but Hollis suspected she didn't give a fig about the Upper Canadian art world. She'd spend her life in New Brunswick following her own muse.

A slide featuring a small boy staring straight at the viewer was conventional but competent.

"Bert Acorn, high school math teacher by day—painter at night and on weekends. I've only sold a few. Maybe I'm not good enough to be here, but I had to come because I felt studying with Professor Hartman would be the opportunity of a lifetime," he gushed.

Oh, dear, was this man, whom she judged to be in his forties like her, as diffident as he seemed? She'd witnessed what Curt could do to those who lacked confidence in themselves or their work.

Curt considered him for a moment. "And where did you study?"

"The Ottawa School of Art."

"Ah, the school for amateurs, where teachers offer no criticism lest students become upset and withdraw, taking their cash with them," Curt drawled.

Colour suffused Bert's face.

The next slide initially appeared to be abstract, but a closer inspection revealed that it could be a cityscape.

"I am Patel—I have decided one name suffices. Originally from Madras, I am now a Torontonian. I share a studio on

King Street and work in my uncle's restaurant. I too have taken a previous course with Professor Hartman."

"Patel. Yes, there are one-name artists. There's Ottawa photographer Evergon and a few others. Your first name is long and unpronounceable—it's a good decision."

His remark could have sounded condescending. Instead, it validated Patel's choice.

The next slide was as complicated as Kate's had been. It was hard to judge scale, but it seemed to be a huge board with fragments of wood affixed randomly. Only if she stared at each piece did she see that they had originally been part of a whole. She guessed it had been a reproduction of a Caravaggio.

"David Nixon. I also was enrolled in Professor Hartman's spring semester course. I'm a fanatical west coaster. I love the sea and sailing." He stopped like a comedian about to deliver his punch line. "But for an ocean sailor, I made the totally inexplicable decision to move from Vancouver to Toronto earlier this year. Occasionally I crew for others, but I plan to buy my own sail boat and live on it. For now I rent a place and run a carpentry business." He reached into his pocket and withdrew a small packet. "These are my cards—I'm in the market for new clients." He passed them around.

David was a chameleon. The hostility she'd seen at the funeral home was gone.

"And where did you study?"

"Off and on at Emily Carr."

"I too attended Emily Carr."

Her own painting of gigantic hollyhocks filled the screen. Why did she always paint everything smacked in the foreground? She'd wondered about this before and attempted to do landscapes, long vistas of distant hills, but without success. Maybe it meant she was a totally superficial person who operated in the present. "Hollis Grant. I studied here many years ago. I teach social history at Algonquin College in Ottawa. I paint as often as I can."

Curt nodded, but he was looking at Sebastien Lefevbre. He made a slight bow to him and addressed the others. "I'm sure you're familiar with the work of Sebastien Lefevbre. He is possibly the greatest portrait artist Canada has ever produced. Seb, I don't know why you're here—I can't imagine there's anything I can teach you."

Lefevbre sat without saying anything until the silence became uncomfortable. Finally, he spoke. "I'm auditing the course. Curt, I haven't painted for six months, not since my daughter, Valerie, died." Pain filled his voice.

Curt stepped back as if Lefevbre had aimed a lethal weapon at him. "Valerie?" he said questioningly. "Valerie's dead?"

"Yes, and I intend to make sure she didn't die in vain." His tone chilled like an Arctic wind. "I'll speak to *you* later."

Curt's gaze fixed on Lefevbre, but he said nothing.

What had this exchange meant? Lefevbre radiated deep, unresolved anger. His statement had shocked Curt and left him speechless. Whatever his connection to Valerie had been, hearing news of her death had unsettled him.

Curt shook himself and squared his shoulders. He took a deep breath and turned away from Lefevbre.

"Before we discuss the materials, I'll talk to you about photographing your work. Some of these slides are not as good as they could be. When you submit slides to galleries or to competitions, it's in your interest to create the best."

He devoted the next forty minutes to the details of taking superb slides. It sounded as if he'd just thought of these things when he examined their slides, but Hollis suspected it was part of the course. Naturally, they all took notes.

"Well, now that you have learned how to take excellent slides, you have improved your chances of having your work accepted in competitions and by galleries." He smiled. "A tip. Pay a professional photographer if you aren't producing superior ones—it'll be worth it, even if you have to beg or borrow the money to pay for them.

"But back to the course. I devote it entirely to the study and reproduction of techniques the Old Masters employed to give their paintings a richness lacking in many modern works. In essence, this course is about light. We'll try to emulate the masters and use light as they did." This was obviously a familiar spiel. "I'm sure you shuddered when you received the materials price list." He nodded at the tables piled with supplies. "The costs are high because I tried to replicate material the masters used. To assure uniformity, I purchased everything. Each of you has a mortar and pestle, along with an interesting assortment of clays, rocks, twigs, dried insects and squirrel fur. You will make your own permanent references to differences resulting from combining various supports and grounds and preparing your own colours. We will paint the same still life set-up for each painting." His lips curved upward in a faintly mocking smile. "Perhaps someday a critic or art historian will study your series and compare them to Monet's haystack studies." His lifted eyebrows and faint smile indicated his irony.

The class, already sensitive to his speech nuances, chuckled appreciatively

"We'll use cotton and linen canvases, along with several species of wood panels for comparisons and..." He paused, picked up a Masonite panel and drew his hand across the surface. "Masonite. Of course I realize Masonite didn't exist then, but it gives us a comparative modern material." He laid the panel back on the table. "Time for a break. When you come back, we'll discuss the relative merits of different materials after we've viewed a few slides. Then you'll prepare a support for your first work."

Kate led the way downstairs to a phalanx of machines dispensing a variety of refreshments. "This will have to substitute for his cocktail party," she said, pointing at the looming behemoths.

The group collected what they wanted and settled around a long table.

"Wasn't his talk on slides useful?" Tessa said. "I'd already realized when he showed mine that I hadn't done my paintings any favours. I apply ten or fifteen transparent layers of paint when I'm trying to capture the feeling that fog gives when the sun is about to break though and burn it off. There's an unearthly light. It's gorgeous but momentary, and hard to capture. Critics have said I've managed to show it, but anyone looking at those slides of mine would never guess. I suppose you don't realize how bad your slides are unless you project them, and I've never done that. That half an hour makes the whole course worthwhile for me."

"I wish he'd talked more about photographing three dimensional work," David said.

"I didn't like his idea of including a ruler to give an idea of actual scale. It might detract from the slide," Patel said. "You always include the dimensions on the slide itself anyway—that should be enough."

"The problem when you're only allowed three slides is that you want to show three different pieces, but unless you photograph a three dimensional object from several points of view, you don't capture its impact," Kate said.

"Speaking of impact, what's the story on Sebastien Lefebvre? And what connection did Curt have with Lefebvre's daughter? He seemed really upset," Tessa said.

"It's upsetting to hear that someone you know has died, and if she was his daughter, she wouldn't have been very old. Maybe he's there for the reason he gave; he wants to jumpstart himself to paint again," Hollis said, although she didn't believe it. Too much emotion had emanated from each man.

"Death." David looked at them. "The impact differs for everyone. The one indisputable fact is that no matter who you are or what your relationship has been, there *is* an impact."

"Too true, and I feel really sorry for Curt," Kate said. "I wish we could do something to make his life easier. It would be hard enough to lose a son in an accident—they do happen. Murder—now that's something else. How do you deal with that?" She turned to Hollis. "You're living with them. How are they coping?"

What to say? That Curt was stoic; that Manon hovered on the brink of a breakdown—none of the above. She didn't even know these people.

"Hard to say. You're right—it must be incredibly hard."

"And to top it all off, he had that heart attack. Someone told me he's on a waiting list for bypass surgery. It's too much for one guy to cope with. It's difficult to imagine how we could help, but if you come up with anything we can do, let us know, will you?" Kate said to Hollis.

Hollis nodded; a sudden lump in her throat made it impossible for her to say anything. What a good group. How lucky she was to be taking the course with them. It was a long time since she'd been part of anything like this. She couldn't think of anything they could do, but the offer had been a sincere one. If Curt ever needed carpentry, Kate or David could do it. She wasn't sure what Patel could offer—maybe he was a superb cook. Anyway, it was good of them.

Patel saw that she was close to tears. "File that offer away. Right now we'd better head back upstairs, or we'll cause him more distress."

Curt stood at the front of the class waiting for them. When they'd taken their places, he ran his hand through his hair. It seemed to be a trademark gesture, part of his cultivated public persona.

"I want each of you to identify your favourite masters of light before we view the slides. We'll choose them from several countries. Begin in Spain, name an artist and describe one of his paintings."

Always "his"—art historians had written women out of art history. When Hollis thought of the Italian artist Artemisia Gentileschi, she hated men's erasure of women. Male art historians simply didn't mention women painters, no matter how valued and well-known they'd been in their own time.

"Velázquez. 'The Infanta' or some such title. There's a little girl, a dog and a dwarf. The light is amazing," Bert said.

"I agree. The title of the painting is 'The Maids of Honour'."

"Goya, 'The Firing Squad', his use of light and shade underline the scene's horror," Kate said.

"It's actually titled, 'The Third of May 1808'. Goya initially admired and recreated the techniques of Rembrandt and Velázquez. We're not discussing content, but Goya's technical skill did heighten the impact of his social comments. Good choice. Italy?"

"Michelangelo, Da Vinci, Botticelli, Gentileschi—the list goes on, but for me Caravaggio was the master of light. I'm thinking of 'The Calling of St. Matthew'," Patel said.

Someone else who recognized the woman's genius, thought Hollis.

"Absolutely true. His use of light makes this a compelling work. He was a master and an innovator. Italy has an abundance of significant painters. What about Holland?"

"Rembrandt—one of his self portraits. All of his work contrasts dark and light. His canvases glow." Hollis paused. "But for me Vermeer is synonymous with light. I think of 'Young Woman with a Water Jug'."

"And before Rembrandt, there was Rubens, although he was Flemish. One more country—France."

"I'll go back to sixteenth century Flanders and choose Hieronymus Bosch and his triptych, 'The Garden of Delight'. I like his vision of Hell for those who succumb to the temptations of carnal pleasure." Sebastien spoke in a deep, even voice.

Curt said nothing, but finally forced his gaze away from Sebastien and nodded to David.

"Chardin, 'Back from the Market'," David said. "His still lifes deceive the viewer. They appear simple, but they're anything but. His use of light is amazing. And after him but before the Impressionists, how about Corbet and his landscapes? I'm thinking particularly of 'The Stone Breakers'."

"Good choice." Curt picked up the slide projector's remote control and asked Kate to close the blinds. The room darkened. A slide identified by Patel as a Caravaggio flashed on the screen. After a spirited discussion, they prepared grounds to apply to their work surfaces.

"Before I leave, I have a couple of things to attend to in my office upstairs. If anyone wishes to talk to me about the course, please drop in," Curt announced as class ended. He grabbed his briefcase and walked quickly ran from the room.

Parking in the neighbourhood was both hard to come by and expensive. As a consequence, Hollis and Curt were sharing the trip back and forth to the college. During class,

Hollis realized she had errands to run and would not need a ride. Since she hadn't caught Curt on his way out of class, she stashed her materials and went upstairs. She walked along the hall to Curt's office but stopped abruptly. The door was ajar and someone was speaking.

"When did Valerie die? What happened to her?"

"You can sit there and ask that."

"I haven't heard anything about Valerie," Curt said.

"She died in February. I can tell you the exact number of days and hours."

"I was in California for reading week, then I had a heart attack and was out of touch for a while."

"You didn't know Valerie was pregnant?" Lefebvre's voice rose.

"I did, but Seb, you have to believe me, I..."

"Offered to divorce your wife? Offered to pay for an abortion? You did neither."

"What do you..."

"You told her life was sacred and counselled her to have it."

"I did. Life is precious..."

"You sanctimonious bastard. Her life was precious to us. You're going to pay in as many horrible ways as I can imagine. I don't care what happens to me, but I want you to feel pain."

A murmur.

"I don't believe you. Every minute of every hour of every day, I intend to make sure you remember."

More indistinguishable words.

"I'll sit in on *every* class you give. I'll attend *any* show. You'll never forget—never. You'll rue the day you counselled my darling Valerie to have the baby."

Lefevbre erupted from the room and stormed down the hall, muttering under his breath.

Hollis waited a few minutes before she knocked softly on the door.

"Curt, I have to run errands before dinner."

He stared at her but didn't quite focus.

"I couldn't help overhearing some of your conversation. It's none of my business, but could Lefevbre have tampered with Ivan's brakes to get back at you?"

Curt started, shook his head and scowled. "It *is* none of your business." He swept papers into his battered attaché case, rose and turned his back on her.

She didn't linger. Despite Curt's refusal to speak about Lefevbre, it still seemed to her that he might have killed Ivan. And might strike again. He had threatened to stop at nothing to hurt Curt. He'd lost his daughter—what better way to retaliate than to kill Curt's son.

Nine

Rhona and Zee Zee had goofed. Initially they'd assumed tampering with motorcycle brakes had to have been a man's crime. Consequently, they'd focused their attention on men with reason to hate the Hartmans. They'd used the men's names in the visitation book as one of their starting points. After Rhona had reported on her lunch with Hollis, they added selected girls and women to the rota. For the rest of the afternoon, Rhona tracked down and arranged interviews with women who had signed the condolence book. Regular work hours disappeared when a murder investigation was ongoing. Who knew how long it would be until they'd finished, and she could go home?

Once at home, she'd feed Opie tuna before she luxuriated under a hot shower. She'd sluice away the day's grime and breathe deeply to clear her lungs of Toronto's bad air. Clean and refreshed, she'd pad barefoot to the kitchen and prepare for her ritual. First, she'd remove the vodka bottle from the freezer and the chilled martini glass from its permanent place on the top shelf of her refrigerator. Then she'd indulge in her private passion—a vodka martini with a twist of lemon. One—she'd only have one before she nuked pad thai or vegetable lasagna. After that she'd recline in her lazy boy and enjoy one of her old Hitchcock movies. She could almost taste the martini as she sat in the office.

Her phone buzzed. To answer or not to answer? She was a cop—there wasn't an option.

"Hollis Grant here. Good thing you gave me your card. Ignore the noise. I'm on my cell outside OCAD. I have something new for you."

The martini faded from view. Never mind—this was what she loved about the job. There was always an unexpected corner to turn, a new trail to follow.

"Go ahead."

"You don't need to sound so excited."

"I don't know what you're going to say."

"The portrait painter, Sebastien Lefevbre, is registered in our class. In case you don't recognize his name, his portraits are world famous. He needs painting lessons like Mozart needed music lessons." She related what had happened in class and what she'd heard in the office.

"That is new information. Thanks, I'll follow up."

She hung up and contemplated the phone. Should they interview him immediately? Of course. She went straight to Canada411 on her computer. Where had Sebastien Lefevbre been on the evening before Ivan's crash, she wondered.

"Mr. Lefevbre, it's Detective Simpson from the Toronto Police. My partner and I want to talk to you. Will you be home for the next hour?"

"You spoke to me after the funeral. I have nothing to add to what I said then."

"It's about your daughter and..."

"Goddamn Curt. He had to go running to you. But what could I expect? Yes, I'll be here."

Sebastien Lefevbre lived in the Annex, a downtown neighbourhood of large old houses. Unlike its well-kept neighbours, his tall, thin semi-detached house was neglected. The garden needed watering and weeding. A black plastic flat of petunias, dried out and unplanted, lay on ragged overgrown grass. Someone had stabbed a rusty trowel into the dirt beside it. The hedge marking the property's edge sprouted a forest of unkempt tendrils.

Duct tape covered the doorbell. Rhona lifted the tarnished brass knocker and heard its banging echo inside. A small man with a bushy grey beard, as untidy as his hedge, peered out before he opened the door and beckoned them in. They followed him down a dim hall hung top to bottom with paintings. He waved them into one of the untidiest rooms Rhona had ever seen.

Too many pieces of heavy furniture crowded the space. Paintings, mostly portraits, hung one above another. Sheer curtains flanked by heavy side panels and overwhelmed by dark green satin swags allowed in little light. Unpolished silver bibelots, framed photos and ornate Victorian china dishes jostled for room on every horizontal surface.

An old spaniel with bleary eyes and matted coat staggered to his feet and barked once. Once he'd performed his guard dog duty, the dog sagged to the carpet. Lefevbre indicated that they should sit on the sofa.

They pushed aside several week's worth of newspapers and lowered themselves gingerly. Zee Zee removed her notebook and tape recorder from her bag.

"I'd offer you a drink, but I forgot to buy anything," Lefevbre said. "I'm the house husband, and I've let things slide since..." His words faded.

"Your daughter died." Rhona finished his sentence

He nodded. Tears slid down his cheeks into his beard.

The claustrophobic room motivated Rhona to get straight to the point. "Why do you blame Curt Hartman?"

Lefevbre's back straightened. His lips turned back in a snarl. "He had an affair with her. The police should have charged him. The school should have fired him."

"How old was your daughter?"

"Twenty-two, but like an innocent, trusting child."

"She wasn't a child," Rhona said mildly.

"Maybe not chronologically. She admired—no, I need a stronger word—she revered Curt. He must have taken advantage."

Rhona wasn't going to argue. But it still took two to tango.

"He told her she should have the baby. Notice I do not say he promised to divorce his wife to marry her, did not offer to go with her if she wanted an abortion."

"Did she identify him as the father?"

"And who else would it have been? Curt this, Curt that, Curt says—blah, blah, blah."

"But you don't know for sure?"

"I do. I confronted Curt this morning." He slumped. "She did finally see sense and went to arrange for an abortion. Too late. No reputable doctor or clinic performs them in the third trimester. She called me, really upset. On the way home she missed a stop sign, crashed into an SUV and died."

"I am sorry," Rhona said. "Where were you on Sunday evening June 26th?"

Lefevbre had disappeared down a rabbit hole in his mind. He roused. "What?"

She repeated the question.

"No idea."

"It's important."

His gaze roamed the room as if he might find the answer hidden behind a candlestick or tucked under a table. Hard to imagine this man painting lively, engaging, psychologically penetrating portraits of everyone from Pierre Trudeau to Pamela Wallin.

"Do you have a date book, a calendar, a Blackberry..."

"I *had* a date book. I can't find it. Maybe Lindsay can tell you."

"Lindsay?"

"Lindsay Inkster—my wife. The comptroller of MFB Corporation and mother of my darling Valerie." His gaze moved erratically, as if he was searching for the two women.

"Where do you think you were? It isn't that long ago. We need the information."

Lefebvre's face closed. "I told you, *I don't know.*" He shrugged. "I only know that Valerie's dead, and I want her killer, not the SUV driver, her real killer, punished."

A man with one thing on his mind, an all-consuming obsession.

"It's important. Try to remember. Call us if you do. And please go to the nearest police station for fingerprinting." Rhona extracted a card from her bag. "I'll call tomorrow to find out if you've found the date book." She removed a pen. "Please give me your wife's work number."

After a long pause, Lefevbre spoke. "She's at their Vancouver office." He dug the number out of his memory.

Outside, Rhona paused on the stoop and exhaled the stale air of the house. She breathed deeply. Toronto's air sparkled in contrast to the musty, sorrow-laced stagnation of Lefebvre's home. His anger ran deep and dark. "Can you visualize him sneaking along Winchester Street to cut Ivan's brakes?"

"Maybe—can you?" Zee Zee replied.

"Yes, I can. I have to attend to a couple of things first. I'll make the call when I get home. Vancouver is three hours behind us, and that will be about right."

Eight o'clock; Rhona shut her apartment door behind her. Time to make a martini. She sighed. Not quite yet. She had to phone Lindsay Inkster.

Opie wound round her legs, grovelling shamelessly as if he hadn't eaten for days.

"You're substituting food for love," Rhona said sternly. "I do it too. We'll both end up lonely roly-poly butter balls." She cranked the can opener around the top of his cat food tin and spooned a portion into Opie's dish. He ignored it and continued to wind himself around her ankles. When she returned to the living room, he followed her. She sank into her high-end sofa. This was one splurge she'd never regretted; she enjoyed the enveloping softness of down-filled cushions. "Come and sit on my knee while I make a phone call. It'll do us both good."

Opie regarded her steadily. He looked as if he understood and was weighing his options. Having made his decision, he leaped up, arched his back, waved his tail in her face and settled on her knees, kneading with his paws.

She stroked him with one hand and punched in the Vancouver number.

"Lindsay Inkster."

Rhona identified herself. "Could you tell us where your husband was on Sunday evening, June 26th? He says he can't find his date book and thought you might know. Were you home?"

"Why do you want to know?"

"We're investigating the murder of Ivan Hartman."

"I can't imagine why you think Seb would be involved, but I'm sure he has nothing to hide. Hang on, I'll check." A pause. "My Blackberry puts me in the Philippines, to be precise at the Royal Hotel in Manila. Sorry, I can't help. My poor Seb has lost his date book and everything else except his obsession with Valerie's death. I mean, she was my daughter too, and I'm carrying on. You have to move on, but he doesn't seem to be able to do that. You can't believe he had anything to do with Curt's son's murder? But that must be why you want this information." She sounded incredulous. Rhona visualized the woman shaking her head. "Listen to me. Poor dear Seb doesn't need police harassment. He needs help, not accusations."

"If you can find his day book, we'd appreciate it."

"And what will that prove? Since I was in Manila, he probably spent the evening alone. He hardly ever goes out, never meets his friends. I'm worried sick about him. I wish I could stay home more—maybe I could distract him, help him find his way out of his black hole. But I can't. We're in the middle of a huge project. But you don't need to know that." She sighed. "I'll find it, but it won't make any difference. You must have better suspects."

Rhona wished they did.

In her tiny kitchen, she prepared the perfect martini, opened the door to her balcony and drifted out, drink in hand. She'd chosen this end apartment because one side overlooked a distant Lake Ontario and the other faced a lane lined with towered maples. Their greenness soothed and cooled.

Months since her arrival, unpacked boxes and excess furniture still cluttered the apartment. Immersed in her first case, she needed a tidy serene refuge—this wasn't it. Time to make a serious effort. She'd start tonight. Pull on her jeans. Unpack the boxes and sort the books. Assemble the two IKEA bookcases still in their cartons. IKEA directions sometimes made her feel like an idiot—like a primate would feel when confronted with a box requiring a tool. Never mind. She'd done it before, and she could do it again. She visualized the white Billy bookcases with neatly aligned books interspersed with interesting bibelots adding colour and personality to the messy apartment.

Such a lot of work. Maybe not tonight.

Back in the kitchen, she zapped a dinner and flipped it onto a plate. What an extraordinary colour. Nothing in the real world except maybe a gaudy sunset came close. It did not pass go but went straight in the garbage. Time for comfort food. She opened the freezer, replaced the vodka bottle and considered the merits of praline, strawberry or vanilla ice cream before she chose vanilla. A rattle through the cutlery drawer located a small demitasse spoon. When she ate ice cream with a tiny spoon, it prolonged the joy. She dropped *The African Queen* into the DVD player and curled up on the sofa. Her hands cradled a cereal bowl filled with ice cream, topped with chocolate sauce and a maraschino cherry.

But the movie didn't do its job.

Cutting the brakes. What a terrible way to plan to kill someone. First he'd pump. Nothing would happen. He wouldn't believe it. He'd cut the gas. If he was on an incline, the bike would accelerate. He might think about jumping off, but he wouldn't have time. She shivered. A killer targeted his victim for many reasons—a robbery gone wrong, self-defense, fear of disclosure. But this was premeditated murder designed to maximize the victim's suffering, to give him time to realize what was about to happen. Whoever had done it had judged the size of cut that allowed fluid to leak slowly and not leave a noticeable puddle. He'd been brazen and sabotaged the brakes under street lights on a public thoroughfare. She hoped the fingerprints they'd taken from the parking pad were those of the killer— evidence not strong enough to convict but certainly enough to sway a jury.

She thought about the suspects. Sebastien Lefevbre, Olivero Ciccio, the SOHD opponents, Arthur White and Lena Kalma. Could it be a Greek tragedy, a Shakespearean tragedy? If Lena had intended to kill Curt then learned she'd killed her son, wouldn't she want to avenge her son's death?

Ten

After she'd called Rhona to report on Lefevbre's presence in class and his confrontation with Curt, Hollis worked her way down her shopping list. She thought about Curt and Valerie while she bought dog shampoo, dental floss and expensive coloured pencils. What was it with Curt? Had Lena also been pregnant when she and Curt married? Did he have a thing about procreation—a need to father children? Psychologists must have written weighty tomes about men like Curt.

She miscalculated how long her shopping would take. Puffing along Winchester Street, she checked her watch, hoping it would reassure her that she wasn't as late as she thought she was. It offered no such assurance. With her shoulders squared, she took a deep breath to relieve the tightness in her stomach and tension in her shoulders.

"Excuse me, Mrs. Hartman, I'm glad to catch you. I'm recruiting volunteers to canvass for the United Way." The speaker, a middle-aged woman, blocked the sidewalk. The woman's flowered summer dress, bouffant hair-do and kohl-rimmed eyes had characterized women in the sixties. Perfume, applied with a heavy hand, enveloped her. Blue Grass—Hollis remembered this scent from her childhood when her mother had used it. At one time, the woman must have been stunning; now she was a caricature of bygone days.

Hollis couldn't pass unless she shoved the woman aside.

"I'm not Mrs. Hartman." And Manon wasn't Mrs. Hartman either—she'd retained her maiden name, Dumont.

"But she lives here?"

Hollis was late and didn't want to talk. "Excuse me." She edged around the woman and headed up the path.

"I wanted to enlist her help to recruit for the United Way," the woman called after her.

The front door banged open. "You're here. We've been waiting for you." Etienne bounded down the steps. MacTee loped after him with his tail waving like a metronome pacing a very fast piece of music.

Etienne promised to become a handsome man. He would combine his mother's dark hair, brown eyes and chiselled features with his father's height and bone structure. Hollis reached to hug him, but Etienne stuck out his hand. He'd crossed the divide between an easily embraceable little kid and a young man who bestowed his hugs more judiciously.

"Not a good time, I can see," the woman said. She pivoted and stalked away.

"Maman, Papa and Tomas are in the garden."

"Hollis is here," Etienne announced when they rounded the corner.

Curt and Tomas, examining a chart spread out on the glass-topped garden table, looked up. Manon rose. She reminded Hollis of a Whistler painting, a woman with perfect porcelain skin and regal bearing. With her dark hair pulled back from her oval face and fastened at the nape of her neck, she could have passed for a nineteenth century gentlewoman.

When they embraced, Hollis felt how little flesh covered Manon's ribs. Stepping back, she noted that her friend's sundress hung loosely, and her collar and chest bones jutted aggressively. The trials of the last weeks had taken a physical and mental toll.

Sometimes she wished she resembled the Manons of this world. They gave up eating when unhappiness or tension overwhelmed them. Hollis guiltily recalled the grocery carts of shortbread cookies, toasted coconut doughnuts and cream-filled chocolates she'd eaten in tense times. Now, to prevent weight escalation, she steeled herself to avert her eyes from pastry shop windows and avoid the cookie aisle in the supermarket. And she tried to maintain a jogging regimen. Sometimes, if she'd held steady for weeks, she rewarded herself with one cookie or one doughnut. It wasn't easy.

Hollis hugged Curt and Tomas.

"I'm sorry I'm late. It isn't much of an excuse, but it'll take me weeks to learn to cope with Toronto distances and traffic."

"No need to apologize, we eat later in summertime," Curt said.

"You need a few minutes to unwind and decompress," Manon said. "How about a cool drink before dinner?"

Manon spoke in an easy voice but looked as if taut elastics that threatened to snap at any moment held her features in place. With raised shoulders, she hunched forward like a boxer pinned to the ropes, anticipating body blows and shielding herself.

It hurt Hollis to look at her. That much tension must do terrible things to a person's metabolism. She resolved to locate a good spa. Soon she'd treat Manon and herself to an afternoon of massage and pampering. She could imagine the massage therapist tut-tutting when her hands encountered the rock hard knots in Manon's muscles.

Manon led them across the flagstone patio to a grouping of teak, brassbound deck chairs with comfortable-looking green and white striped cushions. Large, square white wooden planters overflowing with silver grey licorice plants separated the chairs.

Tomas, tall, tan and dark-haired, folded the chart. He smiled at Hollis. "You'll excuse me. Dad and I didn't know whether to get back to our regular life, but we decided it would be better for us if we did. We were planning a weekend sailing race. But I have to go." He passed his half-brother and cuffed him gently. "You take care of that dog."

Etienne's grin revealed his love for Tomas.

Curt, showing none of Manon's physical stress, sauntered to a chaise lounge and sank into the cushions. Slightly off-balance, he reached for a nearby teak table to steady himself. The table wobbled and threatened to topple an uneven stack of magazines crowned with reading glasses. He grabbed for the glasses, perched them on his nose and smiled at Hollis.

Hollis returned his smile, chose an adjoining lounge and waited for Manon to sit down.

She didn't. Instead she restlessly straightened a cushion, picked dead leaves from potted plants, and bent to wrest weeds from cracks between the patio stones. MacTee didn't settle either. While he paced, his nails clicked a tattoo, his tongue hung out and he panted.

Curt, ignoring his restless wife, pointed to the path that wound through artful plantings of shade-loving perennials and ended at the two-storey carriage house. "Hollis, I didn't invite you to visit my studio when you were here before. As a matter of fact, I can count on my fingers the number of visitors I've had." He drew the fingers of one hand down his chin, smoothing a non-existent beard. "Since you're an old friend, I'm making an exception." He produced a tight, smug smile.

She knew she was supposed to appreciate this honour, but he irked her. The confrontation between Lefevbre and Curt was colouring her attitude. She wondered how Curt could carry on as if it had never taken place. That was irrational, as surely she hadn't expected him to come home and discuss Valerie's pregnancy and death with Manon.

"It's always interesting to see an artist's working space. I love *studio* tours." Her emphasis on "studio" would annoy him. He wouldn't like being lumped in with the art world proletariat who used studio tours to publicize their work. God, she had barely arrived, and she was being ungracious. Why should Manon and Etienne suffer because she resented Curt's attitude. Enough. Curt and Manon didn't need a snotty house guest. She injected warmth and enthusiasm into her voice. "Thanks. I'll enjoy every minute."

If Curt had any idea how Hollis felt, he didn't show it. "The gravel was Manon's idea. *She* wanted it to resemble garden paths in France—our own Petit Trianon." He sniffed. "She failed to consider that we live in Canada, not France. Gravel is a mistake. Impossible to shovel in the winter."

"It's a lovely garden, and it feels ten degrees cooler," Hollis said.

Manon ignored Curt's remark and offered a choice of cold drinks.

MacTee stopped directly in front of Hollis. He stared fixedly at her and gave a single low woof. Hollis had assumed that sometime during the day, someone would have taken him out. Whether they had or not, his message was clear.

"Lemonade, but it will have to wait—MacTee's desperate for a walk."

"Poor dog, of course he is. I should have taken him," Manon said. She shifted her gaze to Etienne, who glared at her. "Etienne wanted to, but I..."

"Wouldn't let him out of your sight." Curt finished the sentence. "You overprotect him—treat him like a baby."

What was this about? Before Ivan's funeral, Hollis had

noticed how grown-up and responsible Etienne had acted. Manon had bragged of his independence.

Manon ignored her husband's jibe. "I'll show you the park," she volunteered. "Etienne, while we're gone, will you bring out glasses, cookies, a bucket of ice and the pitcher of lemonade. And the set of keys on the kitchen counter."

Etienne stroked MacTee's back. He scrunched his lips in disappointment but nodded his agreement.

Shoulders hunched and head thrust forward, Manon left the garden. She halted abruptly at the front of the house.

Hollis, unprepared for her sudden stop, nearly crashed into her. She hauled on MacTee's leash to brake his charge for the grassy verge.

Manon peered up and down the street. "It's okay," she said. Her shoulders relaxed. She repeated, "It's okay."

"What's okay?" Hollis asked. She waited for an answer and allowed MacTee's flexi-leash to extend to its limit. Awash in new scents, he sniffed his way from bush to post to bush.

"Nothing," Manon said.

"Come on. You didn't stop like you were about to fall off the edge of the earth for nothing."

"Did I tell you about Arthur White?"

"No, but I know he was Curt's agent and ran the Starship gallery. I read that he hated the accusations Curt made against him in last year's biography. I met him years ago, but I don't remember him."

"He's short and has white fuzzy hair. He's suing Curt for libel. I stopped because he sometimes hangs around. Don't worry if he says something nasty to you. He's harmless."

"Now that you describe him, I do remember seeing him standing outside when I went for a run the day Ivan died. *You* don't sound convinced that he's harmless."

"I'm not. But I find monsters everywhere. I'm trying to think positively, to consider Curt's troubles with Arthur as his problem."

Hollis hadn't acknowledged her own tension until they left the garden. A knot between her shoulder blades, her clenched jaw and slight feeling of nausea provided ample evidence. She considered her body's reaction and wondered if she'd be more help to Manon if she didn't stay with them. Maybe she and MacTee should retreat to a motel each evening. It would give her the opportunity to recharge her batteries and regain her equilibrium. Maybe Manon would agree.

"It's great to be here, but I worry about our stay. You're contending with a lot. No matter how many times you've said it's okay, three weeks is a long time for house guests, especially when one of them is a dog." With her free hand, Hollis grasped Manon's arm. "Say the word, and we'll book into a motel. I'll totally understand."

Manon covered Hollis's hand with her own. "Not a chance. Nadine is more than a housekeeper—she's like a grandmother to Etienne. She thinks MacTee will be a great diversion for him." She squeezed Hollis's hand. Hollis winced. Manon loosened her grip. "Don't you dare think about leaving." Her voice had risen. "I've been counting the days until you arrived. Life here is hell." Tears brimmed but didn't flow. "I'm losing perspective. I have no one, absolutely no one, to talk to who really knows me."

Manon must have seen doubt in Hollis's eyes.

"It's true. Curt has his own problems. Anyway, he's never understood or sympathized with how much I worry. I talk to my psychiatrist—but it isn't the same as having a friend." She squeezed Hollis's hand more gently. "I'm happy you're here." She tightened her grip. "You *and* MacTee. If anyone can figure out who Ivan was and maybe who killed him, it'll be you."

"Manon, the police will track his killer."

Hollis shut her eyes. There was to be no escape. She felt inadequate, afraid she wouldn't be able to help Manon. She opened her eyes, glanced down and gasped. She'd always admired Manon's smooth, elegant hands and beautifully kept nails. Since their university days, Manon had acknowledged that her nail fixation was excessive. She'd rationalized it as a harmless idiosyncrasy.

But not any more.

Manon's unpolished, bitten nails revealed the depth of her anxiety and despair more clearly than anything she'd said.

Eleven

MacTee tugged on his leash. "Manon, the police *will* find the killer. It's little more than ten days since Ivan died." MacTee's eyes implored Hollis to move.

"It seems like forever. Uncertainty, fear." Manon shook her head as if to clear away frightening thoughts and ventured a smile. "Poor dog, he's telling us it's okay to talk but not to stop."

"We'll walk and talk. I want to hear everything." Hollis used what she called her 'bright cheery voice', although she felt anything but bright and cheery. "Things aren't always as serious as they seem at four in the morning. When you're alone with your thoughts in the middle of the night, they terrify you. Examining them in daylight, they become more manageable." Hollis could have kicked herself for the sheer fatuousness of her remarks. Manon was dealing with murder and the threat of murder. *She* was babbling on like a third rate self-help writer.

"Ivan's murder was terrible. You were with us—you know how awful it was. Now we live with the unknown, the horror..." Her voice trailed off. "You can't imagine," she added.

Since her own husband had died violently the year before, she could have contradicted Manon. Instead she murmured, "The uncertainly must be..." She searched for a word and found nothing.

"Unbearable," Manon said flatly. "If it was our only problem, I might cope better. It isn't. Every new development stresses Curt. If life continues like this, I'm afraid he won't live long enough to have his bypass." She stopped. "Mostly I worry about Etienne. What must it be like for an eleven-year-old?"

"Kids are resilient," Hollis said, knowing that they weren't unless adults intervened and made sure the kids didn't blame themselves. Maybe Etienne felt responsible because he hadn't told his mother Ivan attended George Brown. Later she'd ask Manon if she'd spoken to Etienne and reassured him that none of this was his fault.

They resumed their walk.

"Curt must hate being sick."

Manon slowed. "That's it. Psychologically, it's terrible. Curt believed he was invincible."

"How serious is it?"

"I don't know how they define serious. He grabs for his angina pills at least ten times a day."

"How is he emotionally?"

"Mostly angry. But neither pain nor the threat of another heart attack stops him." She crossed her arms over her chest. "I want to scream when he aggravates the situation. He climbs stairs, moves heavy stuff, sails." She pursed her lips. "It's like he's daring his heart to give up, pushing himself to prove to the doctors that they should have placed him higher on the waiting list."

"I don't suppose he listens if you say anything."

"No. He tells me to stop nagging. He says it's his body, and he'll cope. I feel helpless."

"Would he talk to a grief counsellor or a psychiatrist to sort out his feelings?" Maybe he'd also discuss his unfaithfulness and explain why he impregnated women. How many other

Valeries were out there?

Manon smiled sardonically. "Never. His pride would never let him. He'd rather die. He will if he stupidly insists on straining his heart." She sniffed. "Curt's irrationally overreacting. He's not facing the issues he needs to deal with. Instead, he's blaming other people." She peered at the ground, scraped the hard-packed path with her sandal's toe and didn't look at Hollis. "It hurts me to say this, but he wasn't a good father to Ivan." She raised her eyes. "Not on purpose. He wasn't mean or cruel, but he was always on Ivan's case. He wanted to shame or browbeat him into becoming more ambitious. Now, I assume, although he hasn't admitted it, he's dealing with guilt."

"That's a heavy burden."

"It is. Even more for Curt than for some others. Since he isn't introspective, he hasn't had much practice confronting his feelings—if he that's what he's doing. He's left train wrecks behind him all his life. I don't know if he's ever acknowledged how badly he's hurt people. I don't need to tell you he has a colossal ego and likes to run the show. None of this is new. He's always been hard to live with—it's like co-existing with a volcano." Manon raised her shoulders and shrugged. "I'm never sure when he'll erupt."

Their gazes locked. Hollis agreed with Manon's description but didn't say so. Spouses could make the most awful charges against one another. Woe betide the listener who agreed with them.

MacTee tugged on his leash.

"We're here," Manon said.

A graveyard stretched into the distance on the left. On their right a paved path sloped into a large grassy space.

"Lovely to have open land in the middle of Toronto," Hollis said.

"Long ago it was Riverdale Zoo. At night you heard the lions roaring. Over there, that's the Toronto Necropolis. It's been here almost since Toronto began, and these were the outskirts. Now the cemetery sits in the city's heart. If you have time, it's interesting to stroll around and read headstones."

"I wonder if MacTee's allowed inside. Most cemeteries forbid dogs. I don't blame them. If the owners don't clean up and someone visits a grave and finds..."

"I get the picture," Manon interrupted. "We'll see if there's a sign." She frowned, "I'm sorry, I'm not usually so self-centred. I haven't asked about you and your plans to change your life."

Hollis was amazed that Manon had remembered. Seconds after she'd made this revelation, Manon's cell phone had rung and her world had flipped.

"Don't be hard on yourself. I'm fine and you're not. A lot depends on how the course goes. We'll talk about me later."

They arrived at a long series of wooden steps leading down to a grassy area crowded with dogs and people. Manon pointed. "The dogs' off-leash area."

MacTee lunged down the steps, oblivious to Hollis clutching his leash with one hand and grabbing at the railing with the other. She shouted over her shoulder, "He's seen them throwing balls. He's retrieving-obsessed." Hollis caught her breath after she'd completed the precipitous descent without a fall. She reached in her pocket for a battered tennis ball before she released the dog. MacTee, anticipating the joy to come, jumped up and down on all four feet as if each leg came equipped with its own powerful inner spring.

Hollis tossed the ball and waited for Manon to catch up with her.

"Does your golden suffer from hot spots?" A burly, barrel-chested man, whose red suspenders bracketed his expanding girth like a writer's ellipses, spoke to Hollis.

"If I don't have her clipped every spring." She marvelled at how an interest in dogs united people.

A shaggy golden exhibiting a depth of chest and rotundity corresponding to her owner's galloped over.

"What a lovely dog—does she have a skin problem?" Where had she seen this man?

The man bent and patted the retriever. "It's a he, Gelato, Gelo for short. He does, but I wasn't convinced clipping would help." He straightened and looked over Hollis's shoulder.

Until that moment, Hollis hadn't known exactly what people meant when they said someone's face "lit up".

The man's face brightened, his mouth opened and a huge grin spread across his face. "Manon, you haven't been here since Beau died."

Hollis swung to see Manon extend both hands to the man, who enveloped her in a bear hug. Manon gazed up at him. "Olivero, I've missed you." She stepped away, reached for Hollis's hand and pulled her forward. "Olivero, this is my friend Hollis Grant. She's staying with us while she takes Curt's course."

As she shook Olivero's hand, she remembered. The funeral home—she'd seen him there. She hadn't spoken to him; she'd overheard him saying he'd come to the visitation because of his friendship with Manon. The man he'd been speaking to had implied his relationship was more than that.

"When do you and Gelo walk here?" Manon asked. It was not a casual, polite question; she really wanted the information.

"Often. The term's over. I'm not teaching at summer school. I come whenever I reach a point where Gelo or I need a break. Quite early in the morning, around noon and sometime before six." He smiled conspiratorially. "You *know* what a news junkie I am—always have to catch the six o'clock news."

Time to make herself scarce. "I'm going to give MacTee a run." She called the dog and strode across the field, pulling details of the overheard conversation from her mind. Curt had done something unspecified but dastardly to Olivero. She reached the far side of the open space. While she repeatedly tossed the ball, she considered this complication. On the one hand, as far as she knew, Manon hadn't had any extramarital affairs since she'd married Curt. But on the other, Manon's affair with Curt had led him to leave Lena. She and Manon weren't like some women, who discussed their sex lives with their friends. Hollis doubted Manon would have confided in her if she was having an affair. But maybe she was jumping the gun. Manon's life with Curt was difficult. Olivero might be a supportive friend—no more. Hollis tossed the moisture-laden ball. People should copy dogs—they lived in the present and derived great joy from small pleasures.

Finally, tired and hot, MacTee refused to relinquish the ball. They rejoined Manon and Olivero, who were talking in low tones.

"We must go," Manon said to Olivero. "We'll meet you here soon."

It was a promise.

"Is Olivero also an artist?" Hollis asked as they strolled away.

"An artist and an art historian. When I tired of inviting Curt's friends to dinner and getting lost in their art-centred conversations, I took an evening course from Olivero. He's a twentieth century specialist and a lovely, kind man," Manon said with a dreamy half-smile on her face. "Very, very kind."

Kind or not, Olivero might hate Curt. Rhona had been farther away when both of them had tried to eavesdrop on the conversation at the visitation. Hollis had barely heard what they'd said, and she didn't think Rhona would have heard anything. Although she'd most likely interviewed him, she might not have asked about his friendship with Manon. Another information tidbit to exchange for an investigation update.

Back in the garden, Manon poured lemonade. "We met Olivero walking his dog," she said.

"I wish you'd let me come with you. I love Gelo," Etienne said. He giggled. "Gelo the dog, not Jello the food. It's gross."

Curt lay on a chaise lounge thumbing through a magazine. "Olivero," he said. A small smile twitched at the corners of his mouth. "Has he recovered from losing his bid for departmental chairman?"

"You voted against him, didn't you?" Manon said.

"Of course. Fat little Italian—what kind of an impression would he make representing the department? We need someone with presence."

"Someone like you—is that what you mean?"

"I'm far too busy to take on the chairman's job, but yes, my reputation would increase the department's prestige."

"That wasn't why you voted against him. You've always envied him his charisma—his warm, friendly personality." Tears brimmed in Manon's eyes.

"*You* certainly think so. At the Christmas party, you made an absolute fool of yourself. I'm sure his wife didn't enjoy your performance. *I* certainly didn't," Curt said.

"You are an insufferable snob." Manon's voice trembled.

An uneasy silence followed this exchange.

"Can I throw MacTee's ball in the garden?" Etienne asked.

"Of course not—that's why we have parks," Curt said.

"When I take him for another walk, will you come with me and throw the ball?" Hollis asked Etienne.

Etienne nodded and moved forward to pick up a computer

game lying on the glass-topped table. At the same moment, Manon reached for the keys Etienne had brought out. She held the ring up. "Hollis, these are for you. Front and back doors, Curt's studio and the garage." A shrug and a rueful glance. "You'll think I'm paranoid. Actually, I'm one person who could produce psychiatric witnesses to testify to my exact mental state. I'm not paranoid." She glared at Curt.

Curt ignored her.

"However, at the moment my *paranoiac* point is to *insist* we lock the door every time we come in or go out." She shook the keys, allowing them to jangle noisily.

Hollis again noticed Manon's unkempt nails.

"*Every* time. You must *always* lock the doors."

"*Every* time—*always* lock the doors," Curt mimicked. "The lady who isn't obsessive obsesses yet again."

"I'll bring in my things," Hollis said to change the subject.

Manon hesitated. "Etienne will help you unload your truck."

She paused, because she didn't want to let him go outside on the street. How awful to feel such anxiety. What must Manon's obsessive need to watch his every move do to Etienne?

"The man across the street is Arthur," Etienne said in a low voice as they lugged bundles back to the house. He edged closer. "Did Maman talk to you about him?"

"She did." Hollis's dark glasses hid her eyes and allowed her to observe, without seeming to do so. She'd seen him before. Today he perched on a shooting stick and held a small black umbrella over his head. He seemed more like one of Santa's elves than an evil presence, but he obviously scared Etienne, who stiffened and walked closer to Hollis.

How infuriating it was to see a grown man frightening a child. Maybe she'd give the old goat a taste of his own medicine. She'd find a similar stick and park herself inches from Arthur and sing in his face. She'd choose from the many folk songs she'd collected on her travels through the rural Maritimes. The image amused her. She reviewed appropriate songs that promised death or eternal damnation to sinners.

As Etienne unlocked the front door, Manon called from the kitchen. "Etienne. Come downstairs after you've helped Hollis—I have a job for you."

The guest room was on the second floor. Etienne dropped MacTee's mat in the corner and flopped on the bed. MacTee, immediately recognizing an opportunity for patting, leaned against him. He nudged Etienne's arm to initiate the process.

"How old is MacTee?" Etienne asked.

Hollis heard concern in his voice. Etienne's dog, Beau, had died the year before. Etienne was mourning his brother and fearful for his father. He was probably hesitant to commit to MacTee without reassurance that this dog wasn't about to die.

"Eight and very healthy. Retrievers live to about twelve— he'll be with us for years."

Etienne scratched behind MacTee's ears and smiled.

A disembodied voice floated up the stairs. "Etienne, come down, please."

While the bed invited Hollis to lie back and relax, the navy upholstered chair with matching footstool invited her to pick a book from the stack on the table beside the chair. She examined the titles: mysteries by Mary Jane Maffini, Barbara Fradkin and Peter Robinson; a book on urban renewal by Jane Jacobs; and two art books, one about Greg Curnoe, whose bicycle paintings she loved, and the other about Georgia O'Keefe. How typical of Manon to search for specific books Hollis would like. Manon often sent her gifts, not for a particular occasion but because she'd found something she thought Hollis would enjoy. She dug MacTee's water bowl from her backpack and filled it in the bathroom.

Even before she unpacked, it was time to go through Ivan's belongings. She crept up to the third floor apartment to see what Ivan had left behind.

Everything belonging to Ivan was gone.

Twelve

Hollis joined Manon in the kitchen. There was no way to bring Ivan back or free Manon from her demons, but she could offer a diversion from the ongoing crisis. "You free to take in a movie tonight?"

Manon swung around from the counter, where she was ripping romaine lettuce into bite-sized pieces and dropping them in a clear acrylic salad bowl. "Unfortunately not. We have a commitment, but later in the week would be good. It would be great to go out, to try not to think about what's happening. And you'll be happy to know that there's a new patisserie near the Cumberland. We can indulge and argue about the movie's success or failure."

"Sounds good," Hollis said. "This room reminds me of Claude Monet's kitchen at Giverny—blues and yellows, sunshine and flowers."

Manon looked around as if she'd never seen the kitchen. "You're right. Giverny captured my imagination when we visited. A Giverny kitchen didn't suit our other house, but it's perfect here." She paused. "Give me a second to finish. I *want* to think about something other than the murder, and I need your advice. As an artist, tell me what colour changes would complement the renovations I made this spring." She paused. "But we can't take long. Curt has *honoured* you with an invitation to visit his studio before dinner. We have time for a short tour before the *momentous* event occurs."

"Honoured", "momentous"—not warm and friendly words. The troubles in Manon's and Curt's lives were definitely not drawing them closer.

Manon led the way from kitchen to front hall. "You know how we've changed things." She gestured at the two doorways flanking the entryway. "We had two formal living rooms, but who needs that?" She opened the door on the right. "This is the same." She opened the other door. "I don't suppose you saw this room when you were here last week. Because of Curt's heart condition, I converted the second parlour into a bedroom and used the library behind it for an en suite bathroom for us and a powder room." She grinned. "You probably did discover that. I've added much-needed cupboard space. The work isn't finished. I'm wondering if the colour scheme in the living room and these two rooms should be more or less identical. Martha Stewart says colour should flow from one room to the next. And the other rooms on this floor—the dining room, kitchen, family room and living room—are colour coordinated."

Twin beds. Another new development. Her expression must have revealed her thoughts.

"I don't want to disturb Curt if he's restless," Manon said.

And you don't want to sleep with him, whether he is or not. Which is too bad, because you might be able to comfort one another. But she understood. Everyone coped differently. Some forged ahead and tried to use normal routines to assuage their grief, and others worked their way through sorrow by giving it the attention it demanded. Manon seemed to be in the first category. "It's lovely. I think it would add to the flow if you used a compatible colour in the bedroom." She considered. "On the other hand, if you normally keep the bedroom door closed, it isn't as important. Go ahead and choose lavender or a soothing blue, whatever you fancy." They went upstairs. The den, guest room and Manon's tiny private office were unchanged. Manon stopped before a door with a large sign taped to it: PRIVATE DO NOT ENTER.

"Adolescence is nigh," she said with warmth and no apprehension.

She made no move to climb to the third floor.

"I popped upstairs earlier. You've removed Ivan's things."

"Yes. After the funeral, I figured constant reminders of Ivan would upset Etienne and Tomas."

They might find it more upsetting to see every trace of their brother and his life dispensed with as if no one wanted to remember him. It had given her the creeps. She understood why Manon had swept Ivan's possessions away—she'd reacted the same way after Paul's death. It wasn't a universal reaction. Others often kept everything belonging to the dead person and maintained rooms or desks or workshops exactly as they'd been left. People dealt with grief in different ways.

"I boxed Ivan's stuff. Tomas lugged it to the basement."

"One of the things you asked me to do was to pick through his belongings to find anything that would tell us more about him. Before I actually do that, we should sort something out."

Manon waited.

"I have the distinct impression Curt doesn't want me to do it." Hollis spread her hands wide and raised her shoulders. "What do you think?"

Manon frowned and crossed her arms on her chest. "Pay no attention. You're *my* friend. It's *my* obsession and *my* problem. Knowing everything about Ivan is *my* solution. Go ahead." A malicious gleam showed briefly in her eyes. "And if by any chance you figure out the killer's identity, won't that just fix him."

"Okay, but given Curt's opposition, I'll be circumspect. No point annoying him unnecessarily." She reached forward, grasped Manon's upper arms and gazed into her eyes. She spoke slowly to emphasize her words. "Manon, I hope to tell you more about Ivan, but I doubt I'll finger the murderer."

"Rationally, I realize that, but it comforts me to think you might. The police aren't getting anywhere." Manon's expression was bleak. "I miss Ivan. He wasn't here often, but he was such an easy person to be with."

Hollis recognized the pain. "Do you want to talk about him?"

"No. That will make it worse."

Back in the kitchen, Hollis kept the conversation on a superficial level. "I loved the Toulouse Lautrec posters in your room at U of T. I remember your search for a bakery where you could buy the perfect croissant and baguette." She pulled a yellow stool away from the counter, sat down and smiled at her friend. "And the subtitled French movies you dragged me to."

Manon returned the smile, although her eyes remained watchful. She removed a bowl of hard-boiled eggs from the refrigerator. "Weeks ago, before Ivan died, Curt and I accepted an invitation to a friend's party. She's a puppet-maker and lives in an amazing house. After," she paused, "after what happened, I didn't know whether we should go. I wondered if we'd be able to cope; whether we'd make everyone uncomfortable. But we decided we had to go out and face everyone sooner or later, so we're going. When she heard you were here, she also invited you and Etienne."

"Did you ask her to include Etienne?"

Manon placed the bowl on the counter, picked up an egg, cracked it against the side of the bowl and placed it on a cutting board before she answered. "Poor Etienne. I guess I'm pretty obvious. I told Betty we couldn't come because Etienne refused to have a babysitter." She flicked off a bit of shell. "Every day since Ivan died, I've been terrified to allow Etienne out of my sight. Several times every night, I tip-toe into his room to make sure he's okay." She finished shelling the egg, took a blue-rimmed plate from the cupboard, cut the egg in half and slid the halves on the plate. "It's hard. At eleven, I should permit him to go places and do things by himself. In normal times, he could stay alone for short periods." She picked up a second egg. "Times are not normal. I can't do it. It's impossible."

"I totally understand. Given your circumstances, what mother could? Although your friend was nice enough to invite me, I'll say no. It's been a long day. I'll enjoy staying with Etienne—it'll give me a chance to get to know him better."

Manon cracked a second egg. "Etienne will love staying home with you and MacTee. Parties bore him, unless the kids are his age." She glanced at the kitchen wall clock. "His Royal Highness awaits you. Leave MacTee here. Knock and then go in. Unlike me, he isn't fanatical about locking the door."

At Curt's studio, Hollis faced a carved antique door. It looked as if it had originally graced the entrance to a Victorian mansion. The black enamel paint, ornate brass lion head knocker and polished brass letter slot announced to the world that *this* was the entrance to an important person's building. She knocked and entered. Immediately inside, a steep narrow staircase led to the loft studio.

"Come up," Curt called.

Curt's fame rested on his huge paintings. Hollis gazed upwards. No one lugged them down these narrow stairs. Perhaps someone, not Curt, extracted the staples fastening the canvases to wooden stretchers, rolled the paintings up and brought them out. Unlikely—rolling would damage and crack his characteristic impasto painting. How did he do it?

Curt waited at the top of the stairs. "This is it—the inner sanctum. You're one of a handful of people I've ever invited."

You'd think it was the Sistine Chapel.

"I appreciate the invitation." It was true. Artists love visiting studios to see how others organize their painting lives. Hollis surveyed the open space with its vaulted ceiling and enormous skylights. What she had initially thought were windows in the far wall over the driveway were double doors. She pointed. "Do you remove your finished work through those?"

"I do. Originally this space was for hay; they loaded bales that way. Now I use the block and tackle to move paintings."

There were no large storage cupboards and a single finished painting. "Where do you keep your other paintings?"

"I never have more than one or two here."

"How come?"

"I'm not like many painters." Curt's tight smile and arched eyebrows indicated that he considered this a virtue. "When I finish a work, I hate having it hanging around. Sending it away allows me to zero in on my current work."

"Makes sense. I suppose most of us feel less confident." Since she'd left art school, Hollis had had seven solo shows, received terrific reviews and sold many paintings. Nevertheless, she never felt confident a painting was finished. She could still want to add, subtract or change a painting she'd done years earlier.

Late afternoon light flooded the space. A gigantic canvas, probably twenty by ten feet, rested on a metal support. A moveable hydraulic dolly with a place for Curt to sit or stand allowed him to comfortably reach the highest points on the painting and to move back and forth. Rudimentary paint strokes indicated that this would be a crowd scene with a focus in the upper left corner. The beginnings of a second smaller painting composed of vertical slashes of colour reposed on an extra-large but conventional easel.

Curt walked to the area close to the stairs. "A builder tailored this space to meet my needs. It's as efficient as a ship's cabin." A wall of bookcases filled with art books was adjacent to a granite counter with a deep sink. "Being a fellow painter, you're aware of how much space you need to clean brushes, mix paint and prepare solutions." He opened a storage cupboard above the counter. "And space to store everything."

Hollis peered inside. Brushes of ascending size filled ceramic jars. "It's wonderful and so tidy."

Curt scowled. "I believe in neatness and order. Why the hell can't the cops get themselves organized?"

What was the connection? Curt was equating Ivan's murder with his brushes. She'd always suspected Curt was one of those people who get emotional responses wrong, who miss the mark and never know they have. His comment confirmed her belief.

He pointed to an open door that revealed a miniscule but complete bathroom. A white, prefabricated kitchen unit with more storage cupboards, a mini-refrigerator, espresso machine, microwave, sink and a red Formica-topped table paired with a single folding chair provided more than the culinary basics. Next to the cupboards, a wall phone and an accompanying corkboard filled with neatly aligned messages and reminders completed the efficient arrangement.

"Everything I need. I could live here for weeks or months."

And it was probably what he'd like to do right now. Hide up here, where he could create his own order. She surveyed the large open space. A cot covered with a navy sleeping bag, a slip-covered blue denim wing chair mounted on large casters, a yellow side table, also on wheels, and a tambour, a table for painting supplies, furnished the room.

"I have all the bells and whistles, although I'm not a big electronics fan. No, let me rephrase that. I *hate* cell phones, answering machines, iPods, Blackberries, computers—crap designed to waste your life while the advertisers, the spin doctors, fool you into thinking these things make you more efficient. But *this* electronic stuff is useful." He demonstrated the lighting and the skylights, electrified to release built-in blinds and open at the touch of a switch.

"It's perfect. I'm consumed with envy."

Curt's lowered eyelids and narrowed lips enhanced his resemblance to a falcon, talons embedded in its prey. "If you'd listened to me and devoted yourself to your art, you'd have a place like this. You wouldn't be wasting your time with the community college morons."

Once Curt made up his mind, he seldom changed it. It was pointless to defend herself.

She and Curt joined Manon and Etienne at the wrought iron and glass table in the garden for a cold supper with a perfect menu: Prosciutto ham, smoked salmon, boiled eggs, pasta and tossed salads, crusty rolls and strawberries. After dinner Manon and Curt excused themselves to change.

Hollis restored the kitchen to its original pristine state and waved her hosts off to their party. Her work done, she went out to the garden. Etienne, focussed on a computer game, sprawled on a lounge chair. She planted herself beside him. *"Monsieur, Hollis Grant à votre service."*

"Merci beaucoup, I like that, but I think you should bow or curtsy when you say it." Etienne grinned.

Hollis folded one arm across her stomach, placed the other behind her back and bowed from the waist. *"À votre service."*

"Much better."

"What'll it be, cards, games, a walk with MacTee, TV? Name your poison."

"A walk, but..." Etienne paused. A frown creased his forehead. "I hope Arthur isn't out there."

"With a big, brave dog like MacTee, we won't have anything to worry about."

Etienne glanced at MacTee, who lay on his back with his feet in the air and his tongue protruding from the corner of his open mouth. Etienne's frown disappeared. His grin became a laugh. It was lovely to see him relaxed and happy.

The green portable phone shrilled insistently. Etienne's smile disappeared. He didn't move.

Hollis felt her eyebrows lift.

"I'm not supposed to answer. Weird people phone. Maman said to let it ring—let the machine take messages." He shrugged. "I'm not a baby. I've heard everything. Sometimes I think Maman needs a reality check." He shrugged, perfectly replicating one of his mother's characteristic Gallic gestures, "But, since it makes her happy, I don't do it."

"What about when your friends phone? What have you told them?"

"It doesn't happen much. I'm not alone very often— Maman, Papa, Tomas or Nadine answer." He slid a quick glance at Hollis. "I haven't told my friends about the crazy calls."

Hollis understood. She sprang to answer when the machine rang again.

"You're murderers like Hitler. What gives you the right to say who should be born? Be careful. We plan to finish you off and end your campaign." The line went dead.

Hollis peered at the receiver in her hand as if it might provide an explanation.

"Weird?"

She nodded. More than weird—threatening. Hatred and determination had sounded in the caller's voice. No wonder Manon didn't want Etienne to answer. She shivered. What was this all about? Would the unpleasant surprises ever end? She mustn't allow Etienne to see that the call had upset her.

"Time to take MacTee for a walk," she said.

After a walk, they played dominoes. Etienne trounced Hollis, who had forgotten the intricacies of a game she hadn't thought about, let alone played since childhood. Later, in the kitchen, they opened two cans of ginger ale, poured them into the blender and added scoops of vanilla ice cream. They stop-started the machine and made old-fashioned ice-cream sodas to cool them off before Etienne went to bed.

In her room, she connected to the internet. The *Globe and Mail* came up automatically. She'd subscribed in order to download the cryptic crossword. Now she went to death notices and typed Valerie Lefevbre. There it was—Lefevbre, Valerie Emmanuelle. Died suddenly in a traffic accident in Toronto. Left to mourn her untimely death are her father Sebastien, mother Lindsay Inkster...

A traffic accident. There had to be a connection to Ivan's death. A cold chill—someone had tramped over her grave. Ivan too had died in a crash. It hadn't been an accident. Lefevbre had vowed to make Curt's life more miserable. Would he have known whose bike was whose? Was he the one who had cut the brakes?

Thirteen

Time to go through Ivan's belongings. She collected her notebook and pen. Trailed by MacTee, she flicked the switch illuminating the basement stairwell. Downstairs, cool damp air wrapped itself around her. She examined the space. Light bulbs dangled from the low ceiling. Wooden walls of horizontal boards divided the cavernous cellar into a maze of small rooms. An antiquated many-armed furnace took up most of the first room. Miscellaneous furniture, including an ornate walnut dining room set, almost filled the second. In the third she found stacked boxes. Someone, presumably Manon, had printed "Ivan's clothes" on the top one. Since she didn't fancy sitting on cold concrete while she rummaged through the containers, she collected a heavy dining room chair from the second room, lugged it back and set it under the solitary low wattage light.

The time had come. She acknowledged her own reluctance to dig into the flotsam and jetsam of Ivan's life. No avoiding it, however—she had promised to help Manon. She shoved the clothes carton aside and lined up boxes labelled, "books", "papers" and "memorabilia".

A flip through high school notebooks—messy, scratched-over notes and papers sprinkled with teacher's corrections and low grades told her Ivan had not been a good student. But she already knew this. The question was—why had he kept this material? Perhaps he hadn't intended to. He'd stashed them when high school ended and never considered them again.

Dozens of photo albums filled a second box. One set was dated. The earliest went back to Ivan's teen years. Inside, each plastic pocket intended for a 4 x 6 photo held one or more recipes. Ivan had identified sources and dates. Often he'd paired recipes with a file card describing problems he'd experienced when he'd tried the recipe and added suggestions for improvements or variations. A second collection of photo albums was identified by subject. Appetizers, seafood, desserts—whatever the category, its name was printed on the cover.

A keen cook, she yearned to read what amounted to a chef's diary. Regretfully, she postponed the treat until she finished her investigation. The collection revealed two things; the scope of his passion and his methodical, investigative nature. She thumbed through the last volumes—recipes he'd collected during his year at George Brown. Towards the back she found a hand-written, numbered list of names and phone numbers with asterisks beside some numbers. She recognized the names of some of his fellow students. She'd spoken to these young men and women at the visitation or funeral. She pocketed the card, intending to phone and ask more questions about Ivan.

A wave of fatigue engulfed her. It had been a long day. Upstairs she hooked MacTee to his leash for his before-bed walk. Standing outside, she reconsidered. Manon would have a fit if she thought Hollis had left Etienne alone. She apologized to MacTee and went back in.

Because the dog still needed a walk, she couldn't go to bed. Instead, she unlocked the French doors and moved to the garden. Stretched out on Curt's chaise lounge, she considered his magazine pile and chose *Canadian Art* because the first article, "Painters' Early Influences", caught her attention. The writer paid particular attention to Mary Pratt and her artistic references to her childhood on Waterloo Row in Fredericton. Then he identified artists who had hidden backgrounds. He speculated whether an examination of their art would provide clues to their pasts.

One was Lena Kalma, the drama queen who rode on the edge of hysteria, revelled in conflict and professed to hate her ex-husband. The article hinted that the tabloids would love Lena's secrets but gave no other information.

Ivan had lived half his life with Lena and possessed half her genes. The reasons why Lena hid her past might provide a clue to Ivan's secretive personality. She'd grit her teeth and talk to Lena about her background. She shuddered but knew she had to do it.

When Manon and Curt returned a few minutes later, she didn't mention Lena—time enough for that later. "Why didn't you warn me about the phone calls? They must drive you crazy. Have you reported them? I'm sure uttering threats is illegal."

"Our number's listed under M.C. Dumont. I don't know how those creeps find us," Curt said.

"Not 'us' darling, 'you'. It's you they want," Manon said.

Hollis hoped no one ever would call her "darling" in that tone. "It was a woman screaming about Hitler and murder. What was that about?"

"A SOHD opponent," Manon said flatly.

"Sod—what is it?"

"Curt can tell you—he's the supporter. In fact, as of a couple of weeks ago, he's president of the local weirdos chapter."

"If *your* son died because medical treatment wasn't available, I don't think you'd be quite such a bitch," Curt snarled.

"Please, tell me what you're talking about?" Hollis intervened.

Curt swept his hand through his hair and assumed a "professorial" stance. "I've told you I'm on the waiting list for heart surgery?"

Hollis nodded.

"And the ambulance didn't take Ivan to the nearest trauma hospital—they drove halfway across the city, and he died shortly after he arrived."

Again Hollis nodded.

"Why do I wait? Why did Ivan die?" He glared at Hollis. "Fundamental flaws in our system." He pounded one fist with the other. "Under-bloody-funding. Why do we need so much health care money? It isn't a mystery. First, too many people spend a lifetime overindulging—eating and drinking too much, smoking, taking risks." He shook his head. "I suppose government campaigns to change how people live may help, but..."

"And private ones. AA, Mothers Against Drunk Driving," Hollis said.

Curt ignored her. He smashed his right fist down on his left. "The second reason is the important one. The one we can do something about. Children are born who *never* should come into this world." He narrowed his eyes and jutted his chin forward. "*If* their parents had genetic counselling and *listened,* when doctors told them they carried genes for Tay-Sachs, Huntington's, cystic fibrosis, Gaucher's, Asperberger's, and certain mental disorders. I could go on and on. It's a long list. Anyway, *if* they *listened,* those children wouldn't be born. Thousands of *those* people take up countless hospital beds."

"But not emergency ward beds," Hollis said.

Curt continued as if he hadn't heard or hadn't chosen to hear. "Stamp Out Hereditary Diseases, SOHD, campaigns not only for more genetic testing but also to have those who willingly accept sterilization shoot to the top of adoption lists."

"Surely if a genetic test is available, people take it?" Hollis said.

"Not enough of them. If governments had aggressively adopted this policy years ago, we'd pay lower taxes and have less crowded hospitals. I'd have had my operation. Ivan might be alive."

"And Etienne might never have been born," Manon said quietly.

"Of course he would have," Curt snapped.

"No, I've suffered from mood swings and depression since my teens. My father did too. I think it's pretty clear he died intentionally. He crashed his car on a nice day. There were no skid marks. According to your scheme, someone with my background wouldn't have been allowed to carry a baby to term and risk passing on mental illness."

"Bloody nonsense. You may be neurotic, but it's not an illness."

Hollis didn't want this to escalate.

"Sounds like the Third Reich to me." She immediately regretted her words. Anything connected to Hitler carried so much baggage, it lost its impact. But since she'd started, she'd finish. "Didn't they use sterilization to rid themselves of those they considered undesirable? Didn't they plan to produce the master race?"

"No, this bloody well is not like Germany. Sterilization would be *voluntary.*" He glared at Hollis. "You'd understand if *you* needed surgery, and *your* son had died because the hospitals were full."

"I agree *you* shouldn't have to wait, but I can't see what this has to do with Ivan. Emergency wards are just that—places to deal with emergencies. They treated Ivan immediately. They couldn't save him because his injuries were too severe. How would having fewer patients in the hospital have helped?"

Curt lowered his head like a charging rhinoceros. "You and Manon know nothing. And calling them weirdos, Manon, is uncalled for. They are caring, concerned citizens who want a better society. It's our opponents who are weirdos. They're the same fanatics who fight abortion. They use extreme methods. They harass and firebomb clinics and murder doctors."

Manon shrugged and stepped out of her high-heeled sandals. She picked them up and directed her anger at the shoes rather than her husband. When she swung them hard by their straps, one shoe broke loose and hurtled through the air. The stiletto heel clipped Curt's hand when he reached to stop it.

"Jesus, Manon, you could have killed me. What the hell's the matter with you? You're crazy as a coot."

Manon winced at his words and stared at his bloody hand.

"Sorry," she whispered and crept to retrieve her sandal.

"Sorry, that's all you can say?" Curt strode towards the house, grabbed the French door's handle and stopped. "Goddamn it, why do we lock the goddamn doors when we're sitting right here? Another one of your *crazy* obsessions." He scrabbled in his pocket, hauled out his keys, unlocked the door and disappeared inside.

Manon sank into a deck chair beside Hollis. Neither woman spoke.

Curt reappeared with a wadded paper towel pressed against his hand. "I'm not locking the goddamn door." His voice challenged Manon to argue with him. The phone rang.

"Screw you." Curt slammed the phone back in its cradle.

"I don't understand why, with all that's going on, you're involved with an organization that attracts hatred." Hollis, aware she should allow the hostility to dissipate, forged on.

She wanted to understand.

"It's not my fault the telephone company can't keep our number private."

"And I suppose it won't be *your* fault if something terrible happens to me or Etienne," Manon said over her shoulder. She stomped inside and locked the door.

*　　*　　*

The next morning, Hollis rolled out of bed before six. She forced herself to spend quiet moments meditating. As events and tension escalated at the Hartmans', it was even more important for her to adhere to this morning ritual that helped her to keep centred and focused. As it usually did, meditation restored her, and she congratulated herself for keeping to her routine. She emerged from her room to find Etienne sitting on the stairs.

"I set my alarm for six so I could come for a walk with you."

"Tomas, Ivan and I walked Beau here," Etienne volunteered when they reached the park a little later.

"I've forgotten—what breed was Beau?"

"A mutt. She belonged to Maman before she married Papa. Maman thought she was part collie and part German shepherd. Papa didn't like Beau." His tone changed. "He said when you bought a particular breed, you knew what to expect."

Hollis could almost hear Curt speaking. Etienne had a good ear. Did all children who simultaneously learn two languages as babies have this ability?

"Maman said dogs from the pound, the humane society, were tougher. She said they didn't spend their lives at the vets like purebred dogs." He sighed. "Ivan thought we should go to the pound and pick one out. He said if the dog was right there," his nose wrinkled, "it would be a *fait accompli*—that's French—and Maman would let her stay."

"What would you have called her?"

Etienne grinned. "I told Ivan I'd name her Penny, because a shiny new penny is lucky." He shrugged. "But if we'd picked one out, that wouldn't have been her name. Ivan got all red and said Penny was a girl's name and we couldn't use it." His grin returned. "Did you know dogs are purebreds and horses are thoroughbreds?"

Hollis remembered how, as a kid, she'd loved collecting nuggets of knowledge. Actually, she still did. Every morning she flipped to the back page of the first section of the *Globe and Mail,* where she read "Facts and Arguments", a compendium of miscellaneous esoteric information.

"Grandmaman gave me a book with hundreds of collectives for birds and animals." He pointed up into a nearby oak tree where more than a dozen crows cawed and disturbed the peace with raucous noise. "Did you know they're called a 'murder of crows'? I've memorized the ones in my book. If they aren't there, I make them up."

"Tell me some. A murder of crows is good."

"A pride of lions, a herd of cows—those are ordinary ones. Others, like an exaltation of larks, aren't common. Maybe that one isn't well known, because I don't think there are any larks in Canada."

MacTee, who'd found a dirty yellow tennis ball so old and worn it had lost its fuzz, waltzed up and deposited it at Etienne's feet. The dog's intense gaze told the boy as clearly as if MacTee could speak, "Throw the ball."

"Message received." Etienne tossed and MacTee, his plumed tail waving in delight, charged after it.

Back at the house, Hollis saw she was running behind on

her schedule, but thought she still had time to scoot over to Buy Right and interview Ivan's boss and co-workers. Then she'd race back to walk MacTee before her two o'clock class. A busy morning, and a hot one if she believed the weatherman.

Hollis couldn't enter Buy Right and say she was trying to find out what Ivan was really like. It sounded lame and made her and his family look like idiots. Who went to a young man's employer to uncover his personality? Instead she'd say finding more information was part of an ongoing investigation.

* * *

"I'd like to speak to the manager," Hollis said to a woman manning the cash.

"His office is back there, through the swinging doors and up the stairs."

Hollis followed instructions and entered a cavernous space loaded with crates and boxes waiting to be unpacked. She climbed the stairs and knocked on the office door. Told to come in, she found herself in a small room crowded with filing cabinets and a desk piled with papers.

The man crouched at the desk grunted, "Yah."

After she introduced herself and explained the reason for her visit, he didn't smile, give his name or welcome her.

"We went through this already. You're not a cop. I don't see why I should do it again."

"I'm here as a family representative. I knew Ivan but not well. I want to form a picture of him to help me in the investigation."

"I can't help you. I didn't know him. Talk to Lourdes, she's head cashier and supposed to know everything about everybody. But tell her I said if there's any interviewing done, it better be on employee break time: I'm here to make money, not help a Nosy Parker."

Pleasant man. Hollis had read that Buy Right franchise purchasers had to prove themselves before the parent company agreed to sell them a store. Obviously this "no name" man had a chameleon personality, or he wouldn't charm a puppy, much less an astute executive.

"Thank you for your help." She retreated to the front of the store and asked for Lourdes.

"That would be me." A dark-skinned, middle-aged woman with a round face, eyes and body, the epitome of "round", smiled at Hollis. "What can I do for you?"

"I'm Hollis Grant, a friend of Ivan Hartman's family. The police haven't arrested his killer. The family asked me to see if I could uncover any information that might shed light on the crime. I'm trying to find out what he was all about."

"Poor lad, what a horrible death." Lourdes shook her head. "He pretty much kept to himself after he came here to work last winter. 'Scuse me, a year ago last winter. Stock boys come and go. If they do their work, no one pays attention to them. But in April he drove up on the biggest, shiniest motorcycle. Jocelyn Jones perked up and took an interest."

"Does she still work here?"

"One of our best cashiers. She'll be here in half an hour."

"Your boss said I should talk to employees on break."

"Oh him, Mr. Sourface Delaney, pay no attention. He's a man who thinks if he's ugly-faced and shouts, he'll command respect." She flipped her long, dark hair. "I'm the best cashier he'll ever have, and he knows it. He also knows every senior who shops here *loves,* and I do mean *loves,* Jocelyn. Don't pay any attention."

Item by item, she rang up a meagre order of cat food,

peanut butter, day-old-bread and instant coffee as a withered, stooped pensioner with thin white hair slowly unloaded items on the conveyor belt. "If you're talking about *our* Jocelyn," the woman said, smiling at them with shining white dentures, "*Our* Jocelyn's a sweet, sweet girl." She shook her already trembling head. "I can't imagine how some of us would survive without her."

Hollis returned the woman's smile and perched on the window ledge to wait for Jocelyn Jones. Moments later, a slim, dark woman in her late teens or early twenties advanced or rather danced toward Hollis.

"Hi, I'm Jocelyn. You wanted to talk about Ivan? I'm glad you're here. I often think about him, and I wonder what else I could have told the police."

"Your boss said not to talk to you while you worked. I don't want to get you in trouble."

"Trouble, shmubble—Lourdes and I have his number. Fire away."

"How well did you know him?"

"Not intimately. It would surprise me if anyone knew him intimately." She shook her head. "Confession time. I didn't pay any attention to him at all until he drove up on his Harley. In car terms, his model compared to a fully loaded Jag or Beamer."

Jocelyn not only loved motorcycles, she knew something about them.

"I own a bike, and I love it passionately." She eyed Hollis quizzically. "I know, not many women do. It's a beat-up old Honda. When I was a kid, my brothers hooked me on motorcycles. They own a garage with my dad. I learned mechanics when I was about three."

Hollis pictured the toddler paddling about, handing appropriate wrenches to her father and brothers.

"When we talked about the Harley, I could tell he hated it. I couldn't believe it—why would he ride it? I challenged him. I said, 'You don't like bike-riding, do you?' He wouldn't admit it, but I watched him leave the parking lot. He drove like the old ladies who shop here would if you stuck them on a bike. He puttered away at, like, ten miles an hour. I couldn't see his hands, because he was suited up in the black leather stuff that goes with the territory. I *knew* that if I could, he'd have white knuckles."

"Why would he drive if he hated it?"

"I was more diplomatic when we talked again. I asked if an accident had shaken his confidence. He could have said yes to get me off his case, but he said no and didn't explain. I found it kind of hard to imagine owning a beautiful machine and not loving it. It didn't make sense to me why he drove it if he was scared."

The manager bore down on them. "Here comes your manager. Maybe we should finish this later."

Jocelyn, a prima ballerina at centre stage, whirled gracefully. "Mr. Delaney, just the man I want." She pointed to the wall clock. "Because we're always busy on Wednesdays, I'll punch in twenty minutes later this morning and stay later tonight. My decision, but I knew you'd be pleased."

Mr. Delaney, like a turtle sizing up its environment, allowed his head to swing from side to side. His eyes narrowed, "Good decision," he said grudgingly. He pointedly examined his watch. "Be sure you're on time," he said as he walked away.

Jocelyn giggled. "The best defense is definitely a good offense. Where were we? Oh yes, Ivan and his bike. Anyway, he interested me. I talked to him at break and then asked if he wanted to trade bikes and go riding at lunch. I remember his horror and then what he said."

"Tell me."

"'If it wouldn't completely piss off my father, I'd sell the fucking bike. I hate it. Hate trying to be a macho guy. We want to go to Italy on a George Brown externship, and selling it would finance our trip.'"

We and *our*—that was new.

"The family wasn't aware he attended George Brown, let alone that he planned to study in Italy. I'm interested in his reference to 'we'. Did he say who he planned to go with?"

"Poor Ivan. Imagine how screwed up he was if he didn't share his dreams with his family. He didn't identify the other person, and I didn't ask. I would have if I'd known what was going to happen. It struck me that he wanted his dad's approval. We never talked about bikes again. I figured he had enough problems in his life. I wasn't going to add to them."

A thoroughly nice young woman who'd given Hollis a new challenge—identifying the person with whom Ivan had expected to go to Italy.

Hollis puffed into class fifteen minutes late. Curt scowled. The stool next to Sebastien Lefevbre was empty. Perfect. After the conversation she'd overheard, she wanted to find out more about him. She'd strike up a conversation at break. For now, she focused while Curt spoke about Caravaggio's dramatic life and art.

A voice interrupted his lecture; an amplified, disembodied voice coming from somewhere outside the building. He stopped talking. Everyone listened. "See Lena Kalma's exposé of Curt Hartman and his son's murder at the Revelation Gallery on Parliament Street. Opening tonight. Don't miss it."

Fourteen

Disbelief, total denial—this couldn't be happening. It sounded as if Lena was accusing Curt. Hollis considered running and sticking her head out the open window to see if it was Lena herself shouting into a megaphone. Or was it a truck with a recorded message? She stared at Curt, waiting to see his reaction.

Silence ballooned into the vacuum left by the voice. A witch had cast her spell.

Curt, his face white and his eyes open wide, clenched his jaw and drew in a lungful of air. "God, that woman will stop at nothing." He reached in his shirt pocket, clapped his hand over his mouth and swung away from the class.

Angina—his pills. What should she do if it was a full-scale heart attack? Call 911. Make sure he could breathe and loosen his clothing. Did you do CPR? She couldn't remember. It didn't matter. Learning CPR had been on her "to do" list, but somehow she'd never gotten around to it. She hoped someone else knew the routine.

In the silence, a buzzing fly sounded like a 747.

Curt faced them. His hand no longer covered his mouth. "Take a fifteen minute break," he commanded before he stalked from the room. Lefevbre followed him.

Kate rushed to the window, yanked the cord and raised the

blind. "A tall blonde woman dressed in black is shouting into a megaphone."

Bert and Tessa crowded in beside her.

"Wow, that's a course extra," Kate said.

"I'll say. Curt was really shocked," Tessa said.

"Who wouldn't be?" David asked.

Hollis said nothing.

"I'm going to get a bottle of water," Patel said and headed for the door. The others fell in line and flowed downstairs behind him. David, limping quickly, kept his hand on the railing as he descended.

Downstairs, the group once again clustered around snack and drink dispensing machines, feeding in loonies and toonies and retrieving soft drinks, water, potato chips, Smarties and Sweet Marie bars. They popped tabs, twisted bottle caps and tore open plastic packages.

"Was she implying Curt killed his son?" Bert asked, pulling the tab from a soft drink can.

"Isn't that slander? Isn't it illegal to defame a person? How can she get away with it?" Tessa said.

"He actually turned white," Patel said. "I don't think I've ever seen anyone do that." His lips twitched. "Actually, with most of my countrymen, it would be hard to tell."

"She must have a major league reason for doing such a mean thing. Does anyone know her story?" Kate asked before she stuffed the last chips into her mouth and crumpled her empty bag.

Hollis listened and decided she wouldn't betray any confidences if she shared facts. "Lena Kalma was married to Curt. She's Ivan's mother."

"His mother!" Bert shook his head. "His mother!" he repeated disbelievingly.

"She is. She's an artist and uses her own name."

"A horror story divorce—is that what happened?" Kate asked.

Hollis nodded.

"Do *you* think she's accusing him of the murder?" David asked Hollis. He spoke dispassionately, as if this was an interesting intellectual question.

Hollis didn't want to consider the repercussions. "Not exactly."

"I feel even sorrier for Curt. Everything is piling up on him. That family is suffering, and now it will be worse. I still wish we could do something to help them. But that aside, we absolutely have to visit the show." Kate cocked her head to one side, and a tiny smile flickered at the corners of her mouth. "This is an event—capital E. *Canadian Art* will write it up. Let's meet at the opening, have a drink afterward and talk about it." She pushed her hands through her hair and made herself look even more like an enraged porcupine. "Who's going?"

"I can't," Tessa said

"Poor Curt," Bert said. "My son is five. I won't even think about something happening to him, but if it did, I can't imagine how I'd feel having my wife or my ex-wife more or less accusing me of killing him." He shook his head. "I'm babysitting tonight, but I want to hear all about it."

"I would like very much to join you," Patel said.

"Sounds good. What about you?" David said to Hollis.

"I'm not sure. Maybe." What would the press do with this story? A Greek tragedy and trial by reporters—it could evolve in many ways. And even if the papers and TV didn't blow it up, how would the show affect the fragile Hartman family? And where did she fit in? What could she do? She didn't have any answers, but she'd have to find some.

Their break over, they headed back upstairs.

Curt strode in, head high. "I'm sorry for the interruption. If Hollis, who's a family friend, hasn't filled you in, I'll tell you that someone cut my son's motorcycle's brake lines and he..." He paused. "He died." He expelled these last words as if they'd been trapped inside, and releasing them made Ivan's death a reality. "Lena Kalma is his mother. I'm as anxious as she is to have the criminal who did it identified and punished. It wasn't me. I loved my son." His voice caught, and he stopped speaking. His eyes glittered with unshed tears.

"I loved my daughter," Lefevbre said in a whisper that sounded like a shout in the quiet room.

How would the others respond to this interjection? Would they think Lefevbre was losing his marbles? Because she'd overheard Lefevbre confront Curt, she realized he intended to upset Curt even more.

Curt must have heard the remark, but he ignored it. Instead he bent and fiddled with the slide projector lens before he clicked it on and focused. "Back to Caravaggio," he said.

Analyzing slides seemed irrelevant, but Hollis ordered her mind to pay attention.

Four o'clock approached. Curt had offered Hollis a ride but warned her that he had half an hour's work to do in his office before he could leave. She took her time packing up before she sauntered upstairs. When she reached his office, she glanced in. Olivero, with his arms braced on the desk, leaned forward with his face inches away from Curt's. She couldn't hear what he said, but his stance was threatening. Neither man noticed her.

Not another confrontation? Curt won the prize as the most unpopular man she'd ever met. She strained to pick up the conversation, but it was impossible. She backed quietly away before they realized she was there. When she returned ten minutes later, Curt was alone and ready to leave.

Should she mention Lena and her show or stick to casual conversation? She rehearsed several neutral conversation openers as they walked to the parking garage. Curt stomped along and said nothing until they were in the car.

"Didn't Lena give us a nice little surprise," he said bitterly. The Volvo station wagon squealed out of the underground parking garage.

Hollis gripped the door handle, braced her feet and checked for a passenger air bag. "Was it a complete shock?"

"Absolutely. Why would she humiliate me? If what she's done is libelous, I'll sue the pants off her." He cornered so abruptly, Hollis feared the car would flip. She prayed its frame was as strong and its construction as crash-proof as advertisements claimed.

"I don't suppose you'll go and see the show?" She recognized the question's stupidity as soon as she spoke.

"Of course not," he snapped. His eyes narrowed, and his nostrils flared. Colour flooded his cheeks then drained away, leaving him white-faced. He reached in his shirt pocket, extracted a pill and slid it under his tongue.

"Would you like me to drive?" Hollis feared he would crumple over the steering wheel and die.

"No, I'm perfectly all right. If I did show up, wouldn't it give the press something to chew on? Lena would go ballistic, but she'd love it. You can be damn sure she's set to milk every ounce of publicity from this stunt." Making his right hand into a fist, he banged it on the steering wheel while directing the car with his left. "Let me tell you"—bang, bang—"she'll do it without any help from me." A final series of thumps, before he regripped the wheel. "A great opportunist, our dear

Lena. Obviously her career needs a boost, and she's willing to sacrifice poor Ivan to achieve her end." He glanced at Hollis, who willed his eyes back to the road: he was driving at double the posted speed limit.

"I *would* like a first-hand, unbiased report, not a hackneyed art reporters' views or those of voyeuristic sensationalist press know-nothings." He swivelled his entire torso toward her. "Will you see it and give me a report?"

A quick response to save herself from dying in a flaming wreck. "Private investigator, Hollis Grant, at your service."

The trip, short in time and long in terror, finally ended. Curt reached up and flicked the garage door opener attached to his visor. Once the police had removed the yellow tape on the front yard parking pad, Curt had insisted he and Tomas continue to park their motorcycles there. She wondered why Curt hadn't sold his bike. If she'd had a son and he'd died like Ivan, every bike she saw would be a constant reminder. Obviously Curt didn't agree. He loved relating how his love affair with Harley-Davidson motor cycles began in his teens, when he'd bought a beat-up wreck and restored it to working order. On Ivan's eighteenth birthday, Curt had given him the latest model of his own bike. Two years later, when Tomas reached eighteen, he had received the current model. Being charitable, she had to believe Curt kept it because it reminded him not only of his childhood, but also triggered happy memories of road trips with his sons.

Curt's features contracted, and his face darkened. "Damn Manon—it's all very well she's such a success, but she's never here when I need her."

Hollis considered the converse. Where was Curt when Manon needed him?

After he'd parked the car, Curt slammed toward the stairs

leading to his studio. Hollis hurried through the garden and unlocked the kitchen's white French doors. After walking MacTee, she occupied herself helping Nadine prepare dinner.

While she shredded cabbage for coleslaw, she wondered whether to tell Manon about Lena and Lefevbre. Curt was unlikely to repeat Lefebvre's accusations, and she didn't see any reason why Manon should know. But he would tell Manon about the show—it wasn't something that could be hidden. And after he did, she and Manon would talk about it. Given Manon's obsessive nature, she would beat the subject to death. Hollis knew the retelling would help her, and no matter how many times Manon felt the need to do it, Hollis was prepared to listen.

Manon appeared at six thirty, looking as cool and collected as a banker should. Her nails, raised shoulders and clenched jaw belied her calm façade. Manon clicked the intercom to Curt's studio. "Dinner in ten minutes."

"I'm not hungry. Ask Hollis to tell you what happened today, and you'll understand why."

Manon's eyebrows and voice rose. "Well?"

Hollis met Manon's gaze and shook her head almost imperceptibly. She didn't want to talk about this while Etienne was there. "Nothing too serious. It'll wait until we've eaten."

Eyebrows still elevated, Manon cocked her head to one side. "These days, who knows what's serious and what isn't."

At dinner, Etienne loaded his plate with second helpings of potato and tuna salad along with two slabs of bread. Between large forkfuls, he entertained them with the mythology behind the names of stars, telling them the stories of the Pleiades, Cassiopeia, Pegasus and Cepheus. He spoke about black holes, galaxies, quasars, ion particle clouds and other mysterious subjects.

Hollis marvelled at the quantity Etienne ate. At the same time, she worried about how little Manon consumed. She'd fade away to nothing if her problems weren't solved soon.

After supper, Etienne changed into his baseball uniform. Manon and Hollis carried iced tea outside to the front porch. Restored Victorian gingerbread trim and curlicue-laden black wrought iron chairs contributed to the veranda's period feeling. Etienne joined them. He plunked down on the wide front steps to wait for his baseball carpool.

"Hollis, tomorrow morning will you take me with you again when you walk MacTee?" Etienne said.

"It will be early—shortly after six."

"That's okay. I'll set my alarm."

When his ride arrived, Manon and Hollis waved him off.

"I'm also setting my alarm and coming with you tomorrow morning." Manon said firmly.

Did she fear for Etienne's safety, or did she plan to meet Olivero?

"Okay, what's his problem now?" Manon spoke in the resigned tone of voice one might use speaking about a spoiled child who frequently used temper tantrums to get his own way.

"Today Lena stood outside OCAD with a megaphone and announced that her new show opened tonight at the Revelation gallery. She promised to expose Curt's treatment of Ivan and implied that Curt killed him. I'm heading to the gallery in a few minutes."

"Mon Dieu." There was silence while Manon absorbed this information. "The woman is insane. No wonder you wanted to wait until Etienne left. My poor child does not need to hear Lena accusing his father of murdering his brother." She shook her head. "Lena's never forgiven Curt for leaving her and marrying me." Despite the heat, she shivered. "Let's move to the garden. I feel exposed out here. I'm anxious every time a car slows down. I expect a drive-by shooting."

In the garden, Manon shifted from one foot to the other, started to speak, stopped and finally banged her glass down on the side table.

"I should never have married Curt." Her chin rose, and she tilted her head to one side. "Probably you figured out long ago it was because Etienne was on the way."

"You were what, thirty-one?"

"Thirty-three."

"I wondered how you ended up pregnant. Not that I need a talk on the birds and the bees, but you'd said a million times you didn't plan to have kids."

"I didn't. It was a time when my mood swings and periods of serious depression worsened. My doctor suggested it might be hormonal. He persuaded me to give up the pill." Manon shrugged. "If you've taken them forever and go off sometimes, you forget to take precautions. At least I did."

"But you could have..."

"Had an abortion." Manon finished the sentence. "I could have, but I made the mistake of telling Curt. I thought he wouldn't want a baby and would support me if I took that route. Not so—he was thrilled." Her shoulders lifted again. "In a way, I felt relieved. Depression runs in my family. With my history, it didn't seem fair to bring a baby into this world. But Curt pleaded with me to complete the pregnancy. He said he loved me and couldn't bear the thought of losing the baby."

"And you, how did you feel?"

"Frightened, but I wanted it too. I was afraid to go it alone. I needed Curt. Having a baby without marrying would have horrified my mother." Her eyebrows lifted. "And the banking community is pretty staid."

"Getting better."

"True. I really thought long and hard about marrying him. I

don't have to tell you he's moody and quick-tempered. I suggested living together for a few months. Then, if it worked, we'd tie the knot. Curt would have none of it. He kept repeating, 'the baby has to have a proper father—I've been there—I know where my duty lies'." Manon leaned forward and fixed her gaze on Hollis's face. "I said—'what about your duty to Ivan and Tomas'—but he kept shaking his head and repeating—'living together isn't the same—I know where my duty lies.'" She paused. "I think Ivan was the reason he married Lena."

Sebastien Lefevbre had accused Curt of fathering a baby who'd died along with its mother. Who knew how many more women and babies there were? She considered making a crack about Curt's carelessness, but this was no time for levity. And three mistakes—nonsense. One was allowable, two marginally understandable, but three was unforgivable. A psychiatrist would have a field day with Curt's serial philandering and fathering.

On the other hand, how did Curt's statement about duty fit in with his actions? "Duty. I don't think of Curt as a dutiful man." Hollis frowned. "No, I'm wrong. He gives the course I'm taking because of his sense of duty. He's committed to passing on his knowledge. I understand him seeing his responsibility and wanting to take it on."

"He sounded sincere. I have to confess, Curt's life appealed to me—it contrasted dramatically with mine. I felt sorry for Lena. I suspected she loved him passionately. I expect she still does, although she'd deny it to her last breath." She wrinkled her nose as if her perfume didn't quite camouflage a bad smell. "I've realized something in the twelve years we've been married. Even in the beginning, I never loved him like Lena did. I never will."

Manon's body relaxed after she'd made this admission. They sat without talking, listening to the traffic's distant murmur and twittering birds bedding down for the night. The lights from Curt's studio skylights cast a glow on the chestnut tree overhanging the garden.

"Tell me more about Ivan," Hollis said.

Manon picked up her glass and gazed into its depths. "This will sound unkind, but in my opinion it's the truth. I don't know about this last year." She paused. "No, make that two, or even three years since Ivan's life became a mystery. He didn't have much going for him in high school. He inherited the worst of Curt's and Lena's physical characteristics, along with *terrible,* and I do mean terrible acne. He was *hopeless* at sports and did poorly academically. And to make things worse, Tomas never had a single spot and excelled in sports and school. I'm sure Ivan saw himself as a failure."

She allowed her gaze to meet Hollis's. "Curt likes successful, beautiful people and wanted Ivan to shape up. The more he kept at him, the more insecure and unhappy Ivan became." Her eyes filled with tears. "It makes me sad to have to say that." Her eyebrows rose. "I bet Ivan didn't tell us about George Brown because he believed Curt would sneer and compare his course unfavourably with Tomas's." She shook her head. "Anyway, I did what I could. But Ivan's focus was Curt. Although Ivan realized I cared about him, I wasn't the one who mattered."

"Why did Ivan and Tomas opt for shared custody?"

"I can only guess. I believe they were afraid Curt would shut them out of his life if they lived full time with Lena." She smiled ruefully. "And although it's hard to believe eleven-year-olds would be mercenary or calculating, money probably played a part. Even then, their father made more than their mother."

Not a far-fetched explanation. Children liked their material possessions. Etienne had arrived soon after the divorce.

"How did Ivan respond to Etienne?"

Manon's lips curved upward, but her eyes remained sad. "He worshipped him and didn't resent how much Curt adored the baby. When Etienne was a toddler, he followed Ivan around and asked him to do things for him." She stared into space for a moment. "Etienne's first language was French. His first nanny and I and even Curt spoke French." She tightened her grip on her glass before she set it down. "Ivan didn't have a talent for language, but he listed words he needed to talk to Etienne and practiced them." Tears filled her eyes. "Ivan loved Etienne." She wiped the tears away with the back of her hand.

"To change tack—why would Lena accuse Curt?"

The lights in the studio flicked off.

"We'll talk more later." Manon rose to greet Curt as he emerged from his lair.

Hollis said a quick hello and nipped inside to collect MacTee for a walk.

*   *   *

"I've heard retrievers eat anything," a voice behind Hollis said in a conversational tone.

Hollis shivered. She didn't have to turn around to know it was him—the cherubic little man who perched on his umbrella staring at the Hartmans' house.

Hollis braked and whirled around.

"I'll report you to the police."

A wide, wolfish smile split his face.

"And what will you tell them? I said I've heard retrievers eat anything, a perfectly innocuous remark."

Hollis felt icy cold. It was true. Retrievers would eat anything. It didn't matter if you kept them leashed. They'd lunge at and ingest decaying food or worse faster than an alligator zooming after an unsuspecting bird. Poisoned meat lying on the path, rat poison hidden in old hamburger buns—impossible to keep MacTee safe. She wanted to lash out, to smash the little man

"Well, *you* can go to the police with what I'm going to say. Listen up, you creep. I will kill you if anything happens to my dog."

"Big talk."

Hollis had the satisfaction of seeing his smile fade. Did she have it in her to follow through? She hoped she wouldn't have to find out.

Fifteen

Rhona arrived at the shop, large coffee in hand, shortly before seven on Wednesday morning. For homicide detectives, sleep deprivation during a murder investigation necessitated frequent caffeine infusions. She'd brought in a tin of her favourite brand to brew when she needed a lift. Now she'd get on the phone and set up appointments with the women who'd signed the condolence book. By ignoring the women's names, she had been guilty of gender bias, of the stereotyping she hated. The sooner she corrected her mistake, the better.

Frank Braithwaite approached her desk.

Rhona smiled and pointed to her coffee mug. "No doughnut."

Frank didn't return her smile. Instead he frowned and adjusted his green and black geometrically-patterned tie. A great choice—it deepened the intensity of his eyes. Rhona wouldn't tell him—that could be construed as reverse sexism. She was fixing her first gender problem. She didn't need a second.

"Bring me up to date. What's the scoop on the younger brother?"

"Tomas—he had problems as a young teen. Then he discovered competitive swimming. And marathon swimming. He has records galore and stars with the UNB swim team. He works at Wendy's, where they cooperate with scheduling shifts around swimming practices. Probably wears a Wendy's bathing cap."

Frank frowned.

"I'm kidding—you know how golfers and other competitors wear branded clothing?"

Frank's brows drew together. Obviously he did not consider levity a virtue.

"He does competitive sailing with his dad. No current girlfriend, no dramatic sagas of broken romances or enraged ex-boyfriends. Nothing in his life to explain why anyone would target him."

"Talk to his friends to make sure, but it does seem unlikely that he was the intended victim." Frank crossed his arms. His body language expressed hostility. "What else have you found out?"

Rhona ignored his stance and gave him the facts. "If the killer targeted Ivan Hartman, it may have been because of a woman. There was one in his life, but we haven't yet tracked her down. We're examining phone records from his mother's and father's houses to find her. His cell phone was destroyed in the crash, but we're looking at those records too. We've checked with Sex Crimes, and he isn't on their radar. Still working on him."

"Sex Crimes? Why didn't I hear about this?"

"Because we didn't find any connections. We're searching for his computer."

"Was he the intended victim?"

"Too soon to say."

"You're also considering the father?"

"If it's the father, the line of possible killers stretches as far as the Santa Claus parade." She tapped a pen on the desk. "We've done a door-to-door canvass. One neighbour recognized Arthur White's photo and said he saw him in the lane behind

Hartman's place on Sunday evening. She couldn't pinpoint the time, but claimed it was before she watched the ten o'clock news. White denies it. We're following up."

Frank picked up a small aboriginal sweetgrass basket woven by Rhona's grandmother. Ostensibly, Rhona used it to store paper clips. In reality, she kept it on her desk to remind her to be true to her heritage.

Frank sniffed the basket. "Still a little fragrance left."

"It's stronger in damp weather. My grandmother made it."

"Is she still..."

"Alive. Yes and very well." She might as well give him the details. "She lives on the Oneida Six Nations reserve near London, Ontario." She returned to the business at hand. "Curt Hartman's enemies are legion, but there isn't one person who seems most likely."

Frank replaced the basket. "Have you prepared a summary?"

"Not yet."

"Before you leave tonight, I want a list of what you've done, who you've spoken to and your prime suspects."

Rhona nodded, already busy at her keyboard. She wasn't going to rank the suspects—too soon for that. But she'd give Frank everything they had. It would motivate her to organize her own thoughts and plan their next move.

Later Wednesday afternoon, Rhona trotted to her boss's office and laid their summary on his desk. Frank skimmed the headings. "You've interviewed all of Curt Hartman's colleagues?"

"Not yet. We're working our way down the list. Because it's July, many people are away. They might shed light on his life, but they aren't suspects. We've talked to those we could contact."

"You're new to Toronto. Some cottage country is no more than an hour away. Make sure you don't miss any supposed out-of-towner who might have killed him."

"We won't. We also plan several in-depth interviews." Rhona's cell phone rang. She glanced apologetically at Frank. She'd intended to turn it off before she came into his office.

Frank waved dismissively. "Take it." He ran his finger down the report.

"Rhona, it's Hollis. I have something else for you."

"Go ahead."

"Two things. The first relates to Olivero Ciccio—he's a painter and Curt's colleague."

"I've interviewed him."

"I feel like the schoolyard tattletale. I really like him, and I'm sure he's out okay but..."

"You're helping us speed up our investigation. And you're doing it for Manon. Keep reminding yourself."

Hollis provided Rhona with information about Olivero that Rhona already knew.

"The most important news—Lena Kalma, Ivan's mother, has a show opening tonight. She implies she proves Curt is responsible for Ivan's murder."

"What. Are you sure? That sounds libelous."

"It does. In case you want to go, it's at the Revelation Gallery on Queen Street."

"Sounded interesting," Frank said, clearly waiting for her to give the details.

"I have a mole in the Hartman house—a woman I knew in Ottawa." And she repeated what Hollis had told her.

*   *   *

"Lena Kalma's exhibition opens tonight—want to come with me?" Rhona and Zee Zee were filling out forms and completing paperwork.

"Lena Kalma—isn't she an original? Nothing derivative about her work. It always sets you on your ear, forces you to think differently. Yes, I'll join you. Could she have intended to kill Curt and accidentally killed her son?"

"The boys must have ridden their bikes to her house a million times. And the bikes weren't absolutely identical. She's a visual artist and would have seen the differences. Even at night in the dark, I don't think she'd confuse them. And why would she choose such a method?"

Zee Zee ran her necklace's triple strands of large wooden beads through her fingers like prayer beads. "Did she want her son dead? Mothers do kill children."

"Why now? He was grown-up, out of the nest, embarking on a career. Lena's bizarre, unique—pick your adjective, but I don't believe she killed Ivan accidentally or on purpose." She shrugged. "Maybe I'll change my mind after I see her show. By the way, Hollis provided more info today. Apparently individuals from the anti-SOHD group make threatening phone calls to the Hartmans. The family hasn't reported it because they don't want to press charges or go to court. I've requisitioned their phone records. Knowing what we do about those people, we should take their threats seriously."

The beads sliding through Zee Zee's fingers clacked rhythmically. "Pretty scary when you see the fanatical gleam in their eyes. I expect some Crusaders looked like that when they ran their swords through the infidels. Righteousness. *This* is for god and country. Yah, they're scary." She sighed. "Believe me, I'm well acquainted with scary, with men who see you as the enemy, not as another human being. I wouldn't want the SOHD opponents after me. Let's talk to them again." She fingered the largest bead. "I enjoy interviewing Barney Edwards—he's such a misogynist racist. He has to pretend he isn't when faced with a black woman. It must kill him. Do we have printouts from his computer?"

"Not yet. I'll make it a priority request."

Zee Zee dropped her beads from hand to hand then coiled one strand inside the other. "Now we should talk about Curt's colleagues. I ran their names past friends in the arts community. Everyone agreed poor Lefevbre had flipped out after his daughter's death. The vote was split about fifty-fifty on whether he'd inflict his pain on anyone else."

"He was pathetic. But that doesn't rule him out."

"What about Olivero Ciccio? He's a sculptor and uses tools." Zee Zee continued to play with her beads.

"Would having Curt veto him for chairperson be a motive for murder? He didn't seem like a fanatically ambitious man, but maybe he's hiding his true feelings. And you have to wonder how Curt's death would change things. Curt wasn't chairperson, so it wouldn't mean Olivero would get the job. Maybe he was thinking ahead to the next election. If he's having an affair with Manon Dumont, Curt's death would complicate his life, because he'd have to decide whether or not to leave his wife. I can't see it."

"Someone cut the brakes," Rhona said. "The print on the asphalt isn't a match for anyone we've interviewed. Should we broaden our net? Maybe the show will provide road signs?"

"You're forgetting Arthur White."

"True, and he certainly does have reason to want Curt dead."

Sixteen

The Revelation gallery, originally a turn-of-the-century brick residence, was one of many galleries on Queen Street. Renovators had removed interior walls, opened up the stairwell and hung halogen lights. These details registered subliminally when Hollis stepped inside.

Noise.

A revving motor cycle, the roar of acceleration, a terrible smashing, tearing metal sound and a high pitched scream, broadcast at a decibel level designed to invade your consciousness and fill you with horror. After a few minutes, she recognized that one particular gut-wrenching scream occurred at regular intervals. It was a loop: the track played over and over and over.

Inside the door, on the right, a motorcycle's shattered remains lay jumbled with one intact wheel, upside down and rigged to spin forever. Simulated blood, along with bits and pieces of what appeared to be bone and flesh; a torn black leather sleeve; a cracked and broken helmet; and one black boot splashed with red: all added to a macabre sense that this was an actual accident scene reconstruction. Lena had finished the tableau by adding an aerial dimension—brake lines in the air, looping, black, twisting snakelike hose with nicks cut and marked in white.

Blow-ups of Lena's photos added shock value to the

soundtrack and ever-spinning wheel. These pictures focused on Curt and Ivan, Curt and Tomas or Lena and Ivan. In the initial one, shot soon after Ivan's birth, Curt held the baby away from him like an alien being or a drippy garbage bag. Curt *might* have pulled Ivan close after Lena snapped the picture, but Hollis doubted it. In a contrasting photo, Curt snuggled Tomas in the crook of his arm and gazed at him fondly.

Differences between Ivan and Tomas were apparent in their childhood photographs. Tomas had inherited his father's tall, lean frame, aquiline nose, dark skin, hair and eyelashes which framed pale blue eyes like Ivan's but made them appear entirely different. Ivan was a short, plain clumsy child, who grew increasingly unattractive as adolescence took its toll on his skin and body. It transformed him from a gawky kid to a pudgy, acne-ridden teenager. Tomas held the winning hand in the genetic crapshoot.

Photos relentlessly recorded Curt's dislike. In one, he raised his arm as if he was about to hit Ivan. In another he extended an arm to push him away. In still another, he turned his back in dismissal. Shot after shot underlined his contempt and distaste. They were even more startling when contrasted with the photos of Curt with Tomas. In the final section, Lena had chosen snapshots picturing her as Ivan's loving, caring mother. She'd underlined the difference between father and mother.

Pictures could say anything. In these days of manipulated images, you had to be suspicious. Hollis contrasted these negative pictures with Lena's positive photo boards at the visitation. At the funeral home, each and every one had celebrated Ivan's life. Here, each and every one picturing Curt did exactly the opposite.

Replicas of official documents punctuated the interstices between photos. Curt's dated application for divorce led the way. The court order mandating shared custody for Ivan and

Tomas, with a note affixed indicating the boys' involvement in the choice, followed it. Next, a photo of Curt and Manon's wedding.

The dry, technical police accident report, providing minute details of a young man's horrible death, came next. The documents' magnification enabled viewers to read them several feet away.

Hollis froze as she contemplated a photo from Ivan's teen years in which his longing eyes followed Curt, Manon and Tomas as they walked away from him. Curt's arms draped over Tomas and Manon's shoulders impressed the viewer with the trio's close-knit intimacy. If this was a true picture, Manon *should* have acted—should not have increased Ivan's misery. Her stepson, eleven when he came to live with them, had deserved her protection. In psychobabble terms, she appeared to have played the enabler's role. No wonder she felt guilt-ridden.

A lump formed in Hollis's throat, and tears threatened. It would have been wonderful to have reached out to Ivan and told him how sorry she was that his parents had behaved so badly. And were still behaving badly. How could a mother, no matter how she hated and blamed her ex-husband, have revealed her son's pain?

Hollis, walking to the second room, glanced down, gasped and stepped quickly to one side. She'd been standing on a red shoe print. These crimson records marking someone's passage to-and-fro, in-and-out, wove around the room. It felt to her as if Ivan's ghost had traipsed through the show, examining the evidence.

In the second room, Lena had magnified various other documents: excerpts from Ivan's high school diaries relating to his disastrous relationship with his father; school reports revealing his abysmal marks; and a counsellor's summation of his problems culminating in the remark, underlined in red, "his problems may stem from his relationship with his father."

She had juxtaposed documentary evidence with more photos. Hollis felt like a voyeur when she read the diary excerpts. What an unhappy, unloved teenager Ivan had been. Where had his mother found this private document? How cruel it was of her to exhibit his confessed pain. She hoped his year at George Brown had made him happy.

Beside the exit from the second room, Lena sat in an alcove behind a table draped with a black silk-fringed shawl. An open notebook's white pages, a sign requesting "comments" and a vase of red gladioli, a summer funeral flower, contrasted with the black tablecloth. Hollis had procrastinated—she hadn't arranged to speak to Lena. She promised herself to make an appointment soon but also admitted that she didn't want to. The woman frightened her.

Lena wore a long black voile dress, lavishly decorated with jet and bugle beads. With its stand-up collar edged with lace and its voluminous leg-of-mutton sleeves, it was either an original or a replicated Victorian mourning dress. It underlined Lena's theatrical presentation.

Although she had the same washed-out blue eyes as Ivan, mascara set them off like well-displayed artwork. Acne scars faintly marred her fair complexion, but her over-generous carmine mouth, perhaps enhanced by botox injections, drew attention away from her skin. Her thick blonde hair, again like Ivan's, skewered in a perfect chignon, added to her imposing presence.

The desire to rush over, grab Lena's neck with both hands and tighten her grip until the woman crashed senseless to the floor almost overwhelmed Hollis. While she struggled to control her feelings, she tried to focus on inhaling through her nose, expanding her rib cage and exhaling until she'd emptied her lungs. Distraction intended to diffuse her rage.

When another woman moved close to the table, Lena looked up at her. "Well, did he do it? Did he kill Ivan?"

Did he do it? What a question. The woman was crazy—crazy and obsessed. Hollis shook her head slightly and moved backwards, but not quickly enough. Lena's jaw jutted forward. She rose and pointed a long fingernail tipped with scarlet polish. "You!" Her voice rose.

Nearby gallery viewers moved closer. Probably they anticipated a confrontation, a scene to titillate and provide them with a good dining-out story.

"You," Lena repeated at a decibel level louder than the repeating accident tape.

Hollis took another step back. Lena strode forward, shaking her outstretched finger at Hollis.

"You," she shrieked for a third time and jabbed her sharp nail in Hollis's shoulder. "*You* were there after his murder. *You* were at the funeral. You are *that* woman's friend. *You* engineered their affair." She reared back and launched a gob of phlegm that landed on Hollis's shoe. "I spit on you, and on all women who break up homes, who cause pain and destruction." Her voice dropped. "I will have my revenge." Her sibilant whisper penetrated like a knife.

The mucus insinuated itself under Hollis's sandal's strap and slid between her toes. If only she could whip off her shoe and immerse her foot in a pail of disinfectant. Or defend herself. She wasn't a homebreaker.

There was no point. A rebuttal would antagonize Lena even more and bring on another attack. There would be no apology—she had nothing to apologize for. Imagine anyone forcing Curt to do anything. If the situation hadn't been so embarrassing, she would have laughed in Lena's face. Hollis pushed aside Lena's stiletto finger, rhythmically stabbing a tattoo on her chest. She forced herself to walk away at a measured pace.

Outside, hot Toronto evening air assailed her almost as forcefully as Lena had. She sucked in deep breaths, even though she knew the summer air's high pollution level. Before she moved, she waited for her pounding heart to resume its normal rhythm.

A man aggressively swinging a placard jostled past. A second then a third person carrying signs followed. "Save Our Children", "Parents Against SOHD", "Curt Hartman: Baby Killer"; the slogans varied as widely as the people carrying them. Pedestrians hurried by. Those scurrying into the gallery resembled furtive porn parlour patrons.

"Wow, what a performance! Hey, there's one out here too," a female voice said. Kate, Patel and David clustered on the porch behind her. Inside, wrapped in her own drama, she hadn't noticed them.

Patel took her arm. As if they'd agreed on a course of action by osmosis, her fellow students hustled her away.

"We'll buy you a drink. You look like you need one. Lena Kalma is one crazy woman," Patel said keeping his hand under her elbow.

"Crazy is an understatement. That was a shocking show. Let's make for the Star Tavern. I need a couple of tall cold ones," Kate said and the quartet set out.

"In India, what did you drink?" Hollis asked Patel, to change the subject. "When I think of Asia, I think of the drinks mentioned in novels written about the thirties and forties—Pink Ladies, Side Cars, Black Russians. I imagine a Singapore Sling in Raffles bar or a gin and tonic on the long shady veranda of a tea plantation in Malaysia's Cameron Highlands. I visualize huge fans hanging from the ceiling, operated continuously by servants pulling on ropes."

"It wasn't as glamorous as Somerset Maugham made out," Patel said. "And don't forget how racist those societies were. People like me served the drinks or swished the fans. They'd certainly be privy to all the secrets, because white people didn't see them, didn't think of them as people."

David, walking in front of them, turned. "It was the same in Canada then and even now. Even though it isn't politically correct to use racial slurs, discrimination is alive and well."

Hollis wanted to ask Patel and David if they spoke from personal experience but figured she'd been tactless enough in her romanticized version of life on the subcontinent.

"I've never suffered much," Kate said. "But then I'm younger, and Toronto is so racially mixed." She giggled. "Actually, I grew up in Markham. You guys probably don't know the Pacific Mall, but if your first language isn't Chinese, some stores would be a total mystery."

"You're exaggerating," David said.

"I'm not. And it isn't the only one. There's a herbal store and a restaurant next to it in one of the plazas near my house where nothing is in English—not the menu, not the signs—nothing."

"That's because you're the majority there. Try being the minority. I come from B.C., where there's lots of prejudice, particularly on Vancouver's lower east side," David said.

"It can't be against the Chinese. They've got to be the majority in parts of Vancouver. I know, because I've been there, that sections of Richmond are one hundred per cent Chinese," Kate said.

"I wasn't talking about the Chinese or about Richmond," David said. "You manage to turn the conversation the way you want, but you don't have a clue about a lot of things." He scowled at her.

"Enough of serious topics. I'm drinking Molson Canadian in honour of my new homeland." Patel smiled at Hollis.

No gentrification marked the tavern on Queen Street. Dark mirrors, stained wooden tables and dim lights preserved the atmosphere where the patrons drank beer, sometimes with whiskey chasers, and ordered greasy fries if hunger pangs struck. Hollis looked around with interest.

"Not your usual stomping grounds?" David said to Hollis. "What do you think Curt will do about the show?"

The show. She didn't want to think about it—the horrifying sounds, motorcycle parts strewn randomly, photos and documents recording Curt's failure as a father.

"My guess is nothing. Lena may be out of control, but she was crafty enough not to accuse him directly. She allowed the photos and documents to do her dirty work. He'll consult his lawyer and tape any TV or radio interviews she gives. But unless she flips out and makes specific accusations, what can he do?"

Patel tapped the table. A frown on his normally long and serious face and his repeated clicking signalled his disagreement. "But those damning photos—he clearly never liked the child. And it seems to me..."

Kate interrupted. "Not necessarily. Remember, she also made photo collages for the visitation, and they were totally different. Lena's an artist, a compulsive photographer—she must have thousands of slides and photos. Think about it—in those numbers there were bound to be ones portraying him in a bad light. Curt might have held Ivan at arm's length because he had a dirty diaper. In those later shots, he could have felt angry because Ivan had dashed out in traffic. The before and after are important." She sipped her beer. "And another thing—if his mother was recording true hostility, where the fuck was she in this story? People will wonder why she wasn't protecting Ivan."

Hollis could have added another question. What was Ivan's stepmother doing? Where did Manon fit in this picture?

"Good point, Miss Social Worker. In *your* perfect world, mothers are *supposed* to keep their children safe. Fathers and mothers have responsibilities to be there. They pay a price if they're not." David paused. What could have been the beginnings of a smile marked the corners of his mouth, but his eyes were cold. "Sometimes the cost is very high, but Kate has a point. You *can* make photos say anything you want. How did you all react to the show?"

"It shocked me," Hollis said. "In my opinion, Lena designed it to shock and horrify. She wants the viewer to jump to her conclusions without posing the questions we're asking. She wants viewers to leave the show thinking, 'Curt Hartman is a monster'. How did it affect you?"

David leaned back and said nothing for a minute. The other three waited for his pronouncement.

"It'll stir up a controversy. The art world will love it. Legitimacy will be an issue. Is it legitimate to exploit family and friends in your art? I remember an American photographer who photographed her naked children and almost lost them to a social services agency because the police charged her with pornography. Critics will question whether or not it is art. They'll challenge Lena Kalma's motives—her disregard for her dead son and her obvious intention to harm Curt."

"It's awful that the family has to cope with this," Kate said. She sipped, put down her bottle and looked from one to the other. "In my community, they'd be taken care of. It wouldn't just be Hollis who'd be there to help. There'd be food and visits and support." She fixed her gaze on Hollis. "Is that happening?"

"It did right after Ivan died. They're getting cards and letters." Hollis shook her head. "But it isn't the same. Manon's mother is a widow with her own business. She had to go home. There aren't any other relatives."

"When there aren't relatives, that's when my community really swings into action," Kate said.

"Mine too," Patel added.

"Since they don't have a Chinese or Indian support network, it's a good thing you're there," Kate said.

Hollis didn't want to be painted as the do-gooder. "It works both ways; it's lovely to have a place to stay where my dog is also welcome."

Conversation ranged back and forth. Eventually they talked about their hopes and dreams for the future and shared their insecurities—their difficulties expressing their vision. But they divided into camps: professionals who worked on regardless of obstacles, and amateurs who talked more than they worked. Hollis was beginning to believe she could move from the second to the first group and make it as a professional painter.

The server stopped for repeat orders. Hollis considered a third and reluctantly declined. MacTee drank gallons of water in the summer and would need his evening walk. The others also refused.

They gathered up their belongings, ready to pay and leave. Hollis reached in her purse for her wallet and managed to upend her bag on the floor. She scrambled to retrieve her belongings. A lipstick tube rolled far under the next table. When David crawled to retrieve it, his black T-shirt crawled up his back and revealed a blue tattooed spider hovering at his waist. He handed the lipstick to her.

"I love your spider," Kate said.

David's face registered surprise.

Kate grinned. "I have a daisy in the same place. I planned

to do a daisy chain, but it hurt too much. How come you chose a spider?"

David shrugged. "It was one of those nights. A bunch of guys ended up in a tattoo parlour. They've got books of designs. You pick one."

"Does it have any significance?" Patel asked.

"What do you mean?" David said.

"I don't know. Aren't they supposed to represent how you feel or who you are? Give anyone who sees them a message about you."

David stared at Patel. "You've been seeing too much TV. It's a spider. That's it—a spider."

"I've contemplated a tattoo—maybe a ying yang somewhere inconspicuous. Or a crow—I like crows. But tattooing hurts, and I hate pain," Hollis said.

"You aren't missing anything," Kate said.

David nodded in agreement. The four painters made their way to the street.

"Who needs a lift? Lots of room in my van," David said.

Quickly they arranged for David to drop Patel and Kate at the subway then drive Hollis home.

"You must find it tough to live with the Hartmans. Did you say Curt or his wife was your friend?" David asked as he pulled away from the subway stop.

"Curt taught me when I studied at OCAD. My friendship with Manon dates back further, to the years when we lived in residence at U of T."

"You went to OCAD after your BA?"

"Yes. My mother insisted I study a subject I could use to earn a living. She's an accountant who once aspired to be a professional pianist. She lived in poverty for several years before she decided eating was a bigger priority than art."

"And were you the villain Lena Kalma accused you of being? Did you introduce Manon and Curt?"

"Yes and no. I *did* have a class party and invited my professors and their wives. Manon *did* meet Curt and Lena there. But let's face it—how many people are you introduced to, and how many times does romance result? Not too many. Yes, they met at my place. No, I'm not a villain. I resent her accusations."

"Take care. You aren't responsible, but she believes what she said. She sounded pretty crazy to me. I can't figure how Curt's holding up, and I'm glad he didn't cancel the course, but I sit in class and wonder how much pain he's feeling. What about his other kids—how are they doing?"

"They're sad. Tomas supports his dad. They have a lot in common; they both love competition. Tomas swims competitively, and they compete together in motorcycle rallying and sailing races."

"They're still keen on motorcycles? If my brother died in a crash, I'd never, ever want to *see* another bike, let alone own and ride one."

Her reaction exactly. She'd wondered if she was off base. "Me too, but they often ride together. They also love the sailing races at the RCYC."

"That's a passion I understand. In Vancouver, I crewed whenever I could. Sailing every weekend becomes a way of life."

"I remember you said how much you liked it."

They slowed on Winchester. David searched for a parking spot. Half a block from the house, he found one and insisted on walking Hollis to the door. They passed houses sitting a few feet from the sidewalk. People crowded many front porches, chatting and drinking. Clinking glasses and diverse music coming from different sound systems along with bursts of laughter combined to create a warm, convivial streetscape.

"I love a neighbourhood like this. I lived in one in Vancouver."

"I thought la la land never let people go. When did you move and why?"

"You're right. Vancouver's great. After my mother..." he paused, "...died, I decided to come east and try to make it as a painter in Toronto."

"Sorry about your mom. Is your dad still there?"

"My mythical dad—who knows who or where he is," he said. "I was an only child. For my entire life, she was a single mom."

"My dad died when I was young. I'm an 'only' too. I have a friend who throws an 'only' party once a year. She figures we're special."

David laughed. "That's a good approach."

"This is the house. Thanks for walking me from the car."

"Hey, no problem. If you or the Hartmans ever need me or my van, feel free to call."

*   *   *

Rhona arrived at Lena's show shortly before closing time.

"What a scene." An impossibly thin young woman in a black linen dress whispered to her companion, an older man in a black linen blazer, as chunky as his friend was wraith-like. Did they live together and conspire to appear in matching outfits? Or did it happen the way people grew to resemble their dogs or vice versa?

"She totally surprised the poor woman she attacked. Imagine how she must have felt when Lena spit on her shoe, poked her in the chest and vowed to take revenge," the woman said.

"She's off her rocker. This show depresses me. Let's cut out of here. I don't know why we came."

"Yes, you do, John. You said it would be interesting because both Curt Hartman and Lena are important in the art world. And the police haven't solved their son's murder. You wanted to see the show in case Curt files a libel suit against her." She giggled and fluttered her lashes. "Be honest. You hope Curt will retain you if he sues. And you also said Lena was totally crazy and would stop at nothing to hurt Curt."

Deep in discussion, the couple hadn't been aware of Lena's approach. "You got that right," she said. "He's going to pay, and pay. And so will his wife and her friend Hollis Grant." Hands on her hips, she pivoted and addressed the crowd. "Everyone here is my witness." She scowled at the man named John. "You'd better write down their names if you think you're representing Curt. You'll need their statements." She jabbed a red-tipped finger. "Mark my words. My son Ivan's death will be avenged."

Seventeen

On Thursday morning, Hollis and Etienne sat at the breakfast table after Manon and Curt had raced off to work.

"More toast?" Hollis asked. She passed it to him, and he worked methodically to spread peanut butter over every square inch. He didn't look up from his task when he spoke. "What's the matter with Papa? What did you tell Maman after I went to baseball last night?"

How much should or did eleven-year-olds know? Hollis thought back to her ninth summer, when her family had rented a beach house in PEI. Her parents had spent weeks sneaking off and debating whether or not to divorce. Despite their attempts to keep her in the dark, she hadn't missed much. She vividly recalled the guilt she'd felt when she decided she was to blame for the whole unhappy situation.

"It's about Ivan and your father. Lena has an art show focussed on their relationship, how they got along. She uses documents and photos to prove that your father..."

"Wasn't very nice to Ivan?" Etienne finished her sentence. He reached for the grape jelly.

"Yes."

"No wonder he didn't come to dinner. He must be really mad." Etienne spooned a heaping dollop on his toast and said nothing for a minute. Finally he put his knife down and looked up. "It's true. I hated how he talked to Ivan. He was a great brother. I really miss him. It made me feel bad when Papa was mean to him—made me think Papa didn't like him. Once I said that. Papa told me not to be stupid—Ivan was his son. He loved him, but Ivan needed someone to give him a push, and that was a father's job." He picked up his toast. A gob of jelly slid off and plopped on his plate. He scooped it up with his finger and stuck it in his mouth before he spoke. "I think Ivan would have done better at everything if Papa had been nicer to him."

"You may be right," Hollis said.

"Today, at camp, we're going to learn about black holes," Etienne said, clearly anxious to change the topic.

"Sounds interesting. When did astronomy hook you?"

Etienne drained his milk before he replied. "When I was a little kid, Grandmaman Dumont took me out at night and told me about the stars. She lives in the Eastern Townships. At night the sky is different than it is in Toronto. It's totally black—you see tons of stars you can't normally see. Grandmaman has a star map. When she saw I was interested, she bought me a constellations globe. For my last birthday, she gave me a humongous telescope and a tripod to set it on. Sometimes at her place I saw the northern lights. Have you ever seen or heard them?"

"Heard them?"

"They sing—they really do. Sheets of green and blue light dance across the sky, and you hear them."

"I've never been lucky enough to see or hear them."

Etienne paused and stared down at his cereal bowl. He stirred the milk around and around before he raised his head and met Hollis's eyes. "I like thinking about stars because they're huge and far away. They make me feel small and help me forget about Ivan and Papa—really sad things."

Tears welled. But Etienne had stated a fact. This was his life and how he dealt with it. She mustn't cry, mustn't allow Etienne to see her pity. This was his coping mechanism. She raised her *latte* bowl, and, pretending to choke, gave herself a pretext for coughing and wiping her eyes.

"You'll have to teach me the basics. I can locate the Big Dipper and the North Star, but nothing else."

"Sure. Now in early July, because the days are so long, I don't have much time to study them before I go to bed. But some night I'll give you my A number one first class tour. We can't do it tonight, at least I hope not."

"How come?"

"Tonight, if it's clear, two kids from astronomy camp will come over with their sleeping bags. Papa said we could use his studio. We'll lay our sleeping bags under his geenormous skylight. After we open it, we'll see what we can see, although only the brightest stars will be visible because of the city lights. Maman will give me money to order pizza for a snack. I'll crank up my boom box, and we'll have a star party." Etienne's eyes shone.

It was so nice to see him happy again.

After he'd left, Hollis collected her notebook and went to the basement to continue investigating Ivan's possessions.

She thumbed through George Brown binders and found a copy of a completed application for "Culinary Arts Italian: Post-Graduate" filled out for the following year. Students specializing in modern Italian cuisine could apply for a three-month externship in Italy. This confirmed what she'd learned at Buy Right.

Hollis sat back on her heels with the application in her hand. She could understand why Ivan had not shared his dreams with Curt, at least not before he'd received his acceptance, but wouldn't his plans have fascinated Manon?

Hollis hoped she didn't have blinders on when it came to Manon and her role in Ivan's life and death. She shook her head. Not a question she could answer until she had more information. It was time to check with some George Brown students. She had their names. Now she'd call them.

Two answering machines. She left messages.

Third call to Patsy Correlli.

"Yes, I'm Patsy."

"I'm a friend of Ivan Hartman's family. You took several classes with him. Could you answer a few questions?"

"Why? I've already talked to the police."

Hollis heard suspicion in Patsy's voice. Maybe she'd feel more comfortable if they met.

"Could we meet for a coffee?"

"You expect me to meet some unknown woman and answer questions about a murdered man? Forget it—I'm not talking to you," Patsy said.

She should have anticipated this reaction. She hadn't thought the process through. "I'm sorry to trouble you. If you change your mind, please call me."

Patsy had hung up.

One more call to remove the bad taste of Patsy's hostility.

"Vincent O'Brien?"

She explained why she was calling.

"Sure thing. Ivan and I shared a few brews. He was a good guy. I was real sorry. Can't tell you much."

"If you think of anything, will you phone?"

What did she want to know? Which students were going to Italy? If he had a special friend? Ivan certainly didn't have much personal information anywhere. Maybe that was because he thought Curt or Manon or even Tomas would pry into his affairs. She'd been like that as a child. Her mother had wanted to know every detail of her life, and Hollis hadn't wanted to tell her. Thinking back to her childhood, she remembered tucking things she didn't want her mother to find behind photos in her albums. Her mother had never caught on. Hollis wasn't unique—maybe Ivan, a secretive young man, had done the same thing.

She opened the carton holding his most recent George Brown recipe albums. This would take time. And in order not to miss something important, she'd better discipline herself to be more systematic than she sometimes was. She'd start at the beginning and work her way through.

"Appetizers" yielded nothing, nor did "soups", although sometime she thought she'd try the green chili bisque. Difficult, but not impossible to cut it down from serving sixty to six. She moved to pasta. Linguine alfredo—the edge of a piece of paper behind the card caught her eye. She slid the recipe out. Underneath she found a receipt for a year's rent of a storage locker in North York. The term expired next spring—just when Ivan would have been returning from his Italian cooking course. Now this was a mystery. She knew the where and when, but not the what or why. And she'd need a key to answer those questions. She pulled her cell phone from her bag and called Manon.

"A storage locker—whatever for? I wonder why the police didn't find the receipt."

"Ivan used the same system to hide things that I did as a kid. The police probably weren't expecting to find anything and didn't make a thorough search. Where are his keys?"

"Keys? I dumped all Ivan's things in the boxes."

"I'll do a quick rummage through the cartons."

But before she searched, she thought she'd run through a few more files and look for other surprises. In "cakes and pastries" she stopped at "Sweetheart Cake". She thought the recipe bulged slightly more than it should, slid her hand underneath and extracted a photo.

The girl was beautiful, even squinting with the sun in her eyes. She could have been a model. She had long, dark hair, classically proportioned features and a radiant smile. She looked familiar—perhaps she was a model, perhaps she'd seen the face on a billboard or in an ad in *Fashion* magazine.

Hollis turned the photo over and read, *"for Ivan, all my love, Penny"*.

Penny—she remembered the conversation with Etienne. Ivan had said they couldn't name a dog Penny. Now she knew why. A girlfriend? And a beautiful one at that—this wasn't what she'd expected to find. How would Hollis locate her without a surname? She yanked the card with names and numbers from her notebook, but it revealed only one name beginning with "p", the unpleasant Patsy. She made a snap decision. She'd tell Rhona about the locker, but not about the girl until she'd found and talked to her. If Penny hadn't contacted the family or the police, she hadn't wanted them to find her. Hollis wanted to know why.

Not a model—the girl at the funeral. The one who'd waited outside and tried to speak to Curt? Hollis examined the photo. It had been a quick glimpse on a rainy day, but it could have been.

She had to find Penny. Vincent might know. The phone rang until his answering service kicked in. She left a message.

Trotting through the park later with MacTee, she grabbed for her ringing cell phone. It was Vincent.

"I have something to ask. Have you met Ivan's friend Penny?"

"Penny Pappadopoulos. Sure. She and Ivan took Italian. I think they dated but kept it quiet."

"Why?"

"I'm not positive, but in the fall Penny was pretty tight with a Greek guy in our course. A big tough guy. Apparently he took it hard when Penny broke up with him. I think he'd have been pretty pissed if he found out Penny had replaced him with Ivan, who was generally considered to be a nerd. I'm pretty sure he would have given Ivan a hard time if he'd known. Don't quote me, but that's what I figure."

"I don't suppose you remember his name?" She was holding her breath.

"Mike, John—I'm sorry, I don't, but if you find Penny, she'll tell you."

It must feel like this when the one-armed bandit bling, bling, blings. The jackpot—she'd hit the jackpot. Penny, the beautiful girl, Ivan's girlfriend. And a jilted boyfriend. At last she'd identified someone who had reason to sabotage the bike.

"How did you find out?"

"I saw them together at a restaurant in Mississauga—obviously way off the beaten path. I was there with my aunt."

"You don't think anyone else knew?"

"No one ever said."

"I don't suppose you can tell me where Penny lives?"

"Somewhere over on the Danforth—that's the cultural centre for Greek people in Toronto."

She'd call every Pappadopoulos in the book. It was more important to make those calls than to make it for lunch. Two calls yielded nothing.

"Penny Pappadopoulos—who wants to know?"

Paydirt. The low, guttural and heavily accented voice could have belonged to a man or a woman.

"It concerns the college." Hollis crossed her fingers. It was close to the truth.

"She don't go there no more, and she never should have. She's at work."

"Could I reach her there?"

"No. The restaurant is busy—no time for talking," the voice said and hung up.

A restaurant. Cooking. Hollis wrote Penny's address and telephone number down. She'd keep trying until she connected with her.

Eighteen

Rhona's Thursday morning was busy. She'd agreed to meet Hollis again, although she doubted she'd hear anything new. It would have been more productive to eat with Zee Zee. They worked well together, bouncing ideas back and forth like tennis balls in a rally, but Hollis had invited her for an early lunch at the Art Gallery of Ontario and promised wonderful salads and delicious desserts. And no Frank looming up to spy on her.

"How are things at the Hartmans'?" Rhona asked, once the waiter had poured their water and supplied menus.

"Terrible and declining rapidly." Hollis pushed both hands through her hair. The curls snapped back in place.

Rhona wished her hair behaved like that.

"Where to begin?" Hollis interlocked her fingers, leaned her elbows on the table, rested her chin on her hands and gave Rhona the details. "Manon is afraid for Etienne. He's eleven, you know. Kids are so damn vulnerable. She's frantic that Ivan's murder will push him over the edge and make him a depressive like her."

"Is he depressed?"

"He's upset." Hollis unfolded her napkin and laid it on her lap. "If he wasn't, there'd be something wrong with him. But, generally, he's pretty cheery. He hasn't withdrawn. He plays baseball and soccer and attends an astronomy day camp. If appetite measures your mental state, he's doing fine. Sometimes he seems terribly sad, but that's okay, considering he's lost his brother, his mother's upset and his father's waiting for heart surgery. You can bet Etienne's frightened his father will die. On top of everything else, SOHD's opponents harass the family with threatening calls." She looked surprised. "Given what's happened, he's amazingly cheerful."

"It's illegal to do that. They should have filed a complaint. They don't need to put up with it." Perhaps they'd find the Hartmans' number when they went over Allie Jones's and Barney's phone records.

"The calls come sporadically. The family keeps hoping they'll stop."

"Hard for an eleven-year-old to cope with everything. Doesn't he have grandparents he could stay with?"

The waitress took their order.

"Just one—Manon's mother. He's visiting her later in the summer. Meanwhile, Manon's terrified something else may happen and keeps him on a short leash."

"I don't blame her. They should take the anti-SOHD bunch seriously." Rhona drummed her fingers on the table. "Hasn't Curt considered what his high-profile advocacy is doing to his family?"

"It's an obsession. I don't think he gives a damn. What effect do you think it will have?"

"Aside from the pain Etienne already feels, consider how his friends probably reacted to his brother's murder and Curt's SOHD endorsement." Rhona raised her hand and pointed a finger at Hollis. "Murder would scare and fascinate Etienne's classmates. When you're eleven, you may lose your grandparents, maybe a parent, but seldom a sibling and not by murder. It's scary. Kids worry about bad things being contagious. Think about adults and how they avoid divorcing couples because they're afraid their unhappiness will spread."

"I don't agree. In my experience, everyone doesn't desert you when something terrible happens. I do think the happily-married avoid divorcing couples, but I don't think it's fear of contagion. Couples like that are tense, and they fight—no one wants to be with them." Hollis's napkin slid from her knee, and she scrambled under the table to retrieve it.

Rhona leaned across the table. "You could be right. But SOHD—that's another story altogether. Many kids develop allergies, asthma, wear glasses or have more serious diseases by the time they're eleven." She lowered her voice. "Etienne's friends *will* make the connection. They *will* wonder if they might not have been born if their parents had received genetic testing."

"When I was a kid, I read articles about diseases in my mother's *Reader's Digest* and immediately interpreted any minor symptoms I felt as an indication I had the 'disease of the month'."

"Me too."

They grinned at one another. The waitress brought their salads, offered pepper and left them to continue their conversation.

"Etienne knows his mother suffers from depression and anxiety and sees a psychiatrist regularly. He's probably aware his grandfather died in suspicious circumstances—he's buried in unconsecrated ground. I hope Etienne doesn't think *he* wouldn't have been born if SOHD had existed back then," Hollis said.

"Why did Curt involve himself with them?"

"Who knows? I'm not a psychologist, but I'd guess it might be identified as anxiety or guilt transference."

"Whatever. Curt seems oblivious to what he's doing to Etienne and his wife." Rhona chopped the chicken in her Caesar salad into smaller pieces and popped one small morsel in her mouth. "I presume that's it—there can't be more." Rhona's voice had risen a bit. The elderly couple at the next table, who appeared to have run out of conversation years before, stared at her with interest.

"You've heard about Lena's show."

"I visited it before closing time last night." Rhona leaned forward and fixed her gaze on Hollis. "Something affecting you happened there."

"Shoot."

"I hope shooting won't have anything to do with it," Rhona said. "Lena Kalma and I overheard a conversation between a woman and a man who was a lawyer. The woman said Lena was totally crazy and would stop at nothing to ruin Curt. Lena barged in and said Curt, his wife and you would have to pay. 'Out of control' and 'oblivious to consequences', those are the terms I'd use to describe her."

"Thanks for warning me. She's one scary woman, and I certainly will avoid antagonizing her, although I do want to question her about Ivan. Anyway I'll deal with that when I have to. Right now I have new information for you."

Rhona chewed an extra large romaine lettuce leaf and wished she'd cut it in half. "What is it?"

"I'll trade the information for your promise to take me along when you check it out."

"A ride-along." Rhona considered Hollis. "It depends on whether I think it'll be dangerous. Even if I don't, you'll have to sign a release and wear a Kevlar vest."

The waitress removed their plates and left dessert menus.

"Fine with me. Going through Ivan's things, I found a receipt for a storage locker in North York. I located the place in my gazeteer. It's in an industrial park off Highway 404. You exit on Steeles. I dug around in other boxes and found a key ring. One had a cardboard tag identifying it as the storage locker key."

Rhona absorbed this news. Definitely worth following up on.

The team had broadened the investigation and now considered Curt the probable target. But maybe they'd been wrong. Right or wrong, she'd check out the storage locker. She calculated she had an hour to spare. But dessert first. Murder or no murder, she wasn't passing up raspberry tart with crème fraîche. "How did we miss it? We searched Ivan's belongings."

The waitress hovered. Hollis chose a lemon concoction. Rhona opted for the tart.

"I was secretive as a child and hid papers I didn't want my mother to find inside or behind other things. It occurred to me Ivan might have done that too, and he did. I found the receipt behind a recipe and..."

"And what?" Hollis had appeared to have been about to say something else then reconsidered. "Did you find other documents?"

"No documents, but I found keys tucked in a carton of Ivan's clothes."

Hollis was hiding something. Sooner or later it would come out. "It's twelve fifteen. We'll go after dessert."

*   *   *

In the industrial park, they located the office. The young woman at the reception desk glanced over her shoulder but only half swung around when they entered.

Rhona identified herself and flashed her badge. "We're interested in locker 47," she said.

"Help yourselves." The woman didn't examine their identification. Her office chair squeaked as she wheeled back to her computer.

Rhona peaked over her shoulder. She was playing Free Cell. So much for the pressure of work. Being a fellow aficionado,

Rhona was well aware how one game led to another and gobbled up endless hours.

They followed the path alongside the building until they reached #47. Rhona inserted the key, stepped inside and flicked on the lights. She probably should have arranged for tracking dogs. If anything struck her as odd, she'd close the door and send for them immediately. Inside, she sniffed—criminals used facilities like this to store drugs or weapons. The stale air revealed no telltale scents.

Piles of cardboard boxes lined two walls. Unboxed tables, one upended on another, filled the room's centre. Large oil paintings depicting Italian scenes leaned against the tables. A number retained auction house tags. They read the boxes' labels—industrial cooking equipment, dishes, Paderno pots.

"Everything he needed to start a restaurant," Rhona said and saw Hollis's eyes fill with tears.

A file cabinet sat beside a desk with a straight chair pulled up to it. It was a mini-office. Rhona tried the drawers. "Locked," she said, stating the obvious. She rattled the keys. "Let's see if any of these fit."

One did. The first drawer held file folders. Rhona flipped through one labelled "invoices".

"Poor Ivan." Hollis sounded as if she might cry. "How secretive he was. It must have taken him ages to amass this stuff at bankruptcy and auction sales. He probably dreamed of surprising the family, his father particularly, by inviting them to his restaurant's grand opening—presenting them with a *fait accompli*. It breaks my heart."

"It is sad, but I can't see a connection to his murder." Rhona fanned the receipts. "I'll have our guys verify these to make sure he didn't keep everything secret because these are stolen goods." She shook her head. "But everything I've learned about him tells me we won't find anything like that."

She pulled open the next drawer. *"This* is where it went."

Hollis couldn't see what Rhona was looking at. "What is it?"

"Ivan's computer. We knew he had one and couldn't find it. Now that I see everything here, I'd guess it contains detailed information about his restaurant plans that he didn't want his family to see. I'm glad we've found it—it provides one more answer. I'll take it back and see what else is on it."

"I'll tell Manon and Curt about this locker and its contents. Unless they've found a will, this belongs to them. The fees are paid until next summer, so they won't have to deal with it immediately."

*   *   *

Hollis raced into class fifteen minutes late again. She wondered if Curt had dealt with Lena's exhibition.

Curt ignored her entrance and continued, "…palettes the Old Masters used. Many colours are no longer available. And we've read about the terrible things lead white did to artists and to women who used it for makeup. Today, although we no long use lead white, we still rely on most colours used by the Old Masters. But we also have new synthetics. If you want your paintings to survive, you must pay attention to a colour's fastness, a medium's compatibility with specific colours and the properties of protective varnishes. Probably you've read about Turner knowing and disregarding those who advised him to avoid certain colours because over time they would fade or change. In fact, even in his lifetime, reds in many of his paintings altered dramatically." He picked up a clear glass bottle half filled with amber liquid. "In Rembrandt's time, linseed, walnut and poppy seed oils were common agents for mixing colours." He pushed his unruly hair back from his forehead and regarded them silently for a moment. "But we'll talk more about them another day." He picked up a twelve by twelve panel. "Today you'll work on oak. Rembrandt used it for his self-portrait, 'Artist in his Studio'. Earlier artists used fig wood. We'll experiment with his techniques and aim to achieve his level of luminosity. But first, we'll prepare the panels and allow them to dry." Curt waved the panel at a stand set up amidst the circle of easels.

Hollis considered a disparate collection of mismatched china; dried flowers in a vase; heavy purple satin drapery; and several unrelated objects—a glass apple, a feather and a silver pitcher. "When your panels are ready, you'll paint this arrangement. Later, using different grounds and materials, you'll paint it again to illustrate varied effects."

What an uninspiring collection. She'd never liked painting still lifes. Thankfully, Curt hadn't added to its authenticity by adding a dead hare or pheasant.

While they considered his setup, he adjusted the cords on the window blinds to darken the room. At the podium, he picked up the projector control and flashed the first slide on the screen.

"Caravaggio painted from dark to light, as most oil painters did and do. In this slide we can see..."

"Visit Lena Kalma's show at the Revelation Gallery on Queen Street. See Curt Hartman, a son-destroyer," blared from outside.

"Damn her, damn her, damn her," Curt muttered. As if to rid himself of her influence, he shook himself like a wet dog before he returned to Caravaggio.

Lefevbre drew continuously. He contributed nothing to the class discussion. At break, when the others prepared to troop downstairs for snacks and drinks, he stayed where he was. Hollis looked at his sketch pad. He'd drawn a likeness of Kate that radiated her vitality.

"That's wonderful."

"I can't help drawing people," Lefevbre said apologetically. "I always carry a sketch pad."

"I wish I did. I'm too self-conscious. I hate it when someone peers over my shoulder."

"My daughter, Valerie, felt like that."

"I'm sorry. It must be terrible for you."

Lefevbre's lips trembled. "I'll *never* recover. I raised her. My wife is MFB Corporation's comptroller. She agreed to have a baby because I wanted one and promised to care for it." He wiped his eyes. "Sorry, more information than you wanted."

"If it helps to talk about your daughter, it's okay with me. What happened to her?"

Lefevbre briefly summarized the accident. He gazed at her fixedly. "You're a friend of Curt's?"

"His wife, Manon, has been my friend for many years."

"Does she know about Curt?"

"Know what?"

"He's a womanizer."

Did Manon? An interesting question, given that Curt had left Lena to marry Manon. Did Manon think she'd been the last? It wasn't something they'd ever talked about. She shrugged. "I don't know."

"Someone should tell her. Maybe she'd leave him. Cause *him* pain."

How to respond? She was out of her depth.

He leaned toward her, lowered his voice and told her about Valerie's unsuccessful attempt to secure a third trimester abortion. "Tell her Valerie's story—open her eyes." He rose and stomped out.

Exactly what Manon didn't need—she certainly wouldn't

repeat Lefevbre's story. She hurried downstairs and arrived to hear Kate talking.

"Do you suppose she'll come by every day the show's on?" She pushed her ring-encrusted hands through her spiky hair and made herself look again like an enraged porcupine.

"Probably. She's obsessed, determined to damage him," Bert said.

"I'd be scared shitless about my safety, my house and my family if it happened to me." Kate widened her eyes behind her round black-rimmed glasses. "She came across as totally crazy."

"I agree. I'd worry about family too. You can always replace 'things', but not people. She strikes me as 'an eye for an eye' person," Patel said.

"Many wronged people seek vengeance—it's a natural reaction," David said.

Bert scowled. "I agree. If she holds Curt responsible for their son's death, I bet she wants to hurt his new wife and their child. That would be perfect revenge, wouldn't it?"

Hollis shivered.

"She doesn't look like a woman who'd have a gun. Actually, I don't know anyone who has a gun. Unless she ran them over in the street, she wouldn't attack them outside. But she might sneak into the house and do something awful. I don't know what, but she looks like a woman who would have ideas. But she'd have to get in to do that, and they must have a security system," Bert said.

"They do. When I was there last week, MacTee and I tried creeping out for an early morning walk and set it off," Hollis said. "Believe me, it woke everyone in two seconds."

"Cool. Maybe she wouldn't go after the family. Maybe she'd attack Curt. Didn't I read in *ARTnews* about a separate studio next to the house?" Kate said.

"Yes, above their garage. It's a big space upstairs with

amazing skylights. There are electronic controls to open them or control shades sandwiched between the glass."

She smiled, thinking about Etienne camped out, gazing up at the stars. "Etienne, his eleven-year-old, loves astronomy. Actually, he and a couple of buddies plan to camp there tonight and stargaze."

"They did a photo shoot of his studio in *Canadian Artist*. You know the kind of article I mean—how to duplicate the studio space of the rich and famous. As if we could. I feel lucky to set up in a corner of the living room or the kitchen," Bert said. "The amazing thing was that there weren't many paintings in the studio."

"There never are. Only the one or two paintings he's working on at any given time are there. He has a cartage company collect the others and take them off to humidity and light-controlled storage."

"Why?" Kate said.

"I wondered. Most artists stack canvases around their studios and work on them periodically until they're happy. I asked him how come he shipped his away so soon. He said he didn't like to second-guess himself. When his gut feeling said 'done', he called the company and bundled the painting off before he changed his mind."

"Do you suppose he ever sees his paintings in a show and regrets his decision?" Kate said.

"I asked him that too. He laughed and said he didn't go in for regrets."

"I wonder if he applies that philosophy to the rest of his life," David said, raising his eyebrows. "If he does it's a great way to get by—'no regrets', 'what's done is done' etc. etc. Live for today. Leave your mistakes behind and move on—very Buddhist, very Zen—live for the moment."

Nineteen

It was almost five when Hollis returned from class. She collected MacTee and Etienne and shepherded them outside. She studied Etienne. "Why the long face?"

"They can't come."

Hollis ran previous conversations through her mind. This was Thursday, the night two boys from Etienne's astronomy group planned to stargaze.

"Why not?"

"Their parents *said* to say it was because they had to do something else that their parents had forgotten about. Ronnie told me the *real* reason. His mother thought it was dangerous to come to our house." He sighed. "Nothing will *ever* be the same again."

"Nothing is ever the same from one day to the next. That's life. But it will get better. I promise."

Etienne's expression didn't change—clearly he wasn't convinced.

"I don't suppose I'd do." Here was a perfect opportunity to do something positive. Not only that, she might surprise herself and find the heavens fascinating.

Etienne paused. Two years earlier, he probably would have thrown his arms around her waist and nearly knocked her off her feet. Now he contented himself with a big grin.

"Cool. You want pizza for a snack, don't you?"

"I certainly do. I never pass up a chance for pizza."

"What kind do you like?"

"I'm not fussy—black olives, sun-dried tomatoes, artichokes—feta."

Etienne's nose wrinkled. "We could order a large with different things on each half. I like double cheese and bacon."

"Done. What time?"

"Nine." Etienne quick-stepped beside Hollis. "I'm staying up the *whole* night."

"MacTee and I will learn a thing or two. We'll keep you company for a while, but I can guarantee I won't last all night."

They reached the "dogs off leash" area. Arthur's threat echoed in her mind. She scrutinized the ground. When she saw no litter, she decided Etienne could keep MacTee busy enough with the ball to prevent him from finding or eating any garbage.

"Etienne, you throw it. You're the baseball player. You have a stronger arm than I do. You can toss it further. We'll pocket it if it's too disgusting."

"I don't mind some slime." Etienne pulled his arm back behind his head, wound up like a professional and heaved the ball.

Back at the house after supper, Hollis hoisted a carryall of provisions over her shoulder and tucked two rolled sleeping bags under her arm. Etienne lugged his impressive telescope and tripod. MacTee, sniffing interesting smells and wagging his tail like a banner, preceded them through the studio door. Upstairs, the last daylight rays angled down through the skylights.

"Pretty neat place, isn't it?" Etienne set up his telescope under a skylight before he flopped into the denim-covered chair on wheels. He propelled himself in a big arc coming back to the telescope. "Did you know that this," he pointed at it, "this is an old-fashioned way to look at stars?"

"What's the modern way?"

"To use a computer. You load a stargazing program and connect it to the telescope. You type in what you want to see and the computer aligns it for you. Pretty cool, eh? My grandmaman says it takes the fun away from stargazing. She says you should be as familiar with the heavens as you are with your own neighbourhood." He wheeled around in another circle. "And did you know you measure space between stars or planets with your fingers?" He braked in front of Hollis. "Are you hungry? Should we order the pizza?"

It seemed like two minutes since dinner, but this was Etienne's night, and he wanted it now.

"Let's."

Etienne reached into his pocket and pulled out a flyer folded around several bills. "Here—it's Paola's Pizza menu. Maman and I think it's Toronto's best. They make *really, really, really* good pizza."

The order was placed and delivery promised within forty-five minutes. Etienne trotted down to the garage and retrieved two air mattresses he'd lugged over and inflated earlier in the day. He dragged them upstairs. MacTee, tail in continuous motion, followed him.

"MacTee must need to go out. I'll take him." Etienne reached for the leash draped over the stair railing.

"It's almost dark. You shouldn't go alone. After we've eaten, we'll take him for a quick walk." Hollis expected Etienne, like most eleven-year-olds, to assert his independence, but he didn't protest. Arthur had spooked him.

After the pizza arrived, they settled cross-legged on their sleeping bags. MacTee, watching every mouthful, planted himself next to Etienne. A long saliva string formed at the corner of his mouth.

"Don't give him any," Hollis said.

"He looks hungry."

"He's not. It upsets his stomach. Please don't feed him."

Etienne sighed. "Sorry, MacTee, gotta do what the boss says."

Their snack finished, Hollis snapped the leash on MacTee's collar. In the laneway, she glanced to the right, where a streetlight's beam cast light and thought someone stepped quickly into the shadows, as if he or she didn't want to be seen. Had she imagined it? Was she as spooked as the rest of the family?

Should she call the police? What would she say? She'd seen someone step back into the shadows. Not enough information. But she wouldn't go that way. Instead she headed to Parliament Street's crowds. After an uneventful walk, they trooped back upstairs, where they organized themselves for the night. They both had flashlights.

"I'll open the skylight. Because of Toronto's lights, we'll only see the brightest ones," Etienne said. "Ready?"

Hollis followed Etienne's celestial guide, and they spotted the brightest stars, despite the glowing city lights. After more than an hour, Etienne's commentary slowed and stopped.

"Etienne," Hollis whispered. She received no response. MacTee's snores had punctuated the studio's quiet soon after they'd returned from their walk. Hollis, who'd been aware for some time of increasing hordes of mosquitoes zeroing in to feast on her exposed skin, crept out of her sleeping bag and closed the skylight.

* * *

Hollis jerked awake.

MacTee pawed her shoulder. He was barking frantically with

his face inches from hers. What was wrong? Why could she see him? It should be dark. Light flickered from somewhere.

She smelled smoke.

Fire.

"Okay. Stop. I'm awake." She pushed MacTee to one side and crawled out of her sleeping bag. Flames flickered in the stairwell.

She grabbed Etienne's shoulders and shook him. "Etienne, wake up. There's a fire."

Etienne barely stirred.

She gripped his shoulders and dragged him from his sleeping bag.

"Stand up." No. Wrong thing to do. Close to the floor there wasn't any carbon monoxide. The fire burned below them. They couldn't use the stairs. The double doors—the only escape.

"What? What the heck?" Etienne sat up.

"Pull your T-shirt up over your face and crawl." She clicked her flashlight on and aimed it at the doors. "There. Crawl there. Now. Follow the beam. There's a fire." Panic welled. She pushed it down—she had to stay calm. The block and tackle. She'd lower Etienne then MacTee. Thank heaven for Curt's huge paintings.

"Get going. I'll let you down. Run to the house. Yell 'fire' as loud as you can."

"What about you and MacTee?"

"We're coming after you. Move!"

Etienne scooted across the floor. MacTee and Hollis followed. Smoke drifted through the room. If it hadn't been for last night's mosquitos, the open skylight would have been a giant chimney sucking smoke up to asphyxiate them. She fumbled for the door frame. Her hands locked on the ropes fastening the sling to the wall

She coughed. When the doors opened, there'd be a

draught. Smoke would funnel upward and billow out. They had no time.

"Hang on and jump. I'll keep you from crashing," she said as she fastened the rope around Etienne.

He swung out. His weight nearly jerked her off her feet, and she clutched the rope with both hands.

"I'm down. I'll wake Maman and call 911," he yelled.

Hollis yanked the rope back up. And coughed. The smoke thickened. The T-shirt over her mouth kept slipping. While she fastened ropes around MacTee, she tried to breathe shallowly. Smoke killed.

She shoved MacTee's bulk toward the door. He braced his feet and resisted, but he went.

A yelp. Oh no. Brilliant, really brilliant.

Etienne's gone. MacTee's tied in the sling. How to release him? How to save herself? Hang on to the rope and let herself down? Too thin—not like a knotted bed sheet. She'd jump.

The air mattresses. She'd throw them out to land on. Drop—not throw. Right below. She'd hang by her hands and let go.

She pulled her T-shirt up over her mouth again and crawled back to where they'd been sleeping. The smoke was thicker. She didn't want to breathe. How to pull two mattresses and crawl? Impossible. One would have to do. On hands and knees, she pushed it ahead of her. At the door, she dropped it down.

Ready to let go. Back to the edge, hang on and...

Howling sirens. Flashing lights, trucks roaring down the street. Thank God.

"Help. I'm up here."

Firefighters below.

They leaned a ladder against the wall. Hollis didn't wait. As soon as it thumped into position, she scrambled down, assured them she was okay and raced to MacTee. She freed him from his tangle of rope and urged him away from the fire. He stood up but whined and lifted a front paw. When Hollis, hand on his collar, coaxed him to hobble away, he lurched forward on three legs, refusing to put his weight on the other one.

Something was seriously wrong.

Etienne zoomed toward them. Manon, white cotton eyelet robe flowing behind her, slippers flapping, tore after Etienne. Curt followed more slowly.

"Stand back," a firefighter ordered. Firefighters were everywhere. One wielded an axe to smash the lock on the garage door.

Through opened doors, they saw fire crackling under the stairs and licking toward the vehicles. A firefighter directed a torrent toward the flames.

Curt hugged Manon and Etienne close. His grip appeared to hurt Etienne, but the boy didn't pull away. Curt's white face and wide-eyes betrayed his ill health and his shock. His gaze met Hollis's.

"What the hell did you do?" he said as he pulled Manon and Etienne closer.

"What did *I* do?" Her voice shook with rage. "*I* saved your son's life—that's what I did."

"Curt, stop." Manon commanded. She grabbed his arm. "Stop. Fires start. It happens." She tightened her grip. "Hollis saved Etienne."

"Thank MacTee. He woke us with his barking." Hollis could hardly speak; her teeth banged together like tin cans in a mill race. Her body shook. She was freezing. Shock—a delayed reaction to adrenaline flooding her body. What if MacTee *hadn't* been there? What if he *hadn't* barked? She wouldn't be here—they'd be dragging her corpse from the fire. She and Etienne would be dead.

Had the killer struck again? Had it been arson?

Twenty

Curt muttered an apology. Hollis heard but didn't care. She'd nearly died—the enormity engulfed her.

"I wonder if it was arson," Manon murmured.

An ever-growing crowd watched the hoses pour gallons of water onto the fire, creating clouds of hissing steam and stinking smoke. Flames consumed the door and interior stairs before they flickered out. The firefighters' prompt arrival saved but soaked the remainder of the building.

Arson—a frightening thought. If an arsonist had lit the fire, aware that a person was in the studio, he'd intended to cut off the escape route, to trap them upstairs. Without MacTee's frantic barking... Hollis's stomach churned with nausea. Had the killer intended to murder her and Etienne? Impossible. She didn't have enemies in Toronto. But how could she argue with facts? The fire had started in the stairwell. There was nothing there that would have ignited spontaneously. Someone must have stuffed something—gasoline-soaked rags maybe— through the mail slot in the antique door. One flick of a match, and the dry, paint-laden wood would have exploded. She didn't want to think about it. Practical things—she'd focus on them.

"Our vehicles have had it," she said to Manon.

"Insurance will cover them—the vehicles and the building," Manon said in her practical banker's voice.

"Only the vehicles," Curt said.

Manon's head snapped up. "What do you mean?"

Curt refused to meet her gaze. "I never got around to extending the house insurance to cover the studio," he said apologetically. "But what does it matter—Etienne and Hollis are okay."

No matter how arrogant or insensitive to others Curt might be, he had suffered about as many blows as any man should have to endure. She had worried almost exclusively about Etienne and Manon. In fact, she'd blamed Curt for bringing disaster not only to himself, but also to his family. Whether he had or not, it was impossible not to feel sorry for him and to worry what havoc shock was wreaking on his already fragile health.

"What's done is done—we can't do anything about the vehicles tonight," Manon said.

Hollis focused on MacTee. Although he lay quietly at her feet, he hadn't been able to walk on all four legs when she'd helped him away from the fire. How could she have ignored him when he'd saved their lives? She knelt down and gently felt his legs. He pulled away and whimpered when she lifted the right front one.

"He may have broken a bone." She stroked the dog's head. "Which taxi company picks up a fare accompanied by a dog?" she asked Manon.

Manon bent over and stroked MacTee's head. "Our life saver," she said affectionately. "You need treatment." She shook her head. "None of them do. They only take seeing-eye dogs."

"He has to get to a vet."

Manon straightened up and considered the problem.

"He can't walk with his sore leg." Etienne squirmed from his father's grasp. "Come on, Maman, Papa, you have to know *someone* we can phone."

"We drove Beau to the clinic ourselves, but not everyone owns a car. The SPCA must have a vehicle or know who to call. There's an emergency veterinary clinic on Belmont or Merton. I'll call them," Manon offered.

"I'll call—they'll want to ask what's wrong," Hollis said.

Minutes later, she returned. "Either the SPCA or the veterinary vehicle will take more than an hour to arrive. I didn't want to wait, so I called David Nixon, who's in our class. He brought me home after the show. Since he told me to call him if we needed anything, I took him up on his offer. He drives a van and lives close by—somewhere on the Danforth. Etienne, grab a large towel. We'll improvise a sling and move MacTee to the front porch."

"I want to come with you," Etienne said.

Manon shook her head, but Etienne persisted. "Maman, MacTee saved *my* life. I *should* go with Hollis and make sure he's okay. Anyway, Hollis needs someone with her—someone who really cares about MacTee."

"When you put it that way..." Manon pressed her lips together and half-smiled at Etienne. "Of course you may go."

Manon waited on the front steps with them, while Curt spoke with the captain. The firefighters were gathering their equipment.

Arson. The word hung in the smoky air.

"If it *was* arson..." Manon's voice broke.

"If it was—who was the intended victim?" Curt had returned.

He posed the question Hollis didn't want to consider. Too bad Etienne hadn't gone to bed—he didn't need to hear this discussion. But, being a clever kid, he'd probably already asked himself the same thing. Maybe it was better to have everything in the open. She remembered her ninth summer and how distressed she'd been when her parents had whispered and shut her out.

"Not Etienne or me," Hollis said. "Who knew we'd be stargazing?" Hollis hoped she'd chosen a reassuringly reasonable tone. But, even as she spoke, she flashed back to class break, when she'd said that Etienne would be stargazing. Then she thought back to their walk and her impression that someone who hadn't wanted to be seen lurked in the lane.

"Maybe it was all of us," Curt said conversationally.

"Why on earth would you say that?" Hollis was furious. Manon's fear for Etienne gripped her like a straitjacket; she didn't need it tightened.

"The explosion would have rocked the neighbourhood if the gas tanks had blown."

"But it wouldn't have killed us unless it set the house on fire and trapped us inside. Be serious. If someone intended to murder us, they would have targeted the house." Manon's tone was chilly.

Hollis expelled a deep breath. She'd feared Manon would fall apart when she heard Curt's suggestion. Instead she'd come close to mocking him. Nevertheless, it felt surreal to sit on a Toronto porch discussing how someone might have set out to kill all of them. MacTee, lying at Hollis's feet, whimpered, an ordinarily imperceptible sound but one easily heard in the quiet, windless air. It was almost dawn. Thin drifts of magenta-tinted cloud added colour to the paling sky.

David arrived, and together they half-carried MacTee to the van. Minutes later, they shuttled him into the clinic's waiting room. A faintly antiseptic smell assaulted their noses. Even at five a.m., worried pet owners huddled on the beige molded plastic chairs. They gripped sad-faced dogs or clutched cats bundled in blankets or yowling in cages. After they checked in with the receptionist, whose pallor betrayed her fatigue, Hollis and David sat down. Released from his sling, MacTee hobbled to Etienne and lay down.

"Poor dog, he's as gimpy as I am," David said.

Etienne, a polite eleven-year-old, normally would never have asked David about his limp. David's comment gave him permission.

"How come you're gimpy?"

"I was in the hospital and contracted osteomyelitis. The doctors operated, but I was left with a permanent limp."

"Why were you in the hospital?" Etienne persisted.

David's jaw clenched. His eyes narrowed. "Something or other," he shrugged. "I don't remember."

Clearly, he remembered very well, but whatever it was, he didn't intend to talk about it. Time to rescue him from Etienne's curiosity. She'd focus on animals and veterinary clinics. "I wonder which night they see the most patients?"

"Obviously Saturday and Sunday, when regular vets aren't available," David answered. "Was it arson?"

"Curt talked to the firefighters. They said it probably started inside the front door of the studio but that he'd have to wait for a definitive answer until the fire marshal had done his thing."

"How can they tell where it starts?" Etienne asked.

"From the ashes—they're different where the most intense burning takes place. That's how they pinpoint a spot or spots where a fire originated."

"But a fire *has* to start somewhere. How can they tell if someone used something to start it?" Etienne persisted.

"They have a machine to test for gases and for a residue of whatever accelerant the arsonist used," Hollis said.

"Could Lena Kalma have set it?" David said.

"Why would you say that?" Hollis asked.

"After seeing the show, I believe she'll stop at nothing. If she thought Curt was up there…"

Hollis glanced at Etienne. He'd heard about Lena's show but not about Lena's threats to hurt Hollis and the family—everyone she blamed for Curt and Manon's marriage. She wished she could protect him.

"No one knew *we* were there," Etienne said.

"Not quite true. I saw someone in the lane when you and I took MacTee out."

"Why didn't you tell me?" Etienne said.

"It was only a glance. And it isn't against the law to walk in the lane. Besides, I didn't want to frighten you."

"Man or woman?" David asked.

"I couldn't tell. I glimpsed someone step quickly into the shadows."

"Why would Lena burn Papa's studio?" Etienne asked.

"She's angry at everyone since Ivan died. She swore to avenge his death—whatever that means."

"It sounds like something from Harry Potter," Etienne said.

"It does. If she saw the studio light when we were eating our pizza and didn't see anyone leave, she'd assume Curt was spending the night. On the other hand, maybe she targeted his work, thinking nothing would upset him more than destroying his paintings." She patted Etienne's knee. "I'm sure whoever set the fire wasn't after us." Whether or not this was true, it might make Etienne feel better. Until the police caught the arsonist, no one would know whom he'd intended to kill. It was healthier for Etienne to think he and Hollis had not been the targets.

"Curt must have other enemies." David seemed unwilling to drop the subject.

"He does." Hollis ticked them off on her fingers. "His ex-

200

agent, Arthur White, the SOHD opponents, Sebastien Lefevbre—the list goes on and on."

Etienne absorbed Hollis's words. "Wow, how come I didn't know these things? I'm not a baby, I'm eleven. You or Maman should have told me. I'm good at keeping my eyes open."

"We intended to spare you, to stop you from worrying." Hollis smiled at his intensity and willingness to assume grown-up responsibility.

"MacTee Grant."

The vet, a young man in green operating room scrubs, called them in. David and Hollis lifted MacTee to the examination room. Inside, the vet gently probed his leg.

"It's very swollen. It's a break, a torn tendon or a severe sprain. Probably the latter, but he needs an X-ray. When did he eat last?"

"Six thirty."

"Enough time has passed. We'll anesthetize him to keep him still. He'll stay here until it's worn off. Call tomorrow morning after ten. By then we'll have identified his problem and treated it."

"Be a brave dog," Hollis said to MacTee, giving him a last hug before she rejoined the others.

David returned them to the Hartmans'. His last words were, "Make sure you lock all the doors."

*   *   *

Thursday night or early Friday morning, the phone shrilled. Rhona had trained herself to come awake almost instantly when it rang. She'd had years to perfect the skill and took pride in her ability. She slithered from her king-size bed to reach the phone on the night table.

"There was a fire at Hartmans'." It was the duty officer.

The other shoe. She and Zee Zee were racing to identify and arrest the killer before he struck again. They hadn't run fast enough. Who was dead?

"Give me the details. When did this happen?"

"Shortly after two. No one was hurt. A dog barking woke them in time."

She peered at the bedside clock radio—five thirty.

"Why am I hearing about it now?"

"Initially, fire and police didn't connect it to the motorcycle murder."

"Was it arson?'

"Too early to say for sure, but they've called in the fire marshal. They're running the appropriate tests."

"How badly did it damage the house?"

"It wasn't the house—it happened in the studio out back."

"Anyone inside?"

"A house guest and a kid."

Hollis and Etienne. Had the killer targeted them because Hollis was sharing information with her? Surely not. Curt's studio—the arsonist had thought Curt was there. If he had been, he wouldn't have had a dog to warn him. This was attempted murder.

"Have you called Zee Zee?"

"After you."

"Tell her I'm on my way—I'll arrive at the shop in half an hour."

Rhona hauled herself out of bed, washed and slapped on a minimum of makeup. Yesterday's wrinkled pantsuit would have to do.

Opie twined around her legs, complaining loudly. He was not an early riser.

"I won't forget. I'll fill the bowls—you won't starve," she assured him.

She decanted kibble and asked herself the all important question. Had the killer failed for a second time?

* * *

"I spoke to the fire marshal," Zee Zee said.

"And?"

"They still have more tests to run, but it looks like turpentine was the accelerant."

"It was arson, but was it attempted murder?" Rhona asked.

"Frank told us to proceed as if it was. We'll work with the fire department. We'll investigate as if it's tied to Ivan Hartman's murder."

"Turpentine. That's unusual—most people don't have it hanging around. Varsol or other petroleum distillates have more or less replaced it."

"Not for all artists—oil painters specifically. Now they even have odourless brands." Zee Zee tapped her nails on the desk's edge.

In other circumstances, the repetitive action could drive you crazy, but Rhona didn't mind if it helped Zee Zee think.

Zee Zee stopped. "Could it be a red herring?"

"How's that?'

"We're thinking artist, aren't we? Did the perp want us to conclude an artist set the fire? The perp may have nothing to do with art but used turpentine to divert us—make sure we concentrate on artists."

"Let's head out. Find out who was home and who wasn't. Who uses turpentine and who doesn't? This time we won't phone—we'll just appear."

Arthur White topped the list. Maybe surprising him had been a bad idea—he wasn't home.

Lena Kalma was next.

"I must see if she's changed the dioramas," Rhona said as they arrived at the shop front.

"My God," she jumped away from the window. "It can't be. This is too much of a coincidence." She moved back for a second look and saw a three dimensional tableau picturing people falling into the flames of hell. Surely if Lena had set the fire, she wouldn't have constructed this horrible miniature. Or was she thumbing her nose—challenging them to catch her, to prove she'd done it.

Zee Zee peered in, drew back and raised her eyebrows. "This interview could be interesting."

Lena wore white coveralls splashed with red and black. On the work table, piles of photographs jumbled in boxes left space for black construction paper and pots of vermillion paint.

"Did you look?" Lena asked.

"Very dramatic," Rhona said noncommittally. "What motivated you?"

Lena's eyes glittered. Her lips twisted. "I keep thinking of the bastard—how he was responsible for my son's death. I hope he burns in hell."

Too good to be true. Time to tell her and see her reaction.

"Your ex-husband's studio burned last night."

There was no mistaking her shock. Her reaction was genuine, unless she doubled as an Academy Award winning actress.

"Was he…" She didn't finish the sentence. Instead, her eyes widened. She clamped her hand over her mouth.

"He wasn't there. Two others were—they're okay. Where were you last night?"

Lena's hand came down. "Right here." She pointed toward

the front of the building. "I construct things when I'm so angry I feel like exploding."

"Do you use turpentine?"

"Turpentine. What a strange question. I haven't used it for years." Her chin jutted forward. "Search my studio if you don't believe me. Help yourselves—I have nothing to hide. It's a solvent for thinning or cleaning up oil paints. I use acrylics. Oils make me sick. You clean up after acrylics with soap and water—it's much easier."

"Was anyone else here?"

"Tomas must have come in after I went to bed—I didn't hear him."

Not an acceptable alibi. Lena would remain on the list.

They set off for the Ciccios', where Zee Zee would pose the questions.

Anna let them in. "You again. I suppose you're here about the Hartman fire." She opened the door wider. "We don't need to entertain the neighbours."

This woman cared what the neighbours thought. Maybe that partly explained why she hated Manon. No woman likes to think others know someone is playing her for a fool.

"Olivero, the police are here again," she shouted and led Rhona and Zee Zee to the kitchen. "Help yourselves," she said, indicating stools pulled up under the marble-topped counter. She planted herself in mid-room with her arms tightly crossed.

If Rhona sat there, her legs wouldn't reach the floor. She wouldn't opt for such an undignified position. She leaned against the counter and pulled out her notebook and tape recorder. They waited in a silence that grew exponentially as the minutes passed.

Finally Olivero, barefoot in jeans and a T-shirt, padded into the kitchen. His face was unshaven and his eyes bleary. "Sorry, I was sound asleep." He yawned. "Want coffee? I'm having some. I don't function well without an espresso shot."

"Or with it," Anna muttered.

He spooned coffee into the machine and spoke over his shoulder. "I stayed up until four working on a sculpture—once I start, I keep at it until I fall over. What can I do for you?"

"We're here to ask a few questions," Zee Zee responded and turned to Anna. "Where were you last night?" she asked.

"Me?" Anna's voice rose and her eyes narrowed.

Zee Zee nodded.

Anna glared at her. "What time?"

"Let's say from six last evening until six this morning."

Anna considered her balefully. "Since my husband is *such* good company, a friend and I shopped then took in a movie at nine. I came in about midnight and went to bed."

"I'd like your friend's name. Did you see your husband when you returned?"

Anna looked like she'd like to get Olivero in trouble and say no. She sighed. "He'd asked me to buy granola bars at the 7-11. When he's working, they keep him going. I took them in to him. He didn't stop." She shoved an errant strand of hair behind her ear. "He never does. He was there then. By his appearance now, I'd say he was there all night."

Zee Zee directed her next remark to Olivero, who was pouring coffee into white china mugs. "Do you paint with oils and use turpentine?"

"Of course," he said over his shoulder.

"We'd like to test your turpentine."

Olivero swung around, coffee pot in hand. His brows drew together. "What's this about? Surely it's not about Ivan?"

Clearly he didn't play the radio while he worked.

"There was a fire in Curt Hartman's studio last night."

"And you think it was arson, and I used turpentine to start it." Olivero nodded. "Help yourself to my turpentine. I have nothing to hide. I'll buy more today. Gelo and I'll walk to the hardware store. Was anyone...*hurt?*"

"He means, 'Is darling Manon okay'," Anna said nastily.

Olivero ignored her.

"No one except the dog, and he sprained his leg."

"Poor MacTee." He closed his eyes.

"Isn't that something—he knows the dog's name," Anna sneered.

Twenty-One

Friday at noon, noise from the usually quiet back lane woke Hollis and drew her to the window. Below, three tow-trucks, lights flashing, congregated outside the studio. One hooked Curt's car and hoisted it in the air. Water streamed from the interior. Modern electronic systems react badly to water—the repairs would be costly or impossible. The car and truck disappeared down the lane. The second truck backed into place, ready to remove her vehicle.

Impossible to meditate. Her room reeked. The smoky smell drifted in from outside and rose from the clothes she'd worn the night before. Hollis threw on clean jeans and a T-shirt, bundled the stinking clothes and carried them downstairs.

Curt and Manon sat at the kitchen the table. Curt nodded at her. Manon, flipping through the yellow pages, looked up.

"I'm ordering rental cars—do you want one?"

A businesslike, efficient woman had replaced the desperately worried anxious person she'd been since Ivan's death.

Manon must have read the amazement on Hollis's face. "You're surprised I'm positive." She grinned and shook her head. "Why would you be surprised? It's what you've told me to do. And I'm doing it—moving on." Her lips tightened. "You will never realize how grateful I am to you and MacTee," she said thickly before she shook her head and smiled. "Darling dog—I pray he's okay."

"I'm phoning to see how he is after I dump this stuff in the garbage."

The vet had diagnosed a sprain and treated MacTee with anti-inflammatories. He would be released later in the day.

Curt and Manon shared her relief. Hollis kept peeking at Manon, expecting her to return to her previous anxious depressed state. It didn't happen. Hollis listened while Manon phoned her mother and told her matter-of-factly about the fire. Then she discussed the details of the visit she and Etienne would make to Quebec later in the summer. What had brought about this dramatic change? Maybe when the long-awaited and dreaded attack on Etienne had actually occurred, it had jolted Manon. The worst had happened, and they'd survived.

They collected their rental cars in time for Hollis and Curt to make it to class. Hollis settled in her seat and marvelled at Curt's resilience. Immaculately dressed and perfectly groomed, no one would have guessed Curt was a man with a bad heart who'd spent half the night watching his studio burn and thanking God his son had survived.

"You may or may not have heard about the fire in my studio last night."

Neither Kate nor Patel were radio or TV junkies. Their expressions reflected their surprise.

Curt shook his head and frowned. Long-faced—his eyes, lips, the wrinkles bracketing his mouth, his ears, everything sagged. He told them what had happened. His lips quivered. He clamped them together, walked to the supplies table and gripped the table's edge.

Everyone stopped breathing, waiting to see what he'd do next.

His shoulders rose, he exhaled, straightened, threw his shoulders back and pivoted to face them.

"Today we'll create paint from raw materials. Next week we'll make brushes. Painters in Rembrandt's time had to do both. They did have guidelines. In 1437, *Il Libro dell'Arte* by Cennino d'Andrea Cennini appeared and became the guideline for artists for centuries." His eyebrows rose. "Today art forgers rely on the book." He resumed his lecture. "Paint has not always come in tidy tubes and jars. In Rembrandt's day, a young artist prepared his own. Once he achieved success, he hired an apprentice to make paint." He distributed colour information handouts. "We won't make some paints. We'd risk our health if we dropped vinegar on lead and collected horse manure, if we could find it, to generate the heat to produce the reaction that would ultimately give us lead white, a highly toxic paint."

Had the Old Masters lived long lives or been like the hatters who used chemicals that drove them insane and led to the term "mad hatters"? Rubens had lived to old age. Perhaps his early success had enabled him to hire assistants who risked *their* health mixing up lethal concoctions.

"And we won't make verdigris—a lovely intense green. We'd have to use the scrapings from wine barrels." He looked up. "Possibly if we lived in Newfoundland, we could use screech. The leavings would then have to contact copper. The resulting fumes would make us sick, but eventually we'd have a lovely green. Let's see what we *can* do." He picked up a mortar and pestle. "We can grind the earth tones—ochres— and see what happens when we mix them with the different oils—linseed, walnut or poppy."

Hollis noticed that Lefevbre was absent. Why wasn't he in class? Had he been in the group when she'd said Etienne would be stargazing? She replayed the conversation but couldn't remember whether he'd been there or not. She was pretty sure he hadn't been. And she would have noticed if he'd joined them at break, because he usually remained in the studio. Nevertheless, she'd heard Lefevbre vow to attend every class.

Why wasn't he here?

Despite Hollis's fatigue, the heady smell of raw materials grabbed her attention. She zeroed in on the colours—the rich creamy whites, yellow as intense as the yolks of free range eggs, blues as deep as the North Atlantic on a sunny day. Her fingers twitched, anticipating adding, adjusting, stirring, readjusting and, finally, applying these luscious paints.

"I can see you're anxious to start. Consult the instruction sheets and prepare two colours. Then bring your palettes, load the paint and work over yesterday's under-painting."

The students stampeded to transform dry powders into enchanting viscous colour. Hollis longed to plunge her hands into the paint and smear thick layers on the canvas; to stroke, pull, overlay, wallow in tactile sensations. She envied kindergarten students and understood their unfettered joy when let loose with finger paints.

"Time for a break," Curt eventually announced.

Hollis didn't believe it. The others' expressions mirrored her incredulity. How could time have passed so quickly? Downstairs, the others crowded around her.

"It must have been damn fucking scary," Kate said.

"Not until afterwards. While it was happening, I only thought about getting us out."

"Did you crawl to the stairs like they say you should?" Bert asked.

"The stairs were burning."

"How did you…"

Kate interrupted Bert. "What about Curt's paintings?"

"How many did he have in the studio?" Tessa asked.

"Three, one finished and two that he's working on."

"He paints huge works. How does he get them out?" Tessa asked.

"Through second storey double doors they used years ago to load hay for horses. There's a block and tackle permanently installed, thank goodness. I lowered Etienne and my dog with it."

"Having been rudely interrupted," Bert said, glaring at Kate, "What about you? How did you escape?"

"I was afraid I wasn't going to." She related her story.

"What time was the fire?" Kate asked.

"After two."

"I'm surprised you or Curt came today," Patel said.

"I nearly didn't. But Curt insisted he had to come. I couldn't stay away—couldn't miss the course."

Hollis knew her face had lit up. She felt her lips curve. "Isn't making paint from scratch wonderful? Too time-consuming to do it on a regular basis, we'd need assistants like they had in the Renaissance. But it doesn't compare to squeezing paint from a tube."

Heads nodded in agreement.

"I suppose Curt's insurance company will pay to clean up and rebuild," Kate said.

"You won't believe it, but he doesn't have any—not a single cent."

"You have to be kidding. Everybody has insurance."

"Maybe you do, but lots of people don't. I don't," David said. Whatever Kate said annoyed David. Hollis had first seen it in the funeral home, but he'd picked at her often. Now Kate had irritated him again.

"But how could his wife live in peace if they didn't have any?" Kate persisted.

"Manon, that's his wife, is a cautious banker. She did insure their vehicles along with the house and its contents the moment they moved in." Hollis didn't know if she should be telling them all this, but she hated for anyone to think Manon was a slacker. "At that point, the studio hadn't been renovated. Curt said he'd contact the insurance company when it was, and he knew how much to insure it for. I can't imagine why Manon relied on him to do it. She should have known better."

"Why? Isn't he good at things like that?" Kate said. She shook her head. "He isn't the only one. I know guys who don't pay their taxes because they don't get around to it. I can't imagine living like that."

"You can't imagine much that doesn't fit into your narrow little world," David said. Kate glared daggers at him.

Hollis didn't want this to escalate. "Did anyone read the book about him that came out last year?"

"I did. It was okay, but…" David paused as if he didn't want to continue.

"But what?" Kate said.

"It was too laudatory. It didn't discuss his dark side and the influences in his early years."

"True, but the reason I brought it up was that the writer *did* deal with his document phobia. He has a thing about filling out forms. According to the author, he doesn't even have a will." Hollis wondered if she should have added this piece of gratuitous information. But it had appeared in print. Besides, he'd probably written a will since the book came out.

"He's not alone. I hate bureaucracy." David's brows drew together, and he scowled ferociously.

Hollis was glad she wasn't a bureaucrat. Run-ins with David would be unpleasant.

"Curt will have to arrange for demolition and repairs and cough up money to pay for them." Kate said. "That will be very expensive."

David shook his head. "Does he have fans running?"

"Fans?" Hollis said.

"Yes. You said water soaked everything. Industrial fans dry stuff and make it salvageable. Not having insurance, he'll want to save everything he can. On the other hand, he should keep his books and papers wet until he arranges for a fire salvage company to collect and freeze dry them."

"He has a library of valuable art books. Freeze dry?" She echoed.

"They stash the material in a big chamber and freeze it. Somehow it removes the moisture and leaves the documents in good shape."

"I'm sure he hasn't thought about fans or freeze drying."

"I could arrange to get fans for him."

"Do you want to offer, or do you want me to do it?" Hollis said.

"You know him better than I do. But the sooner they're installed, the better."

"I think we should do more than that," Kate said. She looked from one to the other. "We have a lot of skills. I think we should help."

"It's a good idea," Patel said. "Why don't we delegate to Hollis the job of finding out what needs to be done?"

Everyone nodded.

"Dry the stuff first," David said.

Before class resumed, Hollis relayed David's message to Curt.

"Where would I buy fans?"

Hollis beckoned David over.

Curt listened and nodded. "That's a good idea. I'd be grateful if you'd arrange to rent them and have them delivered."

*   *   *

Arthur let them in, cocked his head and considered them, seemingly without a glimmer of recognition.

"We've already visited you twice," Rhona reminded him after she reintroduced them. "Tell us if you were outside Curt Hartman's house last night."

"Last night," Arthur said, as if they'd asked him to remember something he'd done as a five-year-old child. "Did it rain?"

"No. Where were you?"

"I walked up and down outside their house about nine. I saw a woman and Curt's son walk the woman's dog then go back in. They had pizza delivered."

Rhona considered his information. "Did you see anyone else hanging around?"

Arthur thought for a minute, pursing his lips. "Might have, but my memory isn't what it used to be. Don't think I did."

"Did you hear that someone set fire to Curt's studio?"

Arthur's mouth formed a perfect "o"—he could have blown smoke rings. "Was anyone hurt?"

"We thought you might tell us," Rhona said.

"You think I'd do that?" Arthur's eyes widened. He drew himself up like a soldier standing in front of his commanding officer. "I can't prove this, but let me assure you I would *never* burn works of art. Curt is an asshole, but he's a great artist. It would be a sin to destroy his work." His shoulders sagged. "I've fallen a long way if anyone would think *I'd* do that." He frowned. "You didn't answer my question. Was anyone hurt?"

"Fortunately not."

"I'm sorry I didn't stay longer—it would please me to identify the person who would do that."

"If you remember anything else, will you call us?" Rhona asked.

Arthur took her card. Rhona had little hope he would use it. His vagueness was worse. Perhaps he suffered from Alzheimer's or some other neurological problem.

"Do you think he's faking?" Rhona asked Zee Zee once they were outside.

"Who knows? He certainly has reason to hate Curt. He doesn't have a life—no gallery, no wife and few creature comforts."

"All right, let's keep asking. Time for Sebastien Lefevbre, and then the charming SOHD duo."

Sebastien, towing his ancient spaniel, emerged from his house as they arrived. "I have to keep going. He's old and needs to go out often, or he has accidents," he explained.

"Why don't we walk with you," Zee Zee said.

They formed a snail-like procession, with Sebastien and Zee Zee creeping after the exceedingly slow-moving dog, and Rhona bringing up the rear. She didn't flip the recorder on. If he said something interesting, they'd ask him to repeat it when they returned to the house.

"Where was I last night? You people are so interested in where I go. I should be flattered. No one else cares. My daughter used to look out for me, but my dear wife is so involved with her work, she ignores me." He stopped and allowed the dog to contemplate a grassy patch. "Lindsay suffers too, but she deals with it by immersing herself in work." His eyes widened, his head rose and he smiled. "I'm painting a life-size portrait of Valerie. I intend to make it as beautiful as she was." His smile disappeared. "It's the one thing I do really well. Sitting in Curt's classes, I realized hate was destroying me. Now I'm easing my pain by doing what I

216

do best." He leaned toward them. "I'm having a show and donating the proceeds to a cause Valerie would have liked."

"What a positive plan," Zee Zee said gently. "To return to our question. Where were you last night?"

"At home, and for once my dear wife was home too. Ask her."

"Do you paint in oils and use turpentine as a solvent?"

The dog's glacial pace suddenly accelerated. He pulled them along, nose to the ground, tracking an enticing scent. "Life in the old boy yet," Sebastien said. "Yes to both."

"We'd like to take your turpentine for testing. You can give it voluntarily, or we can…"

Sebastien interrupted Zee Zee. "Why would I care if you took my turpentine? I'll buy more. But what's with the turpentine?"

"There was a fire in Curt Hartman's studio last night," Zee Zee said.

Sebastien didn't seem surprised. In fact, he didn't register any emotion. Perhaps he'd been in pain for so long that he was incapable of responding, or perhaps the news hadn't surprised him.

"If I'd stopped painting long enough to go to class today, I would have heard. Was anyone hurt?"

They told him what had happened. Like Arthur, he swore he would never destroy art.

After they collected the turpentine and drove away, Zee Zee lightly tapped Rhona's arm. "Well, is he the culprit?"

"Could be. We can't rule him out. But we've saved the best for last. On to Barney Evans and Allie Jones."

*   *   *

Later Friday afternoon, Etienne, sitting on the front steps, didn't wait for Hollis to finish maneuvering her rental car into a tight

217

parking space. He rushed down the front walk and flung open her car door even before she'd turned off the engine.

"MacTee's okay?"

"He is, but I stopped and bought him an extra thick dog-bed." She helped MacTee to the sidewalk. He favoured his leg, bandaged and covered with a protective plastic bag. In fact, he held it up and allowed his gaze to swing from Hollis to Etienne and back to Hollis again.

"I think he's going to make the most of being an invalid—what do you think?" Hollis asked.

Etienne grinned. "Smart dog. He knows we'll give him treats to make him feel better."

"Will you bring in his bed? It's in the trunk."

Etienne hugged MacTee before he opened the trunk. He scooped out the bed, nearly his size and covered with soft, dark green Arctic fleece. On the sidewalk, he contemplated it. Finally, he stood it on the sidewalk, squatted down, grasped the short sides and hoisted it on his head. He deposited it on the porch while Hollis unlocked the door.

"The fire investigators have been here all day. They told Papa they'll finish by the weekend. He can't clean stuff out and start rebuilding until they do, but he can set up fans to dry it out. Your friend, David, is coming over to install them."

Etienne bent to pat MacTee. "He said to tell you he's bringing extension cords."

"That was fast." Hollis shepherded MacTee inside. Etienne picked up the new bed and leaned it on the wall in the hallway before he followed her to the kitchen.

Curt sat at the kitchen table, thumbing through the yellow pages. "I'm wondering whether to call a company specializing in cleaning up after a fire or phone the contractor who did the original work."

"I'd go for the fire cleanup specialists. But before you make the call, I have an offer for you."

Curt tipped his head to one side and waited.

"When the class heard that you didn't have insurance…"

"What do you think you're doing running around discussing my business with every Tom, Dick and Harry?"

What an ungrateful, picky man. She wasn't apologizing.

"They were worried about you and asked about your clean-up plans, and I told them," she said, allowing a chill to creep into her voice. "Anyway, when they heard you didn't have insurance, they offered to help. David has construction experience, and if you're interested, I'm sure he would organize the job."

Curt, head lowered, peered at her from under his bushy eyebrows. "I suppose you meant well. I hate people knowing my business." He raised his head and looked thoughtful. "He did introduce himself as a carpenter. Because he's an artist, I assumed he meant cabinetmaker. A generous offer; I wonder why they made it?"

"Possibly they don't have ulterior motives; maybe they want to help because they like and respect you."

"Since I give a credit, not a mark for my course, I suppose that could be true." Curt spoke grudgingly. "We can't rebuild until we clean up, but it's a kind offer—I'll talk to David when he arrives."

"Before he does, MacTee needs a walk. Etienne, are you coming?"

"I'll come too," Manon said.

"I need you here to help make decisions," Curt said.

Manon sighed but didn't argue. No doubt she'd hoped to meet Olivero.

MacTee limped. She didn't bring a ball. Sore leg or not, he wouldn't resist a tennis ball's siren call.

Manon would have been happy if she'd come—Olivero waved and joined them. He reached in his pocket for a ball. Gelo jumped up and down and so, despite his sore leg, did MacTee. When Olivero noticed Hollis gripping MacTee's leash and making no move to release him, he paused. "He can't play ball today?"

"No. He was injured in the fire."

Olivero pocketed the ball. He showed his empty hands to both dogs. "No ball. Not today." He had to repeat the gesture several times before the dogs finally and reluctantly believed him. Gelo trotted away, searching for anyone who might toss something he could retrieve. MacTee sulked.

"I remembered the information that was niggling in my mind," Olivero said.

Hollis tried to recall the conversation. They'd talked about Arthur and Lena. "What?"

"I grew up in Italy. English is my second language."

Hollis nodded.

"The first time I met Lena at a party, she was married to Curt, and they were fighting. I remember he said, 'you're crazy as a coot' and she retorted, 'maybe that's because I'm from the *Koot*enays'. Coming from Italy, I wasn't familiar with either word, and they stuck in my mind." He shrugged, "Probably doesn't help you much, but it's what I remember."

Gelo appeared with a fluorescent pink frisbee in his mouth. He was pursued by an overweight beagle and a panting little boy wearing large droopy shorts. Olivero pried the frisbee from Gelo's mouth and returned it to its owners before he said, "If I think of anything else, I'll call you."

Another puzzle piece. Lena Kalma from the Kootenays. Any article she'd read had said she came from Western Canada. This might help pinpoint the location.

*   *   *

Back at the house, she'd joined Curt and Manon in the kitchen when the doorbell rang.

"That must be David. He's setting up the fans. You can work out the details with him—I never did like the middle woman role," Hollis said as she went to let him in.

David, in work boots, jeans and baseball cap, followed her to the kitchen.

Curt rose and extended his hand. "Thanks for arranging this. Hollis tells me you've offered to help and might even organize the project. However, we'll have to clean up first."

David shook Curt's hand and grinned. "I factored the clean-up into my offer."

David directed the next remark to Etienne. "When we're ready, would you take charge of cleaning up the small stuff?"

The light in Etienne's eyes showed how pleased he felt to have a job.

"You and I can be a team," Hollis said to Etienne. "I'm great at grunt jobs."

Etienne's brow crinkled questioningly.

"Grunts are guys who don't think—who do hard uncomplicated work—I think grunt is a military term for the ordinary soldier."

"Grunts, we're the grunts, the soldiers," Etienne smiled.

Curt shut the phone book. He fumbled in his pocket, withdrew his key ring and pried off a key. "This is for the house—you may need to come in when no one is home. I'll pay you for doing this. Tell me what you charge," he said to David. "And my son Tomas will help. He's available because he's doing shift work this summer. "

"The more workers we have, the sooner we'll finish,"

221

David said, popping the key on his own ring.

"I'm supposed to sail with him tomorrow, but I don't think I'm up to it. I'll discuss it with him." Before Curt could punch in Tomas's number, the phone rang.

When Curt answered, an invisible wrench appeared to be tightening each muscle. His face reddened, and he held the receiver away from his ear. They could all hear what was said.

"Ha, ha, ha—serves you right. Too bad you weren't in it and didn't fry like a catfish in a skillet."

Twenty-Two

"Time to see Barney. Have we finished with his computer?" Rhona asked.

"Awful stuff. Some could be useful if he's the perp—it certainly provides a motive. Did we copy everything?" Zee Zee said.

"We did. Who will interview the delightful Barney?"

"It really bugs him to talk to me, so I'll do it again. What do you think—should we bring him to the station and use the interview room?"

"We could, but let's go to his house." Rhona grinned. "Maybe the warm and friendly Mrs. Barney will offer us tea and a scone with her homemade strawberry jam."

Barney answered the door. Stained khakis sagged beneath his belly. His grey-tinged undershirt drooped from his narrow shoulders and draped over his protruding stomach. An unshaven face and uncombed hair topped the unattractive package.

They followed him to the living room, where they returned his computer and sat down. Rhona made sure not to park herself beside the vile-smelling, overflowing ashtray. You'd think even smokers would find it revolting and empty it occasionally, she thought.

"Where were you last night?" Zee Zee said.

"Last night. Let me see." He raised his hand, drawing attention to his dirty fingernails. "First, it was cocktails at

Sutton Place with oysters on the half shell, then a limo dropped us off at a rock concert at the Air Canada Centre." He ticked off the items. "A late dinner at the Hyatt and music at the Top o' the Senator." He lowered his hands, stopped and sniffed dismissively. "Right here."

"Can anyone vouch for that?"

"The old lady."

Why did it offend her to hear a man refer to his wife as the old lady? Maybe it related to her youth, when she'd heard "squaw" used in the same derogatory tone. Someday she'd go to a psychiatrist and unearth the reasons behind her likes and dislikes.

"Do you have any turpentine?"

This time his eyebrows rose involuntarily. "Turpentine. You're really scratching, aren't you?"

"Do you?"

"Sure, it's in the shed. I don't suppose you'll tell me why you're interested."

"We won't."

"And were you happy with my email?" He cocked his head to one side and smiled sardonically. "Did it get you going? Titillate you? Going to prosecute me?"

"You'll have to wait and see."

In the car, Rhona rolled the windows down. "I need fresh air after all that cigarette smoke."

Zee Zee laughed. "What passes for air in summertime Toronto isn't exactly fresh." She gestured at the CN Tower, hazy in the distance. "That should stand out like a cardboard cut-out. Instead, isn't it like a soft, hazy impressionist painting?"

"Onwards and upwards to visit Allie Jones. After we saw her last time, I wondered about her sanity. Do you think she's crazy?"

"I do. In abnormal psychology in college, we studied a

psychiatric disorder; I forget its scientific name, where the person seems perfectly normal except if you mention one particular topic. I volunteered on the Distress Call phone lines when I ran my gallery. We had regular callers, and if you kept away from their particular obsession, they were rational, pleasant conversationalists. But if their special topic came up, it was as if someone had thrown a switch—they raved. Very odd. Anyway, for me Allie Jones is the same."

"The switch was Curt Hartman's name. I wonder how I can elicit a rational response. I'll try the turpentine angle."

Allie Jones answered the buzzer and reluctantly allowed them into the building. Rhona's first thought when she saw her was that Allie had dressed for a nineteen fifties sock hop. She wore a blue-flowered circle skirt, an elastic waist-cinching blue belt, a pale blue short sleeve sweater over a white camisole, beads, ankle socks and ballet slippers. Her hair, teased into an impossibly stiff bouffant beehive, was rigid enough to withstand a force five hurricane.

"The same two women," she said icily. She allowed them in but didn't invite them to sit down.

"Do you have any turpentine?" Rhona asked.

Frozen in place by too many face lifts, her eyes opened fractionally wider. Her lips thinned. "Why would two of Toronto's finest take the time to come to my apartment and waste valuable man, excuse me, woman power to inquire whether I have turpentine? How stupid. Had you thought about it, I'm sure you wouldn't have come. Living in a high rise, why would I have turpentine? No, I don't."

"May we check your cupboards?" Rhona said.

"Not unless you have a warrant." Allie's body had stiffened to match her face. "I have nothing to say unless I have my lawyer. Shall I call him?"

"Suit yourself. We may be back, or we may have *you*," Rhona paused, "and your lawyer come to the station for an interview."

Allie moved to open the door before Rhona had finished speaking. "Fine. Call me." She as much as pushed them out the door.

"That was useful," Rhona said wearily as they walked down the corridor.

"Actually, I think it was. Let's go for a warrant. She really did not want us to have a look-see. What was she hiding?"

Back in the overcrowded homicide section, desks jammed against desks and stacked boxes made it a hazard to walk. Rhona and Zee threaded their way to their desks. Rhona pulled papers from her in-basket and skimmed them. She removed the third item and took it Zee Zee. "Did you get this?"

"I haven't read everything in my in-basket." Zee Zee paraphrased the document. "This woman's dog had an upset stomach, and she let it out in the back yard about one thirty. The dog barked at someone who darted down the lane. She can't say if it was a man or a woman." She shrugged. "This doesn't help us pinpoint who or even what gender the person was."

Frank was marching toward them. "What's happening?"

"We're following a number of leads."

"You do realize that you'll need to work all weekend."

Both women nodded.

Frank sighed. "I'll be here, and I can tell you it isn't where I want to be."

They waited for him to explain.

An enormous grin spread across his face. "I have a new dog."

"That's terrific," Zee Zee said. "A puppy. What kind? Will you take it to the same classes you took Bailey to?"

"Not a puppy, a rescue dog. He's a retriever. Juno, great

name, and he's wonderful. I'd hoped we'd be finished, so I could take him over to the Island for a good run."

"That's my favourite place in Toronto," Rhona said.

"Well, neither one of us will be there this weekend. Let's get this case solved so we can get over there before the summer's over."

Rhona flashed both thumbs in an affirmative gesture. "We're doing our best."

*   *   *

In the kitchen, Curt smashed the receiver down. "Damn bitch. Damn, damn." His face, rigid with repressed rage, was frightening. He stomped to the fridge, clunked ice in a glass and topped it with cold water. "Bitch," he muttered, draining the glass. "It wouldn't surprise me to find she started the fire. She'd do anything to hurt me. I'll be in the family room if anyone wants me."

"The fans and the extension cords are in my van," David said. He addressed his next remark to Etienne. "Do you have a long ladder?"

Etienne nodded. You could tell he liked being consulted. "We do. It's an aluminum extension ladder, and it's on the inside wall—on the far side of the garage."

David's eyebrows rose.

"The ladder will be okay, because the fire didn't do any damage there," Etienne explained.

"Come and help." David's invitation included Etienne and Hollis.

"Love to, but I have a couple of things I absolutely have to do." Two tasks awaited her, researching Lena's background and tracking down Penny.

David and Etienne left the room. Here was her opportunity for a private conversation with Curt. "I have a question for you," she said.

"Fire away," Curt said.

"You told me you wanted me to stay out of your business, but the fire changed things."

Curt regarded her with a steady gaze and waited. The jury was still out.

"I'm going on the internet to google Lena."

Curt's brows lowered. "Bitch," he muttered.

Hollis ignored the comment. "Can you tell me if there's anything in Lena's past that would connect her to Ivan's death or to the fire."

"I don't want to talk about her. Leave it to the police."

"Your son and I could have burned to death or asphyxiated last night. I'm sure the police are doing everything they can, but I do not intend to sit back and wait for them to solve the crime. Etienne and I may still be the arsonist's targets."

Curt considered her words. "Don't expect the key to the mystery to come from me. We've been divorced for years. I avoid her as much as possible." His voice was petulant rather than angry. He paused. "I wonder how many entries I have. I've never looked myself up on the internet."

Ego, ego, ego. "I'm sure you'll have many more than she has."

"Is that your idea of tactfulness? Your expression is as transparent as a newly washed window. You're thinking I'm an egotist and indulging me in the hope I'll talk about Lena. Am I right?"

She'd never had a gift for subterfuge.

"Okay, you're right," he continued, "you *could* still be a target if someone set the fire because you were there. I think whoever did it was after me—but ask away. First, I'll tell you we married in our twenties. She'd had a smashing show of her amazingly detailed vivid paintings. Almost folk art, but sophisticated. It was at Stemppels, a top-notch Toronto gallery. I'd been studying in New York and hadn't had an exhibition anywhere, let alone in Toronto. I loved her work and envied her success. I introduced myself. We hit it off. By the way, she was as dramatic then as now."

"Was Kalma her maiden name?"

"It was the name on our marriage license."

"Where did she grow up?"

Curt leaned back in his chair and locked his hands behind his head. "This may sound pretty strange, but she only told me she'd grown up out west. She refused to talk about her background—apparently it had been painful. I never met a relative or a friend from her past."

Hollis's marriage to Paul had been the same. They were in their thirties when they married, and they'd agreed to keep their professional lives separate. After his death, she'd discovered facts she should have known before. No, it wasn't common, but sometimes you sensed it wouldn't do any good to pry. Either you accepted the story someone told you, took them at face value or you didn't.

"Thanks—I'll fill you in if I find anything."

In her room, she booted up her computer.

Hundreds of entries—a staggering number but better than plowing through library microfiche. She hoped she wouldn't have to do that—the jumpy lines and out-of-focus edges gave her headaches. Lena had a website, but because of her reputation for invention, her version of her life wouldn't give Hollis the information she wanted. Entries for exhibitions, articles from *ARTnews,* scholarly articles in university publications, reviews in newspapers: the list went on and on.

None answered her questions about Lena's early hidden background.

A new tack. She typed in Kootenays. Again, a host of leads. One triggered a response, something remembered from long ago history classes. And she knew exactly who to go to for help. She typed an email to her friend, Francine Marcot, an Ottawa National Archives employee. Thirty-five minutes later, Francine responded. Hollis picked up the phone and called her.

"I did the tracking," Francine said. "Your timing was perfect. We received a terrific bequest several months ago that we're cataloguing, or I wouldn't have been able to tell you much."

"Who was it from?"

"A woman in Vancouver. The Sons of Freedom Doukobhor sect had fascinated her for years. She didn't have any connection to them but had heard their story since her childhood. She was an amateur historian and feared they wouldn't record their history and everything would be lost. About twenty years ago, she began obsessively collecting information, and she's bequeathed it to us. Are you familiar with their story?"

"They protested by shedding their clothes and setting fires." Setting fires—this was too good to be true.

"There's more to it. I can email you references."

No way. She wanted this information now. "Can you give me a brief synopsis and tell me how it relates to Lena Kalma?"

"Sure, I'll do both. The Doukhobors were a religious sect like the Hutterites. They came from Russia to escape persecution. Initially the whole group settled in Saskatchewan. Later a breakaway sect moved to B.C. That group, the Sons of Freedom Doukhobors, is the one we're interested in. They protested against the Marriage and Vital Statistics Act because they were afraid if they registered births and marriages, the government would use the information for military conscription. When their leader, Peter Verigin, was tried for perjury in 1932, it set off a wave of nude protests. The government prosecuted them for public indecency and sentenced hundreds to three years imprisonment. The existing prison system couldn't cope. They ended up interning them in a special penal colony they built on Piers Island."

"Interesting, but what does it have to do with Lena?"

"Patience—I'm getting there. The government sent Freedomite children to orphanages, industrial schools and foster homes to 'resocialize' them. This program continued for many years, as did the Freedomite protests. In fact as late as 1963, Mary Braun, an eighty-one-year old woman, was convicted of arson for burning down a community college. Anyway, that's Lena Kalma's story." She paused. *"She* was an institutionalized child."

"No wonder she never gave any information about her background. Thank you for doing this—I owe you a dinner when I come home."

"And you can tell me why you wanted the information and what you did with it."

After hanging up, Hollis sat back. Secrets. Everyone had secrets. She had a few herself. Manon did too, if the way she and Olivero looked at each other was any indication. And her classmates—what deep, dark secrets were they hiding? What was the real reason Patel had left India? Had he fled a checkered past? Was Tessa a Grand Manan smuggler who used her art as a cover? She laughed to herself at her flights of fancy. What of David with his tattoos and love of sailing? Tattoos. Patel had asked if it was significant. Someone had told her there was an iconography of tattoos as detailed as that surrounding the windows in Gothic cathedrals. She typed "tattoo" into Google. She wasn't surprised to find hundreds of websites. She checked out three and decided she definitely wouldn't be getting a spider.

But she was wasting time. What should she do about Lena? It seemed only fair to confront her with the information she'd uncovered. Given her volatility, Hollis shouldn't be alone when she faced Lena. She had to admit, the woman intimidated her. There had to be a solution. Lena loved to grandstand. Perhaps she'd be making another gallery appearance to vilify Curt. That would be the perfect scenario. She'd be safe from Lena's rage because other people would be there. Before she had second thoughts, she phoned the gallery and confirmed that the artist would be present on Sunday afternoon. Her mouth went dry thinking about the meeting, but it couldn't be avoided. She'd have to be brave.

* * *

It was Saturday morning, and humidity—the summer curse—hung over Toronto and intensified the stink from the fire. No breeze lifted it: the heat and sun promised to intensify its unpleasantness. David arrived early to reposition the fans and check on the drying process. He came to the kitchen after his survey. The family, finishing breakfast, clustered around the table.

Curt introduced Tomas. "We're in a sailing race this afternoon. Well, we will be if the wind picks up." He sighed. "I hate to admit it, but the damn fire tired me out. I'm thinking of cancelling."

"Why don't you admit you're sick?" Manon said.

"Why do you drag my health into everything?" Curt snapped.

"Because your health affects everything. If you'd look after yourself, we'd all be happier," she fired back.

This had the makings of a major donnybrook. Hollis interceded. "David crewed in Vancouver. Remember the first day of classes. David told us he missed sailing more than anything else. Maybe he could help you out."

Curt sighed but nodded. "What classes of boats have you sailed?" he said to David.

The tension eased as the conversation moved to sailing. Tomas, Curt and David discussed the various classifications, crew requirements and idiosyncratic challenges. They told David that the RCYC scheduled sailing races on weekends and several times during the week. Curt and Tomas competed frequently.

"How would you feel about replacing me today?" Curt asked.

"I'd love to do it. It would be an unexpected treat. Hollis is right—sailing is what I miss most," David said. "And I promise…"

The ringing phone interrupted him.

Curt answered, muttered monosyllables and returned to the group. "Good thing we agreed to do that. For some strange reason, Sebastien Lefevbre insists on coming over this afternoon. I can't imagine why—he said it was important but wouldn't say why."

"That's mysterious," Manon said.

"To finish what I was about to say, I'll come back after the race to see how the stuff is drying," David said.

It was time for Hollis to contact Penny. Most regular restaurants opened at eleven. Assuming that was the case with Penny's, she should still be home. Up in her room, Hollis punched in the number. She crossed her fingers that the dragon she'd spoken to last time was out or asleep, or had moved to another planet.

"Hello."

Definitely not the dragon. "Penny Pappadopoulos?"

"Yes."

"I'm helping Ivan Hartman's family find out more about his life. I found your photo in Ivan's papers. Would you be willing to talk to me about him?"

"I wondered when someone would call and why it took so long," Penny responded. Her audible sigh could have signalled relief or sadness or both. "I think I'd like to speak to you face-to-face."

Whatever she'd expected, it hadn't been this. "Would you like to meet this morning?"

"No. I have to go to work. My family owns a restaurant on the Danforth. I'm off after lunch from two until five. Are you familiar with Java Java? It's also on the Danforth, but since it's a health food restaurant, I'm not likely to run into any family members." She gave a dry little laugh. "To say they aren't into health food is the understatement of the year."

"What time?"

"Some time between four and five. Let's say four."

If Penny had important information, why she hadn't come forward on her own? And why had she sounded so relieved to hear from Hollis?

Java Java, a small restaurant with an eclectic collection of tables squeezed together to provide maximum seating, still hummed at four. One or two baby strollers blocked access to some tables. Teenagers with busy cell phones occupied many others. Hollis paused and surveyed the room, looking for a woman alone. An elderly gentleman, correct in a tweed jacket, tie and worn white shirt, had a book propped in front of him and lemon pie with sky-high meringue waiting. A scholarly woman busy on a computer drank coffee and took cautious bites from a sandwich stuffed with so much tomato and avocado it threatened to fall apart. A pregnant young woman with a large glass of milk sat on a bench that ran along one wall and provided seating for several tables. She waved tentatively at Hollis.

It was the woman who'd tried to speak to Curt after Ivan's funeral.

Pregnant?

This *was* a surprise. She knew she was staring, but it was hard not to. Never in her wildest scenarios had she envisioned a pregnant girlfriend. Was it Ivan's baby? Had they been in love? If they had been, how hard these weeks must have been for Penny. Why hadn't she contacted the family? She'd tried, but why hadn't she called or written? Hollis was nonplussed. She didn't have an approach plan. What would she say? Nothing. She'd give Penny the lead and see what happened.

"You have to go to the counter to order," Penny blurted after they'd said tentative hellos.

Penny, wide-eyed and wary, perched her tense body on the edge of the banquette. Flight was a possibility that might momentarily become a reality. Caution would be the watchword. Hollis rejoined her with an Orangina bottle clutched in her hand and no idea what to say. She'd start with their phone conversation.

"You said you'd expected someone from the family to contact you?" she began.

"Ivan said he hadn't told his family about me, but I figured he would have something in his room or his wallet with my name on it."

"I found your picture, but it was hidden." Why had she said that? No woman wanted to learn that the man in her life had hidden every reference to her. But she was making assumptions. Maybe Ivan had been a casual friend.

"Hidden?"

"You know how Ivan was—he kept things from his family."

"I do. He was afraid of his father. I felt sorry for him, but I have dragons in my own family, so I understood."

"I didn't see your name on the culinary course student lists. I gathered from whoever answered the phone the first time I called that you attended George Brown."

"Definitely *not* the culinary course." Penny smiled ruefully. "Cooking was one thing I was sure I didn't want to take." Her face crumpled, and she shook her head. "I guess you can't avoid your destiny—I'm back in the kitchen cooking up a Greek storm." She patted her stomach. "But not for long. No, I took business, but I did meet Ivan at George Brown."

Sure she knew the answer because of the photo's inscription, Hollis said, "You were friends."

Tears flowed down Penny's cheeks. She swiped at them, picked up her paper napkin and mopped the flow. She opened her mouth to speak. Her face twisted. She gulped and sobbed.

Even the teenagers, self-obsessed and tied to their cell phones, stopped to peer at this noisy display of sorrow.

Hollis slid off her chair, moved to the banquette and hugged Penny, who dropped her head to Hollis's shoulder and wept. Hollis soothed and patted. This was not a friend's grief; Penny had loved Ivan.

"Is the baby Ivan's?" she murmured.

"Yes."

"Did he know?"

Penny took a deep, shaky breath, raised her head and nodded. "We planned to get married and go to Italy while Ivan took his course."

"Did your family know?"

"I'm so afraid," Penny wailed.

236

Twenty-Three

A hot Saturday afternoon. Rhona would have liked to take her bike on the ferry to Centre Island. An Ottawa friend had told her about the island, one of Toronto's treasures. Her first visit had hooked her, and she returned whenever she could. She loved pedalling along the tree-shaded paths watching a kaleidoscope of ethnic groups picnicking and enjoying the outdoors. This population mix was what Toronto and Canada was all about.

The fire had changed her plans. Instead of recharging her batteries, she sat behind a desk piled with paper. It was supposed to be a paperless world, but that hadn't happened, at least not in Homicide. The office hummed. Criminals didn't take weekends off. There had been yet another gang shooting in an afterhours night club. A young woman's failure to return from a shopping trip to the Dufferin Mall had sparked an all-out search. In fact, Zee Zee and Rhona had lost the help of two officers who'd been moved to the missing woman's case.

Rhona shuffled paper from one pile to another. Maybe Hollis had found something new. She punched in her cell phone number.

"Anything new? Did you identify the mystery girl at the funeral?"

A pause. Rhona's antennae quivered. Silence usually meant the person was deciding whether or not to lie.

"My phone's dying—I'll call you from one that works."

Clever evasion. Hollis knew something and didn't want to lie but didn't intend to share the information. Rhona waited for the phone to ring. It did.

"Simpson."

"It's Zee Zee. I have the warrant for Allie Jones's house. I'll be back in a few minutes."

Rhona waited ten minutes, but her phone didn't ring again. She called Hartman's house. Hollis had gone out.

Frank approached her desk. "Just the woman I want to see. Come into my office." He led the way.

"This case is bogging down. Murder. Arson and attempted murder. No suspects. Give me a rundown of the avenues you've explored."

Rhona explained what they'd done. Frank suggested other options. They tried thinking outside the box. Hollis glanced at her watch. Six thirty. Opie wouldn't be too happy. Nor was she—breakfast had been a long time ago. Two coffees and one bottle of water had left a void.

Frank's phone rang.

"At the Hartmans'? I thought we had surveillance there."

"What is it? What's happened?" Rhona said.

*   *   *

"Second place, they came second." Etienne announced to Hollis late on Saturday afternoon as she joined the family in the garden. David and Tomas, windblown and smiling, lounged at the glass-topped table. Their nearly empty Molson beer bottles had left a multitude of wet rings. Etienne stood between them. All three dipped into a large bag of lime-flavoured tortilla chips. Manon and Curt lay stretched out on chaise lounges.

"Great to sail again," David said to Hollis.

"And he's good," Tomas said. "We've made the quarter-finals. We'll practise on Tuesday evening."

Curt raised his diet drink can. "To the winners. I've been dethroned—Tomas and I haven't won anything for months."

"Dethroned? The king loses his crown in a coup and goes into exile. Isn't your analogy a little overdramatic?" Manon said.

Curt frowned. "Manon, don't criticize everything I say. It was a metaphorical remark."

Not again. The way they picked at each other kept everyone on edge.

"You do have a talent for self-aggrandizement, but never mind. It's time to eat. You'll stay and have supper with us?" Manon said to David.

"Love to."

They rose, collected bottles and glasses, and moved to the kitchen, where Hollis helped Manon set out the food. Settled at the table, they passed platters and loaded their plates. The conversation was desultory until the doorbell rang.

"I'll go. It's probably Bobby. We have a new sponsor, Cleanway Window Washers. They're giving us baseball shirts with their company's name on them." Etienne pushed his chair back and headed for the front door.

A thumping bang. The house shook.

For a brief moment, the group around the table froze like figures in a waxworks display.

Manon sprang from her chair and raced from the room. The others were right behind her.

"Oh no, *mon dieu,* not Etienne," she screamed.

Twenty-Four

Etienne lay face down on the porch floor. Manon fell to her knees. Etienne lifted his head and struggled to rise.

"Don't move," Manon said.

Hollis grabbed her cell phone.

A crater fragmented the hedge. Beyond it, a man with a mop of white curls lay face down and unmoving. His arms and legs splayed, his head pushed against a yellow fire hydrant's base, he sprawled atop a woman. A black umbrella like Arthur's stuck out of the bushes. Was it Arthur?

"A bomb's exploded." Hollis gave 911 the address.

The woman squirmed, shoved and wriggled out from under the man's inert form. Without looking at him or anyone else, she scuttled off down the street.

Curt charged to the edge of the porch and stopped.

"If that's Arthur lying there, and he isn't already dead, I'll kill him." Curt's quiet intensity was more terrifying than a shout.

"No, Papa, no, no," Etienne pleaded shakily.

"What?" Curt turned to his son, who had ignored his mother's order and rolled over. Etienne levered himself to a sitting position. Manon's arms, wrapped around him, did not stop his shivering and shaking.

"No, Papa, no!"

Curt focused on Etienne.

"It was *her*, not Arthur. Arthur *yelled* at me." Etienne's teeth chattered.

"What? Yelled what?"

Etienne stared as if Curt had asked a really stupid question. "Get away. Don't touch it."

"And then…"

"Arthur ran to the porch—the box was on the top step. He grabbed it, threw it in the bushes and chased the lady."

"What lady?"

Hollis ran down the steps. The woman had disappeared. They'd all stood like dummies, and she'd escaped. Hollis didn't even think she could give the police a useful description other than that she'd been middle-aged and middle-sized. But right now, Arthur needed help. Not that she could do anything medical. She ran over and stared down. He lay on his stomach, arms and legs splayed out as if he'd been dropped by a giant. No blood. His back moved slightly. He was breathing, but she knew better than to move him.

Wailing sirens drew closer.

Thank heavens. Arthur needed help. A barrage of noise. One after another, police cars, fire trucks and an emergency response vehicle screeched to a halt. Uniformed figures surrounded Arthur. Others approached the porch.

Dèja vu: fire night all over again. They were living in a nightmare. Every time life appeared to be about to return to normal, something awful happened.

Arthur hadn't moved since they'd come outside.

Hollis clutched the nearest police officer's arm. "We saw the woman who bombed the house but didn't know she'd done it until after she'd walked away."

The officer sent a car to look for the mystery woman. But if she'd reached Parliament Street and its crowds, there was little hope they'd pick her up.

The ambulance attendants who had dealt with Arthur hurried back with the appropriate equipment and loaded him into the ambulance. Lights flashing and siren shrieking, it raced away.

More police swarmed the scene.

A female medic clumped up the porch steps and squatted beside Etienne. "Does anything hurt?" she asked.

"No, but I'm really, really cold."

"That's shock. I'll do a quick once-over. Let me help you lie down. When we're sure it won't do any harm, we'll load you on a backboard to move you."

"Move him where?" Manon tightened her grip on Etienne.

A police officer approached Hollis. "Was anyone outside when the blast went off?"

She pointed to Etienne. "He was."

The paramedic crouched beside Etienne looked up and said, "He needs a hospital check-up. Superficially he's okay, but concussion from the blast may have done damage we can't see."

Manon rocked back and forth with her arms clutched against her chest.

"Since the blast didn't blow his ear drums, it probably wasn't huge. I don't think you have anything to worry about." The medic spoke calmly. "But he must go to the hospital."

"I'm coming with him," Manon stated.

Hollis, Curt, Tomas and David clustered on the porch while the police taped off the area. Curt moved back to lean on the wall and slowly slid to the floor. His bleached grey face and sunken eyes told his story.

"My pills," he croaked.

"Where are they?" David said.

"In my shirt pocket or in my bathroom."

Tomas found them in his pocket. "Two. Under my tongue," Curt whispered.

A police officer saw what was happening and called for a third ambulance. Two other officers clomped to the porch. The first one, a man of average height and unremarkable features, spoke to them. "Can anyone give us details of the blast?"

Curt, crumpled on the floor, shook his head.

"We weren't outside. Etienne, the little boy who went to the hospital, saw it. Tomas, David or I can repeat what he told us," Hollis said.

"First, we'll send this gentleman to the hospital. Then we'll talk."

After Curt and Tomas had left, the younger officer removed a notebook from his pocket. "Now I'll take a statement," he said.

"Let's go inside," Hollis suggested.

At the kitchen table, Hollis and David repeated Etienne's story. Then they talked about Ivan, SOHD, Arthur and the fire. When the officer had all the information recorded in his book, he contacted the ambulance service.

"The two men are at St. Mike's. The little boy and his mother went to Sick Kids," he said.

"I want to go to Manon and Etienne, but I don't think I should leave the house unguarded. The bomber could come back." Hollis shrugged. "I know it's highly unlikely, and the door will be locked. Nevertheless, I feel someone should be here."

"Not a problem. Nothing on my agenda. I'll stay with MacTee until you're back," David said.

Hollis drove carefully—she knew shock affected your reflexes. Would Etienne have internal injuries? She dreaded what she'd find. She remembered a program about the 1917 Halifax explosion victims. Initially, many had seemed perfectly fine but died later from the effect of the concussion or whatever they called the waves generated by a blast. The paramedic had thought Etienne was okay. Presumably the hedge and veranda had protected him. But what about Arthur? He'd been in the open and subject to the full impact. And who was the woman? Had Curt suffered another heart attack, or had his collapse resulted from shock? What would this latest calamity do to Manon's fragile emotional state? Ready or not, Hollis had to ignore her feelings and be strong for the entire family.

At Sick Kids, the emergency room nurse directed her to a cubicle. A doctor wearing a non-frightening pink smock and almost young enough to be a patient tested Etienne's ears.

Manon smiled at Hollis. "He's fine. They don't think there are any ill effects." Her eyes shone, and she continued to smile as if she'd found the "on" switch and planned to ignore the "off" one forever. "We are *so* lucky." She tilted her head and peered behind Hollis. "Where are Curt and Tomas?"

Hollis realized the ambulance with Manon and Etienne had sped away before Curt had collapsed. No need to alarm her. Let her hang on to her joy for as long as possible.

"Tomas and Curt are at St. Mike's." She extended her arm with her palm facing Manon—the universal sign telling Manon to wait before she said anything. "Just a precaution, given Curt's heart trouble." She hoped it was true, but even if it wasn't, she needn't worry Etienne and Manon. "Since you're both fine, why don't I slip over to St. Mike's to see how he's doing?"

"What about Arthur?"

"Arthur's also at St. Mike's. I don't think they caught the woman."

Etienne struggled to get out of bed.

"Sweetie, calm down. I have tests to run. We're checking you over." The doctor gently pushed him back.

Etienne resisted. *"She* did it. The woman who left—*she* did it. She was walking away from the porch when I opened the door. It was *her.* She left the bomb."

The doctor reached into her smock pocket and extracted a cell phone. "Have security come to Emerg immediately," she ordered.

"I'm sending you and your son upstairs," she said to Manon. "And I'm arranging for security to wait with you until the police arrive."

Wide eyes and a trembling mouth replaced Manon's smile. *"Mon dieu,* it isn't over. It will never be over," she wailed.

Hollis patted her friend's shoulder. "You'll be fine with police protection. I'll scoot over to St. Mike's now. Do you have your cell phone?"

"No cell phones in the hospital," the doctor said, pocketing her own.

She meant that the plebes couldn't use them—they were fine for medical personnel. "What floor will Etienne be on? May I call the nursing station?" Hollis asked.

The doctor gave her the emerg extension and assured them she'd tell the staff to expect the call.

"I wish you'd stay," Manon said, grabbing Hollis's hand. "But you must warn Curt and Tomas. They may be in danger— she may be planning something even worse."

* * *

Rhona was horrified. "A bomb—the anti-abortionists. We should have pushed for the search warrant sooner."

"Nothing we can do at the Hartmans'. We'll go to Allie's. If she isn't there, the super will let us in."

Frank stared at her. "What's this about?"

245

"We told you. We interviewed Allie Jones. She's obsessively anti-SOHD. When we visited her after the fire, she wouldn't allow us to search her apartment. Her reaction made us suspicious. We applied for a search warrant. It arrived late today," Rhona said. She flipped through her bag to make sure she had everything they'd need. "We'll call the techies if we find anything."

* * *

Before leaving to visit Allie, Rhona and Zee Zee withdrew their guns from their lockers and pulled on Kevlar vests.

"If she managed to evade the police, I expect she went home to pretend she hadn't been out all day," Rhona said.

"I don't think she'll expect us. We're making a pre-emptive first strike. If we're lucky, she may have the same clothes on— we'll send them to the lab for a residue test."

At the site, they buzzed Allie's apartment.

"It's the police. We're back with a warrant," Zee Zee said into the speaker phone.

"Not until my lawyer arrives," Allie replied.

"Let us in," Zee Zee ordered, but Allie didn't respond. Fortunately, the building had a manned entry hall desk. They flashed their cards, displayed their warrant and asked the concierge, a nervous-looking brunette in her mid-thirties, to let them in.

"Early evening is busy. I shouldn't leave my desk," the woman protested, licking her lips. Her gaze shifted from Rhona to Zee Zee and back again.

They waited.

"There won't be gunshots or anything, will there?" Her lower lip trembled.

Rhona and Zee Zee exchanged glances—who knew?

"Give us the appropriate keys," Zee Zee said.

The girl removed one from the ring and passed it to them. In fact, she almost threw it at them before she retreated into her glassed-in office as if it was a bunker in a war zone.

Upstairs, Rhona and Zee Zee drew their guns and knocked. "Police. Open the door," Rhona commanded.

When nothing happened, Rhona inserted the key and pushed. The door swung open. Guns ready, they edged into the hall.

Allie, in a flowered summer dress, her arms akimbo, smiled sweetly at them. "Too much TV watching, girls," she said. She extended her hands. "I don't have a weapon."

Rhona extracted the warrant from her bag. "We're taking you to the station. Have you changed your clothes today?"

"Why would I do that, and what business is it of yours? But, as a matter of fact, I have." She paused for a moment, as if giving herself time to invent a story. "I picked this outfit because it's cooler than the one I was wearing."

"We want you to bring whatever you wore earlier. My partner will accompany you to your room where you will show us what you wore and pick other clothes to take to the station," Rhona said. She waved the warrant. "We've also arranged for our technical experts to come in and go over your apartment."

Allie regarded them impassively. "Is this where I call my lawyer?"

When she'd made the call and shown them the clothes, she retreated to the living room sofa, where she sat erect, ankles crossed and hands folded. Rhona and Zee Zee, gloves on, left her perched on the sofa while they searched the apartment.

In the freezer, they found a bundle of fireworks wrapped in plastic and tucked under a frozen salmon slab.

"That explains why the blast did so little damage—the bomb was really a giant firecracker," Zee Zee said in a low voice.

But beneath the kitchen sink, they found the essentials for serious bomb-making neatly stored in an empty dishwashing detergent box and a large Tim Hortons coffee can.

Zee Zee shook her head and pointed to the can. "This wouldn't do a lot for Tim's image, would it?"

"I think they've become such a part of the Canadian psyche that nothing will damage them," Rhona said.

"We expected to find something, but it still shocks me," she nodded toward the living room, "that she would do this."

"Given what she has here, we can be glad she only used the fireworks. And aren't we glad we caught her?" Zee Zee said.

"We'll leave this to the techies. Let's get her downtown and charged."

Allie smiled as they led her away.

Twenty-Five

Chaos reigned at St. Mike's emergency, where the neighbourhood walking wounded waited for treatment. Their friends and supporters crowded the anteroom. Stretchers lined the halls. The triage nurses worked at full speed.

Hollis surveyed the gurneys in the corridor—no Arthur, no Curt. No Tomas sitting in the waiting room among anxious, murmuring families, women in chadors and street people, drunken or overdosed. She couldn't barge through the door leading to acute care. She also hesitated to enter the area where medical professionals treated the less severely ill or injured. Instead she disregarded instructions fastened to the wall and plunked down on the last empty molded plastic chair. These seats were designated exclusively for those waiting to have their data recorded before medical teams dealt with their problems. Three individuals later, the middle-aged nurse, tired circles under her eyes, beckoned Hollis forward.

"It isn't me. I'm here to find Curt Hartman and Arthur..." She drew a blank. "Arthur who came in by ambulance. He'd been in an explosion."

The woman ran her finger down a clipboard list. "Curt Hartman is down the hall." She pointed. "Turn right past the double doors. The charge nurse will direct you. Arthur White is in there." She nodded to a door leading to the critical care unit.

Curt first. A nurse, busy with paperwork, didn't raise her eyes when Hollis entered. Finally, Hollis cleared her throat. "I'm looking for Curt Hartman."

"Straight ahead to the end and turn right," the nurse said without lifting her head.

Hollis passed a parking lot of gurneys. On the first, a man shackled to his stretcher shouted and muttered. On the next, a grossly overweight man lay with tears running from the corners of his eyes. An equally large woman in a multi-coloured sari stood beside him. Her bulk partially blocked the passageway. She held one of his hands in both of hers and made the consoling sounds one makes when words are useless.

Inside the six-bed ward, curtains enclosed each bed. Hollis tipped the first aside. A tiny Asian woman lay curled in a fetal position while an IV dripped clear fluid into her arm. Hollis dropped the curtain and peered cautiously behind the next one. A man propped on pillows and coats laboured for breath. A woman dressed entirely in black hunched on the bed beside him.

Pulling back the third curtain, she found Curt. He lay with wires running from his chest to a heart monitor. A white-coated man bent over him. Tomas stood to one side.

"No heart attack, but given your history, we'll keep you overnight," the man said.

"Good news," Tomas said to his father.

"Etienne's fine too," Hollis said. "Arthur was seriously hurt, but the woman slipped away in the confusion."

Tomas thought about what she'd said. He shook his head. "If she's out there, Dad is in danger."

"We have police coming and going all the time. You're safer here than anywhere," the doctor said. "The staff will keep an eye on you."

"I'll stay with you," Tomas said.

"Nonsense," Curt blustered. "What a brouhaha about nothing."

"Dad." Tomas bent down and locked his gaze with his father's. "Dad, *someone* killed Ivan, probably thinking it was you. *Someone* torched your studio, probably believing you were sleeping there. *Someone* exploded a bomb on the porch. Dad, this is not *nothing*. A double negative means it's *something*, something serious. It's time you paid attention. You *will* stay, and I *will* stay with you." He straightened up and left the cubicle, returning a minute later with a metal chair that he positioned beside the bed.

Hollis said goodnight and threaded her way through the stretchers, ambulance workers, police and waiting patients. On her way down the ramp from the emergency exit, she stopped.

What had happened to Arthur? She'd forgotten all about him. Arthur had gone to Critical Care. She swung around. If he had survived, she had to warn the critical care staff.

"Are you a relative?" The nurse stooping over Arthur's bed asked Hollis.

Hollis shook her head. How would she categorize herself? An enemy, an acquaintance, a victim—she wouldn't use any of those terms. "No. I was there when the bomb went off. Arthur saved my friend's son by grabbing it and throwing it as far as he could."

She stepped closer to the bed and looked down. Arthur lay very still, except for his chest, which rose and fell almost imperceptibly. Liquids dribbled into his arm from two intravenous bags suspended from an IV pole. His pale skin and shallow breathing did not bode well.

"How is he?" Hollis asked.

"He's hit his head and hasn't regained consciousness. His vital signs are good. He's stable. He carried no information about next-of-kin. Can you tell us who to notify?"

"No."

"It would help us if you could find out if he has relatives."

"Have the police been here?"

"Why would they come?"

"Arthur can identify the bomber. She's still on the loose."

The nurse's eyebrows rose. She peered at Hollis over her half-glasses. "You're kidding."

"Regrettably, I'm not. Arthur may need police protection."

"Lots of that here—sometimes I think we have more police than we do patients. Pretty violent people come in, particularly on Saturday nights. Sunday isn't too bad, but detox is busy. I'll alert the staff."

"I'll call tomorrow to see how he's doing." Hollis backed out of the cubicle and headed for the door.

As she parked outside the Hartmans', the hole in the hedge that the bomb had made shocked her, as did the yellow tape enclosing the site. One or two people loitered across the street, staring at the house. And why not—a bomb in this quiet neighbourhood was definitely something out of the ordinary. Eleven o'clock. Poor MacTee. Unable to enter the front door because of the tape, she moved to the back of the house. A flash of gratitude—David had turned on the outside lights. This was not a night to brave a dark and spooky house. Maybe he was still here. She hurried inside.

"Hollis, I'm upstairs in the den," David called. "I've walked MacTee."

What a relief. She hadn't been looking forward to taking the dog out. In fact, now that she was back, exhaustion engulfed her. It had been a frightening few hours. She trudged up the stairs. David lounged in Curt's leather chair reading *ARTnews*. He stood up, surveyed her for a moment and stepped forward.

"Bet you need a hug," he said, and, to her surprise, wrapped her in his arms before releasing her and stepping back. "Tell me what happened. How are Curt and Etienne?"

"Both of them are okay. Arthur is unconscious."

"Are you nervous about staying alone? Would you like me to stay tonight?"

It would be nice to have someone else in the house, but it would be a responsibility as well. She'd have to offer a drink and figure out where he could sleep. And his hug had made her nervous. "It's a lovely offer, but I'm fine with MacTee."

David examined her face. "You're sure."

"I am."

"What about Monday's class?"

"Curt asked me to lead it if he isn't back. The notes are all prepared."

She closed and locked the door after David. She hoped she'd made the right decision—hoped the madwoman wasn't still on the loose. Hollis could only hope she didn't plan to detonate a bigger bomb.

*   *   *

When she opened her eyes next morning, she groaned. Her body, reacting to the previous day's shocking events, felt heavy, unwieldy and weighted to the bed. Gritty eyes, knotted stomach and nausea added to her discomfort. In the past, vigorous exercise had solved these problems, but with MacTee's recent injury, she had to settle for a short walk. At the dogs off-leash area, she waved at Olivero.

"Am I glad to see you! I've been frantic—phoning the hospitals, the police. No one would tell me anything. Is everyone okay? And Manon, my lovely Manon?" Olivero's eyes brimmed with tears. "She's had so much to bear."

"She's okay," Hollis reassured him. "I think Manon would like, no I'll change that—I think Manon *needs* to see you. If everything works out, we'll bring MacTee over here later today."

"Curt won't be too thrilled."

"Tough. He got them in this mess." She was "aiding and abetting", and she didn't care.

Back at the house, she made two calls. Etienne and Curt had been released and would both be on their way home. Breakfast—something concrete to do. She filled the coffee maker and removed eggs and milk from the refrigerator. French toast could wait in the oven until the family appeared.

The paper—had the Sunday *Star* covered the bombing? She went to the front door, but it swung open before she could unlock it.

"Oh my God," Hollis squeaked before she realized it was Etienne and Manon. Over their shoulders, she glimpsed a police car double-parked at the curb.

She gave Etienne a high five and hugged Manon. Up close, the tell-tale signs of stress—puffy red-rimmed eyes, tense facial muscles and grey skin—revealed Manon's anxiety.

"I gather I look like hell." Manon attempted a smile.

Hollis didn't deny it. "Who wouldn't after the night you've had."

"Maman, I'm starved," Etienne said.

The women smiled. Boys hovering on adolescence's cusp could be counted on to think of their stomachs.

"Let's feed the monster eater," Hollis said.

"How did you feel about everything, Etienne?" she asked, breaking eggs into a yellow bowl. Immediately she regretted her words. Males of all ages disliked talking about "feelings", and "everything" was much too vague.

"Cool, it was cool. The police asked me questions. They said I was a big help."

"What kind of questions?"

"What the lady looked like."

"And what did you say?"

"She was old and didn't dress like Maman or even like Grandmaman."

Intent on the conversation, Hollis swung around with the bowl in one hand and a wire whisk in the other. What did "old" mean to an eleven-year-old? She suspected anyone over twenty-one would be classified as "old".

"How old, and how could you tell?"

"Not old like you and Maman, but wrinkly old like Grandmaman."

"And her clothes?"

"Her clothes were funny—a dress not like anything you or Maman would wear. And she had stiff puffy hair, sort of like the candy floss you buy at the Exhibition."

"You're observant. Anything else."

"She had really red lips and blue stuff around her eyes and two red spots on her cheeks. I told the police her eyes were really, really blue and mean. When I opened the door, she glared like she hated me. She scared me."

The eyes, almost turquoise blue and filled with venom—the description triggered a memory. The puffy hair and the outmoded clothes. How could she have forgotten? "I've seen her before."

Manon, slumped forward with her head in her hands, snapped to attention. "When? When did you see her?"

"The evening I arrived. She stopped and asked me if I was Mrs. Hartman. She claimed she was recruiting neighbourhood residents to canvass for the United Way. When Etienne and

MacTee rushed out, she muttered something about coming back at a better time and left." Hollis whisked the eggs again. She dropped a butter dab in the pan and listened to it sizzle. She dipped bread slices in the egg mixture and laid them in the frying pan. Intent on cooking, she didn't say anything else until she'd finished and carried a plate piled with French toast to the table.

"I bet she's a SOHD opponent. When she asked me if you lived here, she wasn't really sure it was the Hartman house."

"She wouldn't be—it's in my name, and so is the phone," Manon said.

Hollis bit her lip. "I wasn't suspicious, but I'm sure I didn't say you lived here. But after the fire, when photographs of the house appeared on TV and in the papers, the SOHD opponents wouldn't have had a problem figuring out where Curt lives."

Manon's shoulders lifted, and her voice trembled. "Damn Curt. If he hadn't involved himself with that stupid organization..." Her voice trailed away.

Hollis tapped the table. "Manon, look at me."

Her friend raised her eyes.

"This is a good news, bad news story. The bad is that it happened because of Curt. The good is that he *was* and *is* the target. Etienne isn't. Tomas isn't. You aren't. It isn't the family—it's Curt. I'm sorry it's Curt but relieved it isn't you."

Manon had tied her napkin in a tight knot. Her hunched shoulders relaxed, and she sank back in her chair. "I suppose you're right," she conceded. Her face an expressionless mask, she watched Etienne dig into his breakfast.

What could she do to bring Manon back, to make her a participant again?

MacTee, his tail wagging, moseyed toward the front door.

"Papa, you're back," Etienne said happily when Curt, followed by Tomas, walked into the kitchen.

Only his rumpled clothing and the white stubble on his jaw indicated that anything out-of-the-ordinary had happened to Curt. He smiled at them. Not only did Manon not return his smile—she refused to look at him. Her body stiff, her shoulders high, her hands clutched the knotted napkin as if it were a life raft. She said nothing to anyone but stood up and left the room.

"Back, fine, and ready to get on with my life," Curt said, ignoring his wife's precipitous departure. "First things first— we need breakfast—they didn't give us any in Emerg. Even if they had, it probably wouldn't have been edible." He smiled. "Now that they've fingered the bomber, maybe they'll tie her to the fire and to Ivan's murder."

Tied to a fire sounded like Joan of Arc. Curt's assumptions startled Hollis. The woman she'd met hadn't been sure Curt lived in the house. It seemed unlikely she'd either tampered with the brakes or lit the fire.

"I've made French toast. Help yourselves. I'll make more," she said. She dipped bread into the egg mix and dropped the saturated slices into the pan. She'd follow Manon and offer comfort. But before she did, there was something she'd wanted to ask Curt—what was it?

"Do you have the latest on Arthur? I called a few minutes ago. They confirmed that he was there but no more," Hollis paused. "Oh dear, I remember—I promised his nurse I'd find out who to notify about his accident—I totally forgot."

"His ex-wife, Ursula, lives in Montreal," Curt said.

"I wonder if she still uses his surname?"

"Pretty old to go back to her maiden name," Curt said as he and Etienne ate their toast.

Upstairs, Manon slumped at her office desk. She'd folded her hands in front of her and sat totally immobile, her features slack, her eyes unfocused. Her expression alarmed Hollis.

"Manon," she said.

Her friend ignored her.

Hollis massaged Manon's rigid shoulders and spoke in a low and soothing voice. "It's going to be okay. Etienne will be fine. The police will find out who did it. We'll be safe while they keep an eye on the house. The woman won't come back." Her hands kneaded the tension knots in Manon's shoulders. "Olivero's worried about you. I told him you and I and MacTee would walk over to the park later this afternoon. Was that the right thing to do?"

Manon nodded almost imperceptibly.

A task—Manon responded well when asked to do something specific. It had worked before—time to try it again.

"Would you do something for me?"

"What?"

"The hospital asked about Arthur's next-of-kin. They wanted a name and number. Would you phone Montreal information for Arthur White's ex-wife's number? Then call her and tell her what happened. She may want to come to Toronto."

Manon remained immobile for a few seconds until the request registered on her neurological switchboard. She shifted in her chair and faced Hollis. "Ursula. Sure. I can do that." She reached for the phone book and a pad of paper. "It'll be good to do something." She flipped to the reference pages. "Later I'll visit Arthur and thank him." Her tone had changed. Life and inflection had returned. "It's the least I can do. He saved Etienne's life."

Hollis was elated that the strategy had worked.

She admired those who plowed ahead and didn't regard the phone as a malevolent being. She had phone phobia. Email delighted her—she could leave messages and avoid talking to anyone.

Manon didn't hesitate after she found the number. "Ursula, it's Manon Dumont, Curt Hartman's wife."

Even sitting across the room, Hollis could hear the surprised response from Montreal, although not the actual words. She listened to Manon's side of the conversation and tried to fill in what Ursula must be saying.

"I know, but once Curt latches on to an idea, there's no stopping him."

Another pause.

"I didn't realize it was one of the reasons you left."

Pause.

"Yes, I can imagine how difficult it's been. But I'm calling about Arthur."

Ursula's high-pitched voice repeated, "Arthur."

"There's been..." Manon hesitated and caught Hollis's eye. Hollis shook her head—no point giving the details.

"An accident. Arthur is in St. Mike's. I'll give the phone to my friend, Hollis Grant. She'll tell you how he was last night."

How come she got to be the bearer of bad news? What approach to take? Cheerful and positive. After all, they didn't know his prognosis. "Hi, Ursula. Last night he was stable, but semi-conscious."

"Did he have a stroke? I always worried about his blood pressure. His mother died of a stroke. And he had migraines. Some medical literature says people who suffer from those are prone to strokes."

Hollis interrupted the flow. "No, not a stroke. There was an explosion, and he absorbed the impact. When I called the hospital this morning, they would only discuss his condition with a relative."

"I'll phone immediately. Then I'll catch a plane. Poor Arthur, he shouldn't be alone. These days, no one should spend a single minute in hospital without an advocate. They employ far too few nurses, and they give them too much to do. I don't suppose you know I nursed in England. No, of course you don't; you don't even know me. I worked in Canada too. Shocking, it's shocking the deterioration I've seen. Modern medicine may have its miracles, but when it comes to care—Florence Nightingale would spin, absolutely spin in her grave. It used to be that a private room was what you wanted, but not any more. If you're in a double or a ward, another patient or a visitor will call the nurse if something goes wrong. But I'm wasting time. Arthur needs me. I'll make arrangements right away."

Had Ursula always talked like there was a prize for spewing out the most words in a given time period? She must have driven Arthur crazy. Maybe he'd learned to tune her out.

"And thank you, and thank Manon. It was good of you to track me down. Even though I'm not living with Arthur, I care about him. We aren't actually divorced. I left him and came to live in Montreal because I couldn't bear listening to him going on and on about Curt and how he'd done him wrong. Arthur wasn't the best businessman, you know. His gallery's failure wasn't totally Curt's fault. Anyway, it was wearing me out, simply wearing me out, listening to him rant and rave. He was and probably is totally, absolutely totally obsessed with Curt and getting even. It took over his life. In my opinion, life is too short for that kind of nonsense."

When Hollis replaced the receiver, she smiled at Manon. "Wow, that woman can talk. Has she always raced on like an out-of-control chain saw?"

"Ever since I met her." Manon stood up. "Thank you for giving me something to do. I feel better. I'm having a bath before I see Arthur." She raised her hands. "I've seen you staring at my nails. You're right—I've been ignoring them. Time to pull myself together. You go and do whatever you have to do."

"I'm sorting Ivan's things."

"Do you think the bomb lady murdered Ivan?"

Should she comfort Manon and agree? No way. Time for extra vigilance. "No, I don't think so. When she accosted me, she didn't know Curt lived here."

"Maybe it isn't the same woman."

"Wait and see what the police say, but let's continue to be careful."

*   *   *

Back at their desks, Rhona and Zee Zee contemplated the ever-growing Hartman file.

"Before we regroup, I'm phoning Hartmans'. They'll be relieved to hear Allie Jones is in custody." She punched in the numbers and delivered her message. When she hung up, she smiled at Zee Zee. "It's great to bear good news for a change. Let's walk through this." She leaned back on her swivel chair and ran through the chronology. "What do you think the perp will do now?"

Zee Zee interlaced her fingers behind her head and considered. "Nothing at the house. Not for a day or two."

"We're missing something or somebody. Nothing hangs together."

"What about the woman, if it was a woman, who sent the flowers? And the woman who tried to talk to Curt after the funeral?"

"Hollis knows something about her. When I asked, she pretended her cell phone had gone dead. We haven't talked since the explosion." Rhona called Hollis on her cell. She listened, shook her head and snapped the phone shut. "She's turned it off." She snapped her own phone shut and dropped it in her ever-present bag. "Enough. This isn't a game. We're going to find out what Hollis knows."

"What about Arthur White? He was lead number one. Now he's a hero—can we write him out of the script?"

"I believed him when he said he couldn't burn art. But he could have tampered with the bike." Rhona shook her head. "What do you think?"

"In my mind, he's not the perp. What about Lena?"

"There's something very odd about her. I wouldn't rule her out."

"Olivero Ciccio?"

"Maybe his wife, she's a bitter woman."

"Sebastien Lefebvre?"

"Not the fire. Artists don't destroy paintings," Rhona said.

"Hitler burned books and suppressed art and called himself an artist."

"He liked dogs too—he was an aberration."

"That leaves Barney," Zee Zee said.

"What about the mystery woman? I'm sure Hollis knows her identity. She's the key to our puzzle, but we have to contact her first. We'll go through the paperwork, but I'm convinced Hollis can provide the key."

Twenty-Six

Happy that Manon was herself again, Hollis concentrated on what she had to do. First, she'd arrange another meeting with Penny. Then, in the early afternoon, she'd confront Lena. Her heart pounded at the thought.

Despite the fact that Penny hadn't come forward, hadn't revealed her relationship with Ivan or told the family about the baby, Hollis knew she had to reveal Penny's identity to Rhona. It was a legal as well as a moral responsibility. If she didn't, she could be aiding and abetting or making it easier for the killer to strike again, but she'd do it later in the day. Right now she wanted to find out why Penny had been frightened. And find out if she might have changed her mind, might want Manon and Curt to hear about her and the baby. Maybe she hadn't known how to go about it.

"She ain't here—she be back in half an hour." Another gruff voice, male this time.

When she called a second time, Penny answered.

"Hi. My uncle said someone called."

"Can we meet again—I have a few more questions."

"We didn't really finish our conversation, did we? I'm sorry I cried." Penny paused and giggled. "Cried isn't exactly the right word is it—I howled like a banshee. Sure, let's meet again this afternoon—same time, same place."

Perfect—the beast before the beauty. Should she tell Rhona

her plans? If Lena had been involved in Ivan's death or the fire, it would be wrong not to share her information with Rhona. Worse than wrong—it could endanger them all. She had Rhona's cell phone number. She'd meet with Lena and Penny then make the call.

How should she approach Lena? She'd ask outright and see what happened. As she was dressing, Hollis didn't choose sandals—no more saliva oozing between her toes.

At the gallery, the exhibit's brutality horrified her again. Lena sat at the same black-draped table. She had replaced the funeral flowers, the gladiola, with blood-red roses. She sat dressed in flowing black with her blonde hair upswept, bent over the visitors' book reading the comments.

Hollis cleared her throat.

Lena glanced up but kept her finger in the book.

"You. What do you want?"

"To speak to you." Hollis glanced around to make sure no visitors hovered close.

"I can't think I have anything to say to you."

"I found out that you come from the Sons of Freedom Doukhobor colony in British Columbia. While you were growing up, your community protested government policy by setting fires."

Lena rose. Her features drew together, and she puffed like an out of shape mountain climber or a volcano about to erupt.

Hollis continued. "It's my guess you've kept your background a secret because the press would sensationalize it. And familiarity with it would prevent critics from judging your art on its own merit."

Lena stepped toward Hollis, who instinctively raised her hands to ward off an attack.

"I don't intend to tell anyone," Hollis said hurriedly, "but I keep thinking about the fire in Curt's studio and wondering if there's a connection..." Hollis paused, gathered her courage and blurted, "If you set the fire."

Lena reached to grab Hollis, who stepped to one side, but not quickly enough. Lena's fingers locked on her shoulder. "Meddling little shit. Why would you think I had anything to do with the fire? My God, fires, protests, the ravings of fanatical religious zealots ruined my childhood—why would I use their tactics? Never. I don't own a barbecue or a propane lighter, I don't burn candles—I have a fear, a terror of fire." She gripped Hollis's shoulders and shook her. "You set the police on me. They were searching for evidence to link me to the fire. They didn't find anything, because there was nothing to find. I hate Curt, but I would never burn his paintings. Never. Never. Never."

She released Hollis and shoved her toward the door.

"Tell the police. Tell anyone you like. But I had nothing to do with it."

Outside, Hollis collected herself. Not a pleasant confrontation, but Lena had sounded as if she was telling the truth.

When Hollis reached Java Java, Penny sat on the banquette close to the breeze blowing in through the open windows. She made notes while she read a book.

"Studying?" Hollis asked.

Penny closed *Modern Accounting* and smiled. "I don't intend to make a career in the restaurant business."

Hollis ordered a lemon tart before filling a coffee mug from the thermos jugs stationed across the restaurant. When the waitress had delivered the mouthwatering treat and two forks, Hollis offered to share.

Penny patted her stomach. "I think not. I'm trying to eat healthy and not too much. I don't want to have to diet forever after the baby arrives."

Hollis broke off a tiny bit, forked it into her mouth and savoured the ambrosial lemon and cream mix. "Two things I'd like to ask. First, who is frightening you?"

Penny poked her straw up and down in her orange juice bottle. "I exaggerated," she said but didn't raise her eyes.

"You're not convincing me—it sounded like a heartfelt comment."

"What's your second question?"

"Do you want Curt to learn he will soon be a grandfather?"

"The way Ivan talked about him, I don't think he'd care. Ivan said his father didn't believe he was capable of doing anything, not even fathering a child. I'd be furious if he didn't believe Ivan was the baby's father. And imagine my shame if he asked me to take a DNA test." She shook her head. "My emotional state could hurt the baby."

"Ivan said *that?*" Hollis took a second bite; she wanted the tart to last forever. "Have you seen his mother's installation at the Revelation Gallery on Queen Street?"

"I didn't have the courage. I read what the reviewers said about it, and I didn't think I could bear to go—neither of his parents had a clue about him." She pulled the straw from the bottle. "Sure, he didn't do well in high school, and he wasn't great at athletics, but so what. He was a wonderful, warm, caring human being, and that's what counts." Her voice shook, and tears ran down her cheeks. "It makes me furious—I can't tell you how much it upsets me." She wiped her eyes with the sleeve of her denim jacket. "I want my baby to think his father was wonderful." She sighed. "No. I'm going to go it alone."

"Before Ivan died, I think I would have agreed with you, but things have changed. His father feels remorseful about how he treated Ivan. I'd guess the whole family would be overjoyed if you allowed them a chance to make it right."

"Why now and not then?"

"Because when the police came and asked about Ivan, about his life and friends—the family had no answers. No, that's not true. His half-brother, Etienne, knew things the others didn't. Anyway, they're remorseful, very remorseful."

Penny considered and shook her head. "I don't think I could risk it."

Hollis leaned forward. "Penny, what if I broach the subject without revealing your name?"

Penny leaned back against the wall and stared fixedly into the distance.

Hollis looked to see what she was staring at, but there was nothing strange in Penny's line of vision. A shelf against the opposite wall held a large orange thermal water jug, a tray of glasses, two coffee dispensers along with cups and open milk containers.

Penny blinked several times, and her gaze returned to Hollis. "I've met you twice, and you want me to risk everything. Let me think about it. I'll call you."

Hollis nodded. "I see your point. Okay, but tell me why you're afraid."

Penny finished her drink, stuffed her books in her back pack and said nothing.

Hollis waited.

"Do you know many Greeks?"

"No."

"Greek men, and women too, are proud and passionate," Penny said.

"Your ex-boyfriend is Greek?"

Penny smiled. "He is, but he isn't even in Toronto. Months ago he dropped out of school to get a job in Fort McMurray."

So much for him. Hollis had felt sure the jilted young man

would provide a lead. "Your family?"

Penny nodded. "My father, my uncles, my brothers and even my grandmother pressure me to tell 'who done me wrong'. If they lived in Greece, there'd be trouble, maybe even bloodshed. That won't happen here, but they are really on my case to get me to 'tell'. I've refused, because I'm afraid to think what they might do."

"Are you sure they aren't pretending? Maybe they do know, have known, for a long time?"

"You're suggesting they…" Penny's already pale skin whitened even more. Her lower lip trembled, and she shook her head violently. "No! No! No! Of course they don't know. And they would *never, never, never* have done anything to Ivan. What a horrible thing to say."

Her vehement reaction suggested Penny had considered this possibility but refused to entertain it. What if it was true? Another tack, time for another tack. "Would they feel better if Ivan's family accepted you and promised to care for you and your baby?"

Penny shrugged. "The Hartmans aren't Greek."

Hollis had finished the tart. "I'm not going to add to your problems, but call me soon."

Penny clambered to her feet, pulled her jacket around her stomach and patted it gently. "I will."

Back at the Hartmans', Hollis joined Manon and Tomas on the front porch. MacTee lay contentedly at their feet.

"Good news. Ursula phoned to update us on Arthur's condition," Manon said.

"He's going to be okay?" Hollis asked.

"He's out of the coma. They're testing for neurological damage, but Ursula says they don't expect to find anything serious." She grinned at Hollis. "When they spring him, she's taking him home. She says Arthur needs her—that she mustn't think just of herself and has to remember her wedding vows. She says that she feels lonely in Montreal. She's already called her banker and transferred the money she took back to their joint account."

"Arthur got a big buck for his bang." Hollis made a rueful face. "Sorry."

"That's okay. There's more good news." Manon's grin widened. "Ursula is one powerhouse. She came here after she left the hospital and dragged Curt into his study. I heard her going on and on. Eventually, she came out rubbing her hands together as if she'd dealt with 'that' problem and could move on."

"I'm surprised Curt took it."

"I'm not. Recently, I've seen chinks in his feeling of invincibility."

"Really?"

Manon looked thoughtful. "I can tell you this—it isn't a secret. You remember the other day when Sebastien Lefevbre phoned?"

What was she going to reveal? Whatever it was, she didn't seem upset or concerned. "I do."

"Yesterday he came over. Apparently his daughter, Valerie, was one of Curt's students and was totally enamoured with him. In the fall, she told her parents she was pregnant, but she wouldn't name the father. Because of her infatuation, Sebastien assumed it was Curt." She shook her head. "I could have told him different. Curt loves women, but he's not a cradle robber. Anyway, Valerie died in an accident, and Sebastien continued to blame Curt. Yesterday, a totally distraught young man appeared at their door. He'd been Valerie's boyfriend. But before he left for Europe to study for a year, they'd had a major falling out. Apparently, Valerie had written to him, but his mother hadn't forwarded the letter. Because he didn't hear from Valerie, he figured the romance was over. When he came home, he found the letter telling him about the baby. Then he learned she'd died. He told Sebastien how broken up he was. Sebastien came yesterday to apologize to Curt."

"What a story."

"That softened Curt up. It wasn't just Sebastien. Despite his ego and his anger, I think he's missed Arthur. He's one of his few friends, and the only one who goes back to the beginning when they both started out."

"Wow, that explosion had major ramifications."

"It did. Curt has gone to visit Arthur." She shook her head. "We may be crossing the bridge too soon. He may come back as mad as ever. Somehow I doubt it."

Her animation cheered Hollis. Manon appeared to have taken a new course, a positive one.

"Guess what—good news." Etienne raced out of the house to his mother and threw his arms around her. He looked at Hollis. "Guess, guess what."

"I don't have any idea, but it must be really good. Tell me."

"Tomas is taking David and me. Did you hear that—me, taking me tomorrow night when he practices for Tuesday's race."

Manon was allowing Etienne to sail. This was amazing.

Twenty-Seven

At Monday's class, Curt showed no distress. "It seems everybody's out to get me. This time a demented woman tossed a bomb at my house."

The crises in his life seemed to invigorate him. Hollis couldn't believe it. She knew that in his circumstances, she'd be a basket case. She'd be jumping at every unexpected noise, checking behind her to see if disaster was sneaking up. In fact, she was a secondary player in this drama, and she still felt threatened and nervous, still feared something else was about to happen.

Those who hadn't heard about the bomb looked shocked.

"Not a 'serious' bomb—little homemade thing—probably made from the fireworks you buy at those highway stores." His tone was light. He was letting them know he refused to take this seriously. "I'll need a new hedge—blew the cedars to kingdom come, but they were pretty weedy anyway." He shrugged. "Who knows what my enemies will do next? Probably a plague of locusts. Now it's time to talk about impermanent colours."

Curt nodded at Lefevbre, who sat in his usual seat, drawing the other students. "Take my colleague here—it would be a shame if his brilliant portraits faded. The impact of his colour choices and the coordination with his psychological insights would diminish if the colours lost their intensity. In this age of synthetics, the long term properties of many are unknown. Perhaps untested would be a better word. We must assure ourselves they are colourfast before we use them." His mouth lifted into a smile. "I expect my colleague will have enough material from the drawings he's made in class to mount his own exhibition."

Lefevbre nodded in acknowledgement of Curt's compliment.

"As I said in an earlier lecture, Turner was a serious offender when it came to using fugitive colours. In fact, Mr. Winsor of the well-known firm of Winsor and Newton wrote and warned Turner not to use certain colours because they would fade. Turner told him to mind his own business. But buyers did bring paintings back to Turner and request that he repaint beautiful red sunsets that had turned grey. He refused. He told them if he did one, he'd have to repaint them all."

At the break, Lefevbre made no move to join the others on the food and drink trek. Should she stay and talk to him? She didn't want to field the questions that would come her way downstairs. However, her throat felt like she'd spent a week in a Sahara sand storm. She opted for water.

Downstairs, Kate led the charge. "Tell us about it." She pursed her lips. "You have had more excitement in your life in a week than most people have in a lifetime."

"Believe me, I wish I hadn't. The police have arrested the alleged bomber. She's a militant SOHD opponent."

"Did she set the fire?" Kate asked.

"They didn't charge her.""

"The poor Hartman family. There must be something we can do," Kate said. "Flowers. We could send flowers."

"What a stupid suggestion. Why would they want flowers?" David said.

Kate stared at him. "You really are insensitive."

"You must have talked to Tomas when you were sailing. Did he say anything about what the family needs?" Hollis said.

"You went sailing with their son, and you can say my suggestion is stupid. Well, Mr. Smarty Pants, what do you suggest?" Kate said.

David glared at her. "I suggest we help with the rebuilding just like we said we would. They don't need us milling around trying to be useful." He faced Hollis. "If you're staying there and are Manon's friend, why would you think that I know anything you don't know? Tomas and I did not, get this, *not* talk about his brothers or his father. We did discuss the rebuilding and how much we could do and what Curt will have to hire contractors to do." He turned back to Kate. "Why don't you concentrate on painting?"

"Thanks a lot, jerk," Kate said and turned her back on him.

"Speaking of painting, that's what I'd like to focus on. Actually I'm doing the ostrich routine—I'm trying to ignore everything except painting while I'm here," Hollis said.

"Okay, but let us know what we can do to help," Kate said to Hollis.

*   *   *

"Which suspect should we concentrate on?" Zee Zee asked after hauling a chair over to sit beside Rhona's desk. She'd brought paper from her inbox with her.

"I intend to pin Hollis down. I'm *sure* she can identify the woman at the funeral and tell us her connection to the crimes." Rhona thumped her desk in frustration, making her mug jump and coffee splash. She mopped the spill with a wad of tissue she pulled from her bag. "Hollis has been in this situation before. She should realize how important it is to identify every puzzle piece. Sometimes the oddest items lead you in unexpected directions. I think she's protecting someone." She dropped the sodden tissues in the waste basket. "That said—the fire has anti-SOHD hallmarks. Arson is an anti-abortionist specialty, and the two groups are pretty well interchangeable. One problem—the turpentine we took from Barney's and Allie's wasn't the accelerant."

"Maybe we should give them credit for not being total idiots and keeping it around, or maybe they chucked the container. Did we do a garbage search in the alley?" Zee Zee said.

"We did and didn't turn up an empty turpentine can. Have you had a gander at the Hartmans' incoming phone records?"

"They're in here," Zee Zee said, reaching for her in-basket. She waved a sheaf of paper before she zipped through it. "The calls came from phone booths," she said.

"It's going to be trickier for anonymous callers in the future—phone booths are an endangered species."

Zee Zee agreed. "We're recording their calls, but it's a bit late."

"Have you read this?" Rhona held up Curt's biography.

"Skimmed."

"And?"

"I'm wondering if we should have pushed to find disgruntled students. We concentrated on peers and colleagues."

"It's another angle to explore," Rhona said.

"We should ask his wife and the other professors about students." Zee Zee shook her head. "Although I think we would have heard about a crazy former student gunning for him."

Rhona interlaced her fingers, locked them behind her head and stretched her tense neck muscles. "I'm wondering if we're on entirely the wrong track."

Zee Zee raised her eyebrows. "How's that?"

"What if, after all, Ivan, Etienne or Hollis was the intended victim? We should be looking at who would want *them* dead."

* * *

Monday evening, Hollis and Manon had settled in the garden. MacTee stretched out for a deep and serious nap. The leaves of the tall trees overhanging the garden rustled in the cool breeze.

Hollis folded the paper she was reading to stop it from blowing. "Wonderful wind. The men will enjoy their sail."

"I hope it isn't too strong," Manon said. "Sailing in a stiff breeze can be a challenge."

Curt, carrying a tray with glasses, vodka and tonic bottles and a jar of salted peanuts joined them. "Time for a little R and R," he said.

In the kitchen, the phone rang.

"I'll get it." Hollis, closest to the house, ran for the French doors.

"Manon," the voice squeaked.

"It's Hollis Grant, I'm a house guest. Shall I call Manon?"

"It's David."

His voice had been unrecognizable. Alarm bells rang.

David, what was wrong with his voice? Why was he phoning—he was supposed to be sailing. "What's happened?"

"You won't believe it. I don't believe it myself..." His voice trembled.

"What is it?"

"An accident."

"Oh, my God. Etienne."

"Etienne is fine, but..."

"Tomas?"

"He's missing."

"What happened?"

"The boat sank."

"Sank! It's a lovely evening. How could it sink?"

Manon entered the kitchen. She stopped. Her mouth moved but no words emerged. Not the time for Manon to faint. She needed to talk to David, to hear that Etienne was alive.

"Here's Manon. Better talk to her."

Manon's wide eyes reflected her fear. She grabbed the phone as if it were a lifeline holding her back from the precipice.

"Etienne," she gasped and listened. "Can I hear his voice?" Her face softened. "Etienne. Thank God…"

She listened again. "Yes, yes, don't worry about that. Let me talk to David."

"How could it have happened? What do you mean you *think* Tomas may have swum for shore?" Manon's eyes filled with hopelessness. "You're telling me you're *hoping* he swam to shore, but you don't know." Another pause. "Everyone knows you don't leave the boat. Even though Tomas is a champion swimmer, he would have stayed with you and Etienne."

Manon clutched the phone and leaned on the wall as if she'd fall to the floor without its support.

"Listen. We'll be there soon. Take care of Etienne."

Hollis pried the phone from Manon's hands and replaced it in its cradle. Manon, her face slack and her mouth open, didn't react.

"I'm sure Tomas made it to shore, or a boat picked him up," Hollis said.

Manon shook her head. "I'd like to agree, but the water's rough and cold. David would have heard if the Harbour Police or a rescue boat had found Tomas."

She took a shaky breath. "David and Etienne are waiting in the Royal Canadian Yacht Club lounge. It's over on Toronto Island—you have to take their launch to get there. Wouldn't you know it—Etienne's worried about Curt's reaction to losing his folkboat." Her lips curved into a caricature of a smile. "How typical for Etienne to think about Curt. David will stay with him until Curt and I arrive." The smile disappeared. "I'll tell Curt."

"Should I come?"

Manon shook her head again. "No, I'll do this myself, but it would help if you'd follow us to the RCYC. In case we have to…" She didn't finish the sentence. An awareness of the terrible circumstances that would keep Manon and Curt at the RCYC flashed between them. "If necessary, you could bring Etienne home."

Tomas. A few hours ago, he was alive and well. Had the killer struck again? But that was silly: how could anyone have predicted Tomas would try to swim to shore and not make it? If someone had sabotaged the boat, he probably hadn't intended to murder Tomas.

Although Curt seldom mentioned his heart problems, they weren't a secret. Anyone who knew him might have thought that immersion in Lake Ontario's always-frigid water would cause Curt's heart to fail. The saboteur would have assumed Curt would be aboard and also know Tomas, a strong swimmer with a normal heart, would wear a life jacket. He wouldn't have known that Etienne and David would be in the boat that day.

Twenty-Eight

In the RCYC lounge, Etienne, a soft drink in his hand and a bag of chips on his knee, sat close to Manon who had her arm around him. Cartoons filled the wide screen TV, but no one paid any attention. People crowded the room. Individuals came and went. Manon and Etienne sat isolated from the room's activity as surely as if someone had erected a wall around them. David was not with them when Hollis arrived.

"I'm here," Hollis said, touching Manon's shoulder.

Etienne jumped to his feet and raced to Hollis. The fact that he publicly flung his arms around her revealed his anguish. "It was awful," he said. She hugged him tight and murmured sympathetically into his hair.

"Any news?" she said to Manon.

Manon shook her head.

"News?" Etienne repeated.

Oh lord, she'd put her foot in. Maybe David hadn't told Etienne that Tomas's whereabouts were unknown. Quick save needed. "The boat—did it come to the surface or float in or anything?"

"It's a keelboat. When they turn turtle, they sink like stones." Etienne said. "Maman wanted Papa to give it up and buy a safer fibreglass boat, but Papa loved it."

A vessel guaranteed to sink: what better way to kill someone. The sabotage evidence would lie on the bottom of Lake Ontario forever.

"Curt and David have gone out in the search boats," Manon said. "Will you drive us back to the house? We'll wait there."

It was close to nine o'clock when David brought Curt home.

"They've called off the search until first light tomorrow. David will pick me up at four thirty tomorrow morning." Curt hovered uncertainly in the kitchen doorway. Manon, Etienne and Hollis sat at the kitchen table, picking at sandwiches.

"We must make plans," Curt said.

Manon shot to her feet. Her lips quivered. "Plans?" Her normally tidy hair was no longer pulled back from her face but hanging in a tangled mass. Her face pale and her lips trembling, Manon repeated the word as if came from some unknown language. "Plans for what?" Her face crumpled, she hugged herself and rocked back and forth. "I'm sorry. It's too horrible. I'm sorry, but I can't stay here. Can't risk anything happening to Etienne. I am sorry, but I can't stay."

Curt didn't move.

"Who's next? Not Etienne. I'm not allowing Etienne to stay one more day."

Curt's head rose slowly, as if the weight was almost too much for him to bear. "Please. I need you," he said.

Manon's eyes opened wide, and she shook her head from side to side. "I don't think that's true. I don't think you've ever really needed anyone." She clasped her hands over her heart. "If it is true, then I'm sorry I have to go. But I do."

"Tell her to stay, not to leave me," Curt implored Hollis.

Curt had lost his second son. And Manon was leaving with Etienne. How terrible for him. But how horrifying for Manon to think she and Etienne would be next.

Manon whirled and pointed a shaking finger at Hollis. "You're my friend. Don't you dare take his side." Her face seemed to fracture and break into a thousand bits. A drawn-out wail shattered the air. Tears flooded. She staggered to a chair and collapsed, sobbing deep ragged sobs.

Curt lurched forward. He bent down, encircled her with his arms and pulled her to her feet, where he cradled and soothed her.

Hollis beckoned to Etienne. They crept into the garden.

"What happens now?" Etienne asked. With his arms hanging at his side, his shoulders sagging—he'd taken the stance of a defeated old man. "What will they do when they find Tomas?"

Poor kid. How unbelievably awful for a child to have to go through this again. "We don't need to cross that bridge yet. We'll hope Tomas is still alive."

Etienne glared at her. "He should be. It's not fair. Tomas is a champion swimmer."

If Etienne wanted to talk about the accident, she'd give him a chance. Whenever something terrible had happened to her, she'd wanted to tell and retell the story.

"Why wasn't he wearing a life jacket? Come and sit down and tell me what happened."

Etienne dropped onto a chaise longue. Hollis pulled a second one around until they sat knee to knee.

"We were a long way out. The boat started to take on water. It washed over my feet. As more and more water filled the boat, it sank lower. It was rough, and waves splashed over the sides. Tomas and David dropped the sails. Tomas said he'd take a look. He ripped off his life jacket, jumped in and dove down to see what had happened under the boat." Etienne bit his lip. "He was hardly down there a minute before he popped up. He said there was a jeezly big hole. When we hauled him in, he said he'd get the caulking stuff from the cabin locker…"

He gazed away as if he was seeing a replay of the accident on an interior TV screen.

Hollis waited.

"It comes in rolls. Usually you stick it on and paint over it. Anyway, Tomas said it would slow the water pouring in and give the bilge pump a chance to work. Then we would have time to signal for help or make it back to shore." Etienne expelled the words in one long rush as if they'd been dammed up inside him. "David warned him it was dangerous—we might sink at any moment. Tomas said it would only take a minute to push himself down into the cabin and get the caulking." Etienne's eyes filled with tears. "He didn't have a minute. The boat shook." He paused "It was like when my dog Beau died—she did that too, sort of gave up. One minute, my feet were braced on the bottom. The next minute there was no bottom. David yelled at me to swim away, so the rigging wouldn't trap me and suck me down."

"My God."

"The waves were high. It was hard to swim wearing the life jacket. When I figured I was far enough away, I treaded water and shouted to Tomas and David. Only David answered. I waited for Tomas, but he didn't come." He stopped.

"How long were you in the water?"

"A long time. It was freezing. We had whistles on our life jackets and blew and blew. A boat came close. It was a sailboat—they couldn't stop, but they must have had cell phones. The harbour police came right after. They pulled us in."

Hollis wanted to hug him, but she didn't know if it was a good idea when he was working hard to be brave and rational. "Horrible," she said.

"If Tomas hadn't been diving, he would have had his jacket on."

"Even a life jacket wouldn't have saved him if he was in the cabin." What a stupid thing to say. She could have ripped her tongue out. "We won't give up hope."

"I'm getting my Game Boy," Etienne said. "It's like the stars—it makes me forget bad things."

*   *   *

Sleep did not come that night. The image of Tomas trapped in the boat haunted her. At four, she heard Curt rise and leave. Half an hour later, there was more noise. MacTee, who hadn't been interested in rising at four, staggered to his feet and trotted off to investigate.

Hollis rolled out of bed and threw on her dressing gown. Whatever they were doing, they might need her. She padded to Etienne's room. He had just added his telescope to the pile of clothing on his bed.

"What are you doing?"

"We're going to Grandmaman's when Maman finishes packing." He patted his telescope. "I don't want to go until we find out what happened to Tomas. Papa will need us."

"I'll talk to your mother."

Downstairs, she rapped on Manon's door.

"Come in, but don't try to change my mind—I'm leaving."

One suitcase sat inside the door. Manon had a third one on the bed. "I'm not sitting here waiting for the killer to pick us off."

"I wasn't arguing. What can I do to help?"

"Nothing. I promised Etienne we'd stop and eat breakfast at a highway restaurant." She continued to move back and forth. At the bureau, she scooped underwear from an open drawer and returned to dump it in the suitcase. She stopped with a bra dangling from her hand. "Would you stay in the house? If they phone about Tomas, call me on my cell phone."

That she could do. "I'll take MacTee for a quick walk while you're still here. Then I'll make coffee. You can take it with you. It'll keep you going until you reach the first restaurant."

Twenty minutes later, Hollis helped Manon and Etienne load the car and waved them off. Back in the house, its emptiness engulfed her.

If she assumed sabotage, this was the fourth, no, the third attempt to kill someone in the family. She could rule out the bombing—the alleged perpetrator had been apprehended. What about the other three crimes? The police considered motive, means and opportunity. Motive was a stopper. Had the killer targeted Ivan? Was it one of Penny's relatives? Or had the murderer meant to kill Curt or Tomas? Would Sebastien Lefevbre, Arthur or Olivero have hated Curt enough to murder him or his son?

No matter what happened, Curt wouldn't teach today. She phoned the college and left a message guaranteed to disappoint her fellow artists. Artists tended to be single-minded.

Artists. She thought of Lena. Had her passion led her to attempt to kill Curt and end up murdering her son? Did Tomas have enemies they didn't know about? Had the arsonist intended to kill Curt, Etienne or her? She shivered. Who had been the saboteur's target?

She couldn't find a motive, but what about means? That wasn't hard. Cutting the brakes required minimal knowledge—nothing complicated. Setting a fire and making a hole in a wooden boat hull didn't require muscle or special knowledge. A man or woman of any age could have committed all three crimes.

Opportunity. Who had all three? She reviewed the list. She scratched Arthur; he hadn't risen from his hospital bed to punch a hole in the boat. One after another, she eliminated suspects, until finally she arrived at a name that shocked her.

Twenty-Nine

The phone rang. The harbour police at first light had found an unconscious young man, whose lifejacket had kept him afloat, and plucked him from Lake Ontario. They assumed it was Tomas. Would someone come and identify him?

Hollis couldn't phone Curt—he didn't have a cell phone. David's had been in his pocket when the boat had sunk. He had intended to replace it later in the day. Nothing for it—she'd have to go to the hospital herself. Should she call Manon? No, not until she made sure it was Tomas and learned his prognosis. She headed for the hospital.

Nursing staff surrounded the young man, still unconscious and inches from death. The room was filled with machines and staff as they worked to restore his core temperature. They allowed Hollis to view him and confirm that it was Tomas.

"Because he's young and healthy, he should recover, but it will be touch and go," a young intern said. "His life jacket kept him floating—his youth and vitality kept him alive."

His life jacket—but he hadn't worn one. That was a mystery, but they'd hear the explanation when Tomas regained consciousness. He would; she knew he would. Hadn't the doctor said he was young and strong? She'd rush home to wait for Curt and to call Manon.

Her euphoria faded. Before she did that, she had a more important call to make. If her speculations were right, she knew the killer's identity, but not why or whom he'd intended to kill.

Upstairs, she called Rhona, who was "in the office but on another line". Should she call back or leave a message? It wasn't an option—she considered her words carefully. She didn't want to make an unfounded accusation, but if she was right, Rhona needed to know.

* * *

"They've picked up Tomas Hartman, and I had to hear it on the radio. He's alive, but barely," Zee Zee shouted at Rhona when both detectives emerged from their cars in the basement parking garage. They race-walked toward the elevator. "Why the hell didn't someone phone us last night after the accident happened? You'd think the Harbour Police might have made a connection or two. I'd say it was a conspiracy, but more likely it was plain stupidity."

Rhona sent an officer to pick up the security tapes from the RCYC. Zee Zee phoned and learned they'd located the sunken boat with sonar and would send divers down later in the day. Rhona called the hospital, made several inquiries and hung up.

"He's suffering from hypothermia and hallucinating. He drifts in and out of consciousness. Hollis has identified him. His father and the other guy in the accident, David Nixon, were out with the search boats, but not in the one that picked him up. They're on their way home."

After she shuffled through her in basket, Rhona held up a file. "The fingerprint info is finally here." Simultaneously she opened the file and checked her phone messages.

"It's Hollis. Come to the house. I've connected the dots. I don't believe what I found, but if I'm right the killer is… No,

I'm not even going to say it until you hear how I figured out who it is."

She hadn't said what time it was when she called. Rhona whipped over to Zee Zee's desk waving the file. "Never mind what you're doing. Let's go. Hollis has fingered the killer. If she confronts whoever it is, she'll endanger herself. We have to stop her before she does something stupid."

Thirty

As she finished her message, Hollis heard the front door open downstairs. MacTee, who considered himself off duty because he'd risen early, paid no attention and continued to snore. She stepped into the hall and shut the door behind her. About to shout her good news, she stopped when she heard David speaking.

"Do you know who I am?"

Strange question. Of course Curt knew who he was.

"You don't, do you? Does the name Rita Brown mean anything to you?"

"Rita Brown?"

"Rita, the Haida woman who studied at Emily Carr College with you. She made the briefcase you carry everywhere. Surely you can't have forgotten? What an unreliable memory you have," David said mockingly.

"I knew Rita years ago. It took me a minute to remember. This is an odd conversation. What does Rita have to do with anything?"

"Rita was my mother."

Hollis tiptoed closer to the stairs.

"Why didn't you say so earlier? What do you mean 'was' your mother?"

"She's dead."

"Poor Rita. What happened to her?"

"Never mind *poor Rita*. You're my father. I found out before she died."

"Whaaat?" Curt's amazement sounded genuine.

"Don't tell me when you flew off to New York to become a big-time star, you weren't aware she was pregnant. You left her alone to have the baby, to have me. You never contacted her again. She told me she thought you didn't want to hear about me, so she didn't tell you. But she should have—you should have come and rescued me from her."

"I had no idea. Truly I didn't. She can't have been very pregnant when I left, or I would have known. What happened to you?"

"What happened? Were you aware that she was crazy, or did you just think she was fey and artistic? She had something called Munchausen's syndrome. Do you know what that is?"

There was a pause.

"You *hurt* your children to give you an excuse to take them to the hospital, where everyone pays attention to you and tells you what a loving, concerned parent you are. Eventually the authorities caught on. The child protection people removed me, but not before she'd broken my leg. Osteomyelitis has made me a permanent cripple."

"My God."

"Oh, but there's more." David's tone was bitter. "Did you read about the battle between social services and the tribal councils? The First Nations demanded to have native children in white foster homes returned to native homes on the reserve. I can see by your face that this is news to you. It was bad news for me. My mother had long disappeared in Vancouver's east side. Thanks to interfering social workers, I went from one terrible foster home to another on the reserve."

"If only I'd known. David, finish your story, but I have to

sit down. Come into the living room."

While they moved, Hollis crept down the stairs.

"Not much else. At one point, my dear mother came home. Someone told her about me. That's when she told me that you're my father. I figure you owe me big time. I'm your eldest son—your legitimate heir. A blood test will prove it. Since you don't have a will, I intend to inherit everything."

"You killed Ivan."

"Bingo."

"And set the fire to kill Etienne."

She'd told David they were watching the stars. She had obviously been dispensable. Hollis slid down two more steps, where she could see into the living room.

"Without her miserable dog, they'd have died."

"And you sabotaged the boat and killed Tomas. You are a monster." Curt reached into his shirt pocket.

David laughed—a chilling sound.

"Those won't do you any good. You didn't notice, but I switched them from their normal brown glass bottle to a clear plastic one. They've lost their potency. Grab away. It's going to seem perfectly natural—a heart attack—everyone knows about your bad heart."

Hollis couldn't sit still. She slammed down the stairs and into the living room. "He won't have another heart attack. I've heard every word. Curt's right—you are a monster. Whatever your mother did to…"

David leaped across the room, grabbed her and threw her onto the floor. He sat on her back and twisted her arm behind her back. Excruciating pain filled her mind.

"The meddler. You're about to join the others—you're not family, but you know too much."

A searing pain in her ribs. She jerked involuntarily. Her

arm felt as if it might break, might tear away from her body.

"That was nothing," David snarled. "To get biblical—I'm cutting to the quick, cutting the quick out of my life. The quick will die. I'll inherit everything."

Curt, clutching his chest, moved to help her.

"Don't even think about it, old man. I'll slice you to ribbons."

"Drop the knife. You're under arrest."

Hollis lifted her head. This was what salvation felt like.

Rhona stepped into the room with her gun pointed at David's chest.

David didn't move.

Rhona repeated the command.

"I won't go to jail again," David said. He twisted to one side and lunged forward. "Never." The knife blade glinted as David drove it into his own chest.

A guttural grunt.

Hollis rolled over. David, his hand under him, lay jackknifed on the floor, his face an agonized mask. Then his features softened and sagged. His body collapsed.

Rhona reached for her cell phone. She requested an ambulance before she and Zee Zee rolled David over. An elaborately carved knife handle protruded from a growing crimson stain. Rhona placed her fingers against his throat.

"No pulse."

Curt, who lay gasping for air, became her priority. She loosened his collar and took his pulse.

Hollis raised herself to her knees. David had almost fooled her. Certainly his references to the price negligent parents would pay and the hostility in his voice when he said his mythical father hadn't been there for him had triggered a question in her mind. And his spider tattoo—a mark that meant he'd been in prison. It hadn't been much, and it had taken a long time and a combination of circumstances for her to figure out that David was the one person who'd had the means and the opportunity to tamper with the brakes, set the fire and damage the boat.

"This morning we matched the fingerprints on the parking pad. They belonged to him." Rhona nodded at David. "A B.C. prison released him earlier this year after he served time for murdering his mother when he was a juvenile."

"And intended to kill his half-brothers and his father," Curt gasped.

Wailing sirens heralded the ambulance's arrival.

*   *   *

Hollis went with Curt to the hospital. After they had admitted him, she went outside to phone Manon and tell her to start back for Toronto. By noon, she'd learned the odds were good that Curt would survive until his heart surgery the next day. She tried to visit Tomas, who was out of intensive care but not allowed to have any visitors. Outside again, she called Penny and related the unbelievable story.

"I'm having a hard time grasping it, and I was there," Hollis said.

"It won't bring Ivan back, but it's good to learn the truth." Penny paused. "Speaking of truth, I've thought about the baby and made a decision."

Hollis surreptitiously crossed her fingers.

"You can inform Ivan's parents about me without giving my name. Then tell me how they react, and I'll decide whether or not to meet them."

"Fair enough. I promise to give you a true and unbiased impression," Hollis said.

Hollis had one more task. It was one o'clock and time to hustle to OCAD, a few blocks from the hospital, and tell her tale again. She knew Curt's class would be assembling, unaware that he was in the hospital.

Tessa, Patel, Kate and Bert stopped talking when she appeared.

"I'm here with bad news." This wasn't going to be easy. Might as well get it over with, but where to start? "Curt is in the hospital. He's scheduled to have a quadruple bypass tomorrow."

A collective groan.

"There's more. David Nixon was not what he seemed. He murdered Curt's son Ivan and tried to kill me and Curt's other two sons. Earlier this morning he killed himself."

"What?" Kate said. Her face and the other's faces reflected total incredulity and shock.

Absolute silence.

"Wow," Bert said, his eyes wide. "He seemed so normal."

"I didn't think so—I thought the way he reacted to things was creepy," Kate said. "And the way he attacked me, I think he knew how I felt. I didn't like him, but I never would have picked him out as a murderer." She ran her hands through her spiky hair. "More than just a murderer—a mass murderer."

"And a terrific artist," Patel said. "Remember the slides of his work?"

"I remember what he said when we had to introduce ourselves. Does anyone else?" Kate asked.

The others shook their heads.

"This isn't word for word, but he said he shattered something that was whole, that he was interested in what was left after a cataclysmic event had occurred. That was the word, 'cataclysmic'. He was telling us what he was doing in his painting but also his real intention—to destroy the family. Very weird."

"What happens now?" Patel said.

Hollis had wondered the same thing. "OCAD will let you know. I have to get back to the house."

Kate impulsively hugged Hollis. "You have all our emails—keep in touch."

Hollis promised she would and headed back to the Hartmans' to care for MacTee. She walked in the door and had to race to answer the ringing phone.

"Hollis, Zee Zee and I want to take you to lunch tomorrow at Little Ethiopia. It's our thank-you for your help."

"I'd love to come. And I'll have more to tell you."

*　　*　　*

Rhona looked up to see Frank approaching.

"Well done," he said, giving her two thumbs up.

"Thanks." Should she tell him what she thought? Why not? "I've been told you are opposed to responding to gut feelings, to intuitions, to anything but scientific data."

Frank nodded.

"If we'd listened to Curt Hartman's wife early in the investigation, we might have nailed the perp sooner."

Frank waited.

"She told us she believed her young son, Etienne, was in danger because the whole family was being targeted. We dismissed her as high-strung and neurotic. But she was right."

"I think you misunderstood me. No police officer with any experience denies the importance of intuition. I acknowledge that, but I also emphasize the need to be familiar with and use all the latest scientific tools." He smiled and shifted uncomfortably.

Rhona wondered what was coming next.

"You said you loved the Island. I'm taking Juno there on Saturday. Would you like to come?"

Was he asking her for a date? Not likely, that wasn't allowed. Senior officers did not date junior officers. Maybe it was the equivalent of an apology for his attitude. But why second-guess him—it might be fun.

"Nothing I'd like more."

*   *   *

At Little Ethiopia, a restaurant off Yonge Street north of Wellesley, the three women chose not to sit outside on the patio, because the temperature hovered around thirty, with the humidex pushing thirty-five. Indoors, Zee Zee spoke Amharic to the waiter, whose face brightened as soon as she began. She ordered Ethiopian beer to cool them down while they considered the menu.

"The sample platter is best for newcomers to our food," Zee Zee said. "When you've tried many items, you find which ones you prefer. I'm having *yedoro infille,* chicken in hot sauce, and *ye'atakilt alich'a,* vegetable stew, but they're an acquired taste."

Hollis and Rhona took her advice and opted for the platter.

"We make quite a ritual of washing our hands before we eat. That's because we don't use cutlery."

The waiter delivered a basket of what looked like spongy pancakes or uncooked crumpets.

Zee Zee picked up a piece. "This is *infera,* Ethiopian bread. We use it in place of cutlery. When you're presented with a platter, small quantities of whatever you're eating—lentil, split pea or meat curries along with *lab,* a spiced mixture of cottage cheese and yogurt—these are ladled on top of a layer of infera." Zee Zee demonstrated how to tear small pieces of *infera* and scoop up the food.

Hollis and Rhona followed her lead and shovelled their way through the offerings on their platters.

"This is really good. Some of it is spicier than I'm comfortable with," Hollis said.

"You get to know which you prefer. By the way, I have to tell you that Ethiopian cuisine developed completely without sugar. In fact, it's traditional to put salt in your coffee."

Rhona and Hollis had demolished the toppings.

"The bottom pieces of *infera* are best, because they've soaked up all the juices," Zee Zee said. "We won't do the coffee ceremony today. Actually, because it takes about three hours, Ethiopians usually only prepare it on holidays or weekends. Coffee drinking and cultivation began in Ethiopia about a thousand A.D., so we've had lots of time to work on the ceremony."

They sat back with regular coffee and discussed the case.

Hollis told them about Penny.

"Not telling us was irresponsible, you know," Rhona said.

"I planned to do it. The boat accident intervened."

"Not good enough. You didn't know whether or not she was covering for her family. They could have murdered Ivan. It turned out okay, but if you're ever in a similar situation, you're morally obligated to share information." Hollis was suitably chastened.

The conversation turned to David.

"Not being part of a family is devastating to a child," Rhona said. "Families are the foundation, aren't they? In First Nations culture, the government until recently wouldn't allow women who married white men to keep their Indian status. If the woman was divorced or widowed, she couldn't go back to the reserve, and her children were not considered to be Indian. The law affected thousands of women and was very destructive. It kept my grandmother from returning to her reserve until she was an old lady."

"Sort of a continuing but more subtle version of what the

slave trade did to families?" Zee Zee added.

"With David, it was more than that—but I'm sure all those separations as well as his mother's abuse helped to make him the way he was," Hollis said. "Was he a sociopath or a psychopath?"

"Hard to say," Rhona said.

"Whatever he was, he nearly killed me. From now on, I only want to meet a man like him on the pages of a novel."

Rhona glanced at her watch. "I'm going home to put together an IKEA bookcase and unpack a few boxes. The decision has been made—I'm in Toronto to stay."

*　　*　　*

Two days later, Hollis joined Manon in Curt's hospital room.

Curt lifted a hand in greeting. "Hell of a way to get a bypass," he said. "Seriously, thank you for saving my life."

Manon moved a second chair next to Hollis's. "We're grateful. I still find it hard to believe David would plot to kill us all in order to inherit Curt's money."

"I've been thinking about his motivation. Who will ever know for sure, but I think it was more than that. David wasn't stupid. He must have realized early on that his plan wasn't going to work out, that suspicions would arise when everyone died. That sooner or later he'd be caught. I don't think he cared. He kept going because he wanted to pay Curt back for *his* suffering by making Curt feel pain and fear. I doubt if he rationalized those feelings—I think he was obsessed and cunning. A couple of things he said triggered alarm bells, but I really wasn't paying attention. I mean, who would have thought Ivan's killer would be an artist, let alone that he'd be taking Curt's course?"

Curt nodded. "He took us all in. We've arranged for his cremation. Late in August when I've recovered and Etienne returns from camp, we'll take his ashes back to the reserve. I'll carry them and bury them in the briefcase his mother made me."

Tears rolled down Hollis's cheeks. Curt appeared to have made a Saul on the road to Damascus conversion. She didn't know if it would last, but it was great to see.

Curt's eyes shone with his unshed tears. "I wonder if he would have been different if I'd gone back." He shook his head. "My parents lived in Prince George and died in a car accident while I was in New York. I flew home to bury them and never wanted to see British Columbia again. But I feel guilty."

"His mother could have called you. She must have been aware that you would have at least paid for his support. She was to blame too," Manon said.

Hollis held her hand up. "Enough with the blame. I have some news."

Manon and Curt waited.

"Ivan intended to marry a girl he met at George Brown. When he died she was pregnant."

"No," Manon exhaled.

Manon and Curt stared at one another.

Finally, a smile crept across Manon's face. Her eyes sparkled, and her head lifted. "How wonderful. When will she have it?" She grasped Curt's hand. "We'll be grandparents. Isn't this marvellous news?"

Curt looked thoughtful. "I never visualized myself as a grandfather." He frowned. "What would I like to be called?"

Manon laughed. "Curt, you're incorrigible. Somehow you always put yourself at centre stage." She leaned forward, looking at Hollis. "Who is she? When can we meet her? Has she had the baby?"

Hollis responded to Manon's enthusiasm. It was going to be okay. "She didn't want me to tell you her name until I told her how you reacted to the news. She hasn't had the baby, but it's due very soon."

At that moment, Etienne and Tomas knocked and came in. Both hugged their father. Tomas did not look like a young man who'd recently hovered between life and death.

"Dad, you look like you've won the lottery," Tomas said.

"I have. We all have," Curt said. Uncharacteristically, his voice trembled.

Etienne examined their faces. "What's happening? Did we really win the lottery?"

Manon nodded at Curt. "Tell them."

"Ivan had a serious girlfriend, and she's having a baby. Manon and I will be grandparents, and you two will be uncles."

"An uncle. Way cool," Etienne said. "I'll teach him about the stars." He looked thoughtful. "A puppy would be really good for a baby. Can we get one?"

Manon laughed. "What a good idea. I'm sure the baby will love a puppy." She reached over and squeezed Hollis's hand.

Her nails were short, but the manicure was perfect.

Joan Boswell was born in Toronto and grew up in Ottawa, Edmonton, Oakville and Halifax. As a member of the Ladies' Killing Circle, she has had stories in each of their six books: *The Ladies' Killing Circle, Cottage Country Killers, Menopause Is Murder, Fit to Die, Bone Dance* and *When Boomers Go Bad.* She has also co-edited the last three books. In 2000, she won the Toronto Sunday Star short story contest. *Cut Off His Tale,* her first novel, was published by RendezVous Crime in 2005.

Joan lives in Toronto with two flatcoated retrievers and enjoys life with her grown sons, their wives and her grandchildren.